Praise for *The Best Place on* [obscured by barcode]

"Remarkable. . . . A potent examination of the quotidian devastation wreaked by continuous bombings in the city. . . . Tsabari writes with a clear yet compassionate eye about characters attempting to wrest meaningful lives out of an environment that strongly opposes them."—*National Post*

"Impressive. . . . Brutally honest. . . . Smart, sad and sincere. . . . The characters imagined by Tsabari are achingly human and almost flawlessly fashioned."—*Winnipeg Free Press*

"*The Best Place on Earth* is a book to begin an informed discussion of the social differences between Middle East and modern west, a well-crafted literary snapshot of love relationships amid shellfire and suicide bomb, and a frequent challenge to one's moral sense of what is and what should be."—*Vancouver Sun*

"Powerful. . . . Brilliant. . . . The stories depict minorities so skillfully, with such a light and accurate touch."—*The Daily Beast*

"This short story collection is a fiction debut for Tsabari, but it demonstrates that she is already a talented storyteller. Her writing has an immediacy and power that invites readers into her characters' psyches. . . . Tsabari's characters will step off the page to captivate readers."—*Publishers Weekly*

"Penetrating. . . . The author [possesses] superior skill at excavating the internal and external conflicts encountered by her characters."
—*Quill & Quire*

"Tsabari's characters represent the complexities that really define Israel, the differing people jostling one another in this tiny plot of land on the Mediterranean. Their tales are fascinating."—*Toronto Star*

"A notable debut. . . . Issues of assimilation and belonging . . . are approached here in specific ways that both trouble the underlying cultural conversations and tell moving stories."—*The Globe and Mail*

"Tsabari's stories pulse with raw energy as they unfurl along the fault lines within modern Israeli society. The compelling urgency of this collection reflects the multi-faceted culture it brings to life; its quiet wisdom speaks to the universality of the hopes and conflicts it depicts."—Nancy Richler, author of *The Imposter Bride*

"Frank, bold, sexy, Ayelet Tsabari's voice astonishes with its vitality. *The Best Place on Earth* offers stories of love and displacement set against a backdrop of military conflict, told through the lens of being young and Israeli of Middle Eastern descent. These tales feel torn from the heart."—Catherine Bush, author of *Claire's Head* and *The Rules of Engagement*

"The most restrictive border may be the most primary one—the distance between two human minds; between one person's inner world and the subjective life of another. In *The Best Place on Earth*, Ayelet Tsabari shows us literature's power to cross this essential divide, and to shatter simplistic notions that tempt us when we think in cultural, regional, or historical terms. This book marks the debut of a brilliant and ambitious literary voice, and Tsabari's rich and subtle fiction gives us the world as it is—complexly multicultural, messily beautiful, and painfully wise."—Wayde Compton, author of *After Canaan*

"Tsabari's debut collection is cinematic. Her vivid descriptions and insights on the intersections of love, hope and war are thought-provoking and challenge the reader to engage with a conflicted world with a new understanding."—Gurjinder Basran, author of *Everything Was Good-Bye*

"Stories are survival. Fiercely alert, Tsabari's Israeli-Mizrahi inspired stories—where nothing is a given—deserve our fierce attention. Her deft evoking of the sensate vibrancy of Israeli daily life locates us inside its very vectors of violence and intimacy. There is no turning away. Elating, wrenching, *The Best Place on Earth* is on the cutting edge of our literature; our deeper comprehension of global life."
—Betsy Warland, author of *Breathing the Page: Reading the Act of Writing*

AYELET TSABARI

THE BEST PLACE ON EARTH

STORIES

HARPER PERENNIAL

For the readers
of Beth Emeth
Library
Best wishes,

Ayelet Tsabari

For Sean
And for my mother, Yona
In memory of my father, Haim Tsabari

The Best Place on Earth
Copyright © 2013 by Ayelet Tsabari.
All rights reserved.

Published by Harper Perennial, an imprint of HarperCollins Publishers Ltd

First published in Canada by HarperCollins Publishers Ltd in a hardcover edition: 2013
This Harper Perennial trade paperback edition: 2015

The stories "The Poets in the Kitchen Window" and "Warplanes" were previously
published in *Prairie Fire* and *Grain* magazine, respectively.

The author gratefully acknowledges the support of the
Canada Council for the Arts.

HarperCollins books may be purchased for educational, business,
or sales promotional use through our Special Markets Department.

HarperCollins Publishers Ltd
2 Bloor Street East, 20th Floor
Toronto, Ontario, Canada
M4W 1A8

www.harpercollins.ca

Library and Archives Canada Cataloguing in Publication
information is available upon request

ISBN 978-1-44341-196-7

Printed and bound in the United States
RRD 10 9 8 7 6 5 4 3 2

CONTENTS

CONTENTS

TIKKUN

I'm just about to cross the street to Café Rimon when I see Natalie sitting on the shaded patio and my heart skips, trips and falls over itself. I stop walking, pull my squished cigarette pack out from the back pocket of my jeans, tap it and dig out a half-smoked cigarette. Then I lean against the stone wall behind me and light it.

Downtown Jerusalem is busy at midday. Cars creep along the congested street, music pouring out from their open windows. The narrow sidewalks—made narrower by the goods overflowing from the storefronts—are swarming with people, lugging bags from the Mahane Yehuda Market. Orthodox high-school girls in long skirts saunter by me, giggling when they pass three young soldiers with kippahs on their heads, M-16s slung over their shoulders. Across the street, a group of pink-faced tourists— probably Christian pilgrims who have disregarded the warnings against travelling to Israel in these dangerous times—take photos

1

of themselves next to an unremarkable alley. Natalie is hidden and revealed in intervals, glimpsed in the gaps between the vehicles and faces, through bus windows, a choppy sequence of still images, like a stop-motion video.

It's been seven years since I last saw her. After we broke up— and by broke up, I mean she ripped my heart out of my chest and stomped on it with both feet—she sort of disappeared. She lost touch with all of the friends we had back then. No one knew where she lived or what she was up to. No one ever ran into her. She was just gone.

I flick my cigarette butt on the asphalt, my eyes trying to register what they see, my brain slow to compute. At first I try to convince myself that it doesn't mean what I think it means. Of course she would look different. She's thirty-five now, no longer the twenty-something Natalie from my memories, with the thick black curls she used to braid with shells and beads, the flimsy wrap skirts she had brought from India, the tie-dyed halter tops that exposed her delicate, jutting shoulder blades. There must be a perfectly good reason—other than the obvious—why she'd be covering her hair, wearing a skirt down to her ankles and a long-sleeved shirt on a summer day. Orthodox women don't usually wear glittery and bohemian-looking scarves like that as a head scarf, don't let strands of hair fall out on the sides. They definitely don't look that smoking hot in clothes designed to make them invisible to men like me.

A part of me wants to walk away, pretend I haven't seen her, keep my memory of her undisturbed. But then a businessman jaywalks into traffic while speaking loudly into his phone, setting off a series of honks and yells, and Natalie looks up at the commotion, and her gaze wanders over and fixes on me. I've been staring for so long that I've almost forgotten she can see me too. Her face broadens in surprise, then brightens. She extends her arm for a wave. I cross the street, wishing I had shaved this morning.

"Lior." She stands up, her eyes glinting like two spoons. We don't hug, the space between us thick with past embraces, with a history of touching.

"Wow, Natalie, you're . . ."

"Dossit," she completes my sentence, smiling as if she's swallowed sunshine.

"This is huge," I say, and she laughs. I quickly give her the once-over: her skirt is embroidered with flowers at the hem, her shirt is a vintage tunic with a floral print. Of course, she's a hippie-dossit: one of those cool New Age Orthodox Jews—often former Tel Avivians—who found God but didn't lose their chic. "Wow." I stroke the stubble on my chin. "I had no idea."

"Seven years now. Baruch Hashem." She gazes up. God bless.

"Seven years," I repeat. Right after we broke up.

"If you're shocked now you should have seen me then." She laughs again. "I was much stricter in the beginning. I had myself covered from head to toe."

"No kidding," I say. My mind is struggling to reconstruct the past seven years, replace the set of imaginary lives I'd created for her in my head. An ashram in the desert, a commune in the Galilee, a temple in India. Never this.

"Your hair," she says with a quick jerk of her chin.

"Yeah." I rub my shaved head, the smooth patch in the middle I'm grateful she can't see. "All gone."

"You look good like that."

"And you're married." I gesture at the head scarf.

"Yes." Her smile seems to fade a little. "Remember Gadi?"

I frown.

"Sure you do. He was in my Judaism class in university."

Natalie used to complain about being forced to take Judaism classes as a part of the curriculum at Bar-Ilan University. Gadi—an American who had moved from New York to find his inner Jew—came over to our house a couple of times to help her study.

"We've been married for six years now."

"Wow." It's like she's dug her fingernail into a scab, unearthing an old wound. Fucking Gadi. I knew he was trying to get into her pants. Natalie said I was crazy.

"It was after we broke up," she quickly adds.

I nod and smile because I don't know what else to do. "And kids? You probably have a troop by now." By the way her face crumbles, tightens around the lips, I know I've asked the wrong question. "Sorry," I say.

Her tan cheeks turn burgundy. "It's okay."

We both look away. I use the opportunity to scan the patio, which I would have done earlier had I not been distracted. A couple holding hands over a half-eaten Greek salad, a young mother rocking a stroller with one hand while flipping through a magazine with the other, an old man bent over a notebook, two female soldiers sharing a cigarette. One of them glances at me, sizing me up. We are all trained to identify potential threats.

"So what are you doing in Jerusalem?" Natalie asks.

"House-sitting in Ein Kerem."

"Alone?"

"Yeah." I slide my hands into my pockets and hike up my jeans. "My girlfriend stayed in Tel Aviv. Listen, can I join you?"

"Actually, I was just leaving."

"It's a public place," I say. "It's not like we're in a closed room or anything."

She glances around the patio, checks her phone and finally says, "Why not? A cup of coffee. It's been so long."

I slide into the chair opposite her and she heads to the washroom. I follow her with my gaze, the outline of her hips against her skirt. Shelly, the young waitress-slash–film student whom I met here earlier this week shakes her head at me with a smile.

Natalie and I were twenty-two when we met. We had both just moved to Tel Aviv, me from the suburbs, her from a kibbutz in the Galilee. We worked at the same bar on Sheinkin—back when Sheinkin was the place to be—saving money for the big trip after the army. We fell in love like you do in your twenties, drowning into each other, blending until the boundaries of our selves blurred. It was the nineties: the Gulf War was over, Rabin was elected prime minister and everyone thought peace was possible, and that soon we'd be partying in Beirut, eating hummus in Damascus and driving along the Mediterranean coast to Turkey. Tel Aviv was just gaining a reputation for being a party capital—ir lelo hafsaka—the city that never stops, and magazines in London and New York began covering its nightlife, including it on lists for the best clubs, the best beaches. Natalie and I rented an apartment on Shalom Aleichem, not too far from the beach, with old painted tile floors and a rounded white balcony, which we decorated with furniture we found by dumpsters. We smoked sandy grass from Egypt in bongs that we had bought at a twenty-four-hour kiosk, had sex in the washrooms of bars, and sat at a beach restaurant at four in the morning drinking hot water with mint leaves and eating hummus between swims in the dark, velvety waters of the Mediterranean. On weekends we hitched rides to trance parties in forests and did ecstasy, and on holidays we went to Sinai, slept in a straw hut by the sea and played backgammon with the Bedouins. We felt like we were a part of a generation, and that life had been made just for us and we'd never be sick and never grow old and nothing bad would ever happen to us. Now, more than a decade later, Rabin is dead after being assassinated at a peace rally; suicide bombers explode in buses and cafés; our friends have all moved to the suburbs, bought apartments and had kids; Natalie is a married Orthodox and I'm unemployed and dating a twenty-four-year-old.

We order coffee. Cappuccino for her, Turkish for me. I try not to stare but it's hard. Her face is the same, heart-shaped and smiling—her default expression—and her skin flawless, tiny wrinkles just starting by her eyes. Maybe it's my staring but she seems restless; she fiddles with everything on the table, her eyes darting around the patio. She checks her messages. "Gadi is in New York till tomorrow," she says. "His mom is not doing so well."

"Sorry," I say. "Why didn't you go? I'd kill to get out of here right now."

"Work," she says. "Couldn't get out of school. How about you? Still in computers?"

"Actually, the company just folded."

"I'm sorry."

"Whatever." I flick my lighter on and off. "Maybe I'll move to New Zealand or something."

She laughs. "And do what?"

"I don't know, herd sheep?"

She waves her hand. "You love it here."

"Not as much as I used to."

She studies the table. I squint up at the stone balconies hunched over the street, their wooden shutters crooked and blackened with car exhaust. I realize that things have changed, that there are certain topics we better not talk about, things we'd probably never agree on. Our fathers' right to this land, for one, which rules out both politics and religion, since in this country the two are joined in a suffocating embrace. But then again, we almost never talked about these things when we were together. We were pseudo-hippies; we wanted everyone to get along so we wouldn't feel guilty for the terrible things that were happening in the world while we made love not war. Sometimes it's better not to know; it can make you crazy. On the way here I saw people huddling around the TV screen at a convenience store, the air around them rigid with alarm. Mouths open, heads shaking, tongues clucking. A pigua in Haifa, they said. Nine dead. I didn't bother to stop. The only advantage to knowing that there was a suicide bombing earlier today is that it makes me feel safer now. It's a warped logic, based in fear. You take what you can.

Natalie grabs a packet of brown sugar, rips the edge of it and dumps its contents into her cappuccino. She then spoons the sugary foam into her mouth just as it starts to melt. No stirring. I sip my coffee and hold back a smile. Some things never change.

"So why are you really in Jerusalem?" she asks, pulling the polished spoon out from between her dark lips.

I lean back in my seat. "How much time do you have?"

It has been a rough few months. Since the second intifada started, the entire country has been going through a mid-life crisis: the economy crashed, the high-tech bubble burst, the hotels on the seawall emptied, their windows dark. When I was a teenager, the city was full of tourists; my friends and I used to hit on them on beaches, offering to help when we saw them carrying backpacks on street corners, fingers to maps.

While I avoided reading the newspapers or watching the news, carefully constructing a bubble in which I could function without losing my mind, my girlfriend, Efrat, pored over every page, was glued to the screen, the cold blue light washing over her face. She stopped using public transit, rarely went out, stayed away from the crowded, open Carmel Market, shopping instead at a smaller, pricier mini-market, where the produce wasn't as fresh but where no suicide bomber would waste his ammunition. It was as though she was in a perpetual state of waiting—for the next news flash, the next bomb to explode, the next series of phone calls to friends and family to make sure no one had been hurt. On top of it all, the anxiety medication she had been prescribed reduced her sex drive to nil. When she refused to go out with me in the evenings, I went by myself, finding reasons to stay out later, pushing her out of my bubble—my safe zone—the gap between us widening.

Then, on my way back from my parents' place I ran over a kitten. I was driving south on the right lane of Ayalon Highway, under bridges and overpasses, when I saw the little bugger—its eyes like tiny headlights—coming out of nowhere into my lane, as if on a suicide mission. I came to a screeching stop, turned my distress lights on and stepped outside. The kitten was splayed on the asphalt, not much bigger than my palm, mouth open in mid-scream, the blood still red and warm underneath it, its insides purple and pink and brown. He probably belonged to no one, another stray that would eat from garbage cans and one day impregnate another cat and make a litter of redundant kitties no one would ever give a shit about. But seeing it there, its blood soaking into the asphalt, something broke in me.

I drove home sobbing; the city's skyline loomed ahead, giant ads with skinny models draped on the sides of buildings. The radio played sad songs because there had been two attacks that day. I was sniffling and howling, snot and tears running down my chin. When I walked through the door, eyes red, face wet and wrinkled, Efrat jumped off the couch, a hand over her mouth. "Oh my God. What happened?"

"I ran over a kitten," I said, and saying it aloud made me burst into another series of ugly, unmanly sobs.

"A kitten?" She stared at me, confused, then she tried touching me, saying, "I'm so sorry, baby," but I shook her off, shuffled into my office, played video games till two in the morning and smoked all of our grass.

I spent the following week in my sweatpants. I smoked too much pot, watched TV, slept into the afternoon. Outside our apartment, life went on, the city carried on its incessant buzzing, while I was frozen inside. Something was wrong. I realized that every step in our relationship had been initiated by Efrat, as if she was holding the road map and I was just tagging along. She asked to be monogamous; she suggested we move in together. I started to wonder: Now what? Was I supposed to be an adult? To know what I wanted? To marry Efrat? Have children? And some nights—I don't tell Natalie this part—I thought of her. Over the years, in her absence, she had become mythical. Every woman I'd ever dated was required to fill her enormous shoes, and failed.

A friend was going away to India and needed someone to watch his house in Ein Kerem, a neighbourhood on the outskirts of Jerusalem—more like a village, really—where artists lived in old Arabic stone houses covered with vines. It was the end of summer, and Tel Aviv was steeped in its own juices, smelling of ripe garbage and swathed in dust and sand. Even the nights were sticky, offering no reprieve. I had been dreaming about getting away, wishing I could afford a flight somewhere. Anywhere. Jerusalem, with its dry air and cooler nights, was the closest thing to Europe.

Natalie is listening to everything without saying a word, nodding in the right places. She's no longer fidgeting, as if listening to my problems makes her forget about hers.

"Do you love her?" she says.

"Well, yeah," I say. "I think. I want to."

"You want to?"

"I don't know," I say. "They're not new, these doubts. They've just been getting worse. I've been asking myself these questions pretty much from the beginning. How do you know when someone is right? How do you know when it's over? Is a mediocre relationship better than being alone? Do I love her enough? What's enough?"

"That's the problem with you seculars," Natalie says. "You ask too many questions."

"I always thought I'd know more at thirty-five. I'm not where I thought I'd be."

"Clearly, neither am I," Natalie says. She empties a sugar packet onto a saucer and draws in it with a toothpick. A flower. A heart.

"I'm sorry," I say. I still can't get my head around it. I got Natalie pregnant twice. The first time was in the alley behind Haminzar, her unshaven legs wrapped around me, scratching my bum. We were wasted on arak and lemonade, and she wasn't on the pill and I guess I pulled out too late. Natalie was very businesslike about the abortion: there were no tears, no talk about options; she wanted it done.

It was different the second time around. We were on her parents' bed in the kibbutz when we discovered that if I did a little motion, a little in and up, I hit her G spot and it drove her wild. We didn't use anything because she was on the last day of her period. The night we found out she was pregnant again, we sat on the dingy couch that took up most of our balcony, bare feet against the rusty railing, and for about an hour or two we entertained thoughts of keeping it: talking names, buying a minivan, renting a little house by the water with a porch and a hammock. But we were twenty-four and had bodies full of drugs and alcohol and cigarettes, and we had no money and still hadn't gone to university. We sat on that couch until morning, drank red wine straight from the bottle and cried for what would never be.

"There must be a way," I say.

"Trust me, at this point I'd do anything." She looks into her cup, swirls what's left of her coffee. "It's complicated. We've been trying for six years. Gadi is waiting for a miracle. Our relationship is . . ." She trails off, stiffens. "I shouldn't be talking to you about this."

"Come on. You're talking to a friend about your problems. I just talked about mine for like, an hour, and they don't seem quite as important as yours."

"What about you?" she says.

"What, children?" I snort. "You're kidding, right? Look around you. Why would anybody want to raise children in this country?"

She looks at the street, fingers the silver chain around her neck—its pendant buried under her collar—and says quietly, "God has a plan."

Natalie had always had some sort of faith. When we were travelling in India, it was the holy cities where she wanted to stay the longest. In Varanasi she started meditating; in Pushkar she went on a silent retreat. All I wanted to do in India was get high, preferably on a tropical beach. Natalie found solace in yoga, meditation, a bit of Buddhism, a dash of Kabbalah. She believed in a supportive universe, in things like manifestation, karma and tikkun: the kabbalistic idea of repairing or correcting past mistakes in order to achieve balance in the world. A part of me admired her for that; I loved that it was her own thing, that it wasn't rooted in religion. Another part of me thought it was a hippie mishmash of spiritual nonsense, with holes large enough to drive a truck through.

"Maybe I don't have the believer chip," I tell Natalie. "I'm just not wired that way, I'm too cynical. Don't know if I can change it."

"You can't force it," she says.

"Can I get you guys anything else?" Shelly saunters over, a whiff of cocoa butter and coffee beans. "A halvah Danish?" She winks at me.

"Not today." I smile.

"Just the bill," Natalie says.

We watch Shelly walking away and Natalie says, "She likes you."

I shrug it off, examine the hardened remains of my coffee, finding patterns in the muddy grounds. An ambulance speeds through the street, and everyone on the patio turns to look. Natalie's neck lengthens, revealing a Star of David pendant hanging on her silver chain.

"Do you ever think about our time together?" I say.

Natalie turns her head quickly, giving me an alarmed look. "Don't do that, Lior."

"I'm just curious," I say.

She holds her cup in both hands, choosing words. "To be honest, I don't think about it much. Sometimes I remember things, but it's like remembering a dream, something that happened in a movie. To a different woman."

I swallow; my mouth is dry. I feel like such an idiot.

She glances at her phone and says she must go. "It was good to see you, Lior. Take care of yourself, will you?"

I stand up, raise my hand to touch her and then tuck it into my pocket instead. "Good luck."

"Be'ezrat Hashem," she says. God willing.

I watch her disappear into the crowd, and my heart crumples in my chest. Shelly strides over, piles our plates and coffee mugs on a tray. "What was that about?" she asks.

"What?"

"You and this . . . dossit." She raises one eyebrow.

"Long story." I smile tightly.

"So . . . I'm almost done." She shifts on one hip, the tray perched on her arm. "Want to grab a drink?"

"At this hour?" I laugh.

"I thought you were from Tel Aviv." She stares at me without blinking.

I eye her, contemplate the possibility. She has warm hazelnut eyes, and she's wearing a vintage blue dress with a gold belt and gold ballerina shoes. She's probably twenty-two, in her experimental slutty phase. I try to pretend I'm single; slip it on like a new shirt. I'm curious if I still have it, if I can do it without feeling guilty, if I'd think about Efrat at all.

"Here." She grabs my wrist, pulls a pen from the pocket of her apron and scrawls a number. "If you change your mind."

The bus is full of passengers with their grocery bags. It smells like cilantro and fish. I stand by the back door, a quick escape route, and watch through the smeared glass as the city lets up, gives way to valleys and hills. It's hard to believe Jerusalem is only forty minutes away from Tel Aviv because it feels like another world. Efrat hates it, says it's too busy and dirty and rundown, the streets too crowded, the people too intense. She gets migraines whenever she's here.

The bus is almost empty by the time it drops me at Ein Kerem, the rush and chaos of Jerusalem left behind. Ein Kerem, tucked up in the city's sleeve, is bathed in warm afternoon light. I walk to my new home, sit on the couch outside and watch the valley, spread open like the palm of one's hand. I turn on my cell, glancing at Shelly's number on my wrist when the phone rings.

"Thank God," Efrat says. "I was going crazy. Your phone was off."

"Sorry," I say.

"You can't do that. There was a pigua in Jerusalem. And your mom was looking for you. She didn't even know you were in Jerusalem."

"Shit," I say. "I forgot to tell her."

"Well, it's irresponsible, Lior. The least you can do is leave your cell on."

"I said I'm sorry."

She's quiet. I can hear her sucking cigarette smoke. "I miss you," she says.

"Efrat, we talked about this. I just need time to figure shit out."

"I just said I missed you. Why do you have to be such a jerk?"

I sigh, suddenly exhausted. "I came here to take a break. Please."

"Fine," she says. "Whatever."

It's almost evening by the time I drag myself off the couch and decide to go for a walk, be a tourist, anything to distract me from my head. I climb up the path to Hama'ayan Street, where three narrow roads meet at Mary's Spring. It's quiet before sunset, the pilgrims and tourists and idling buses all gone. A mosque towers over the spring, with a crescent and a star perched on its spire. I follow the trickling sound of water under a stone archway, disturbing a nun who's bent over the shallow pool, washing her face in the stream from the rock-hewn tunnel. It's musty and cool underneath the curved, low ceilings. On the wall, a sign advises visitors against drinking the water many of them consider holy. I have seen pilgrims fill plastic bottles with this stuff. I wait until the nun leaves and lean over, let a few icy drops into my mouth. It tastes like rain: earthy and fresh.

I hike up the wide, stone-paved stairs to the Church of the Visitation. The road is empty, except for a young souvenir vendor leaning against his modest stall: wooden crosses and rosaries dangling from hooks, fluttering scarves tied over a pole, postcards stacked on a rotating stand. He nods at me and continues to play on his phone. The valley yawns to my right, lush with olive and cypress trees, and the hillside is terraced and capped with clusters of stone houses. The setting sun is bouncing off distant car mirrors and water heaters on roofs.

I'm breathless by the time I make it all the way to the top of the stairs, where a large wrought-iron gate leads to a stone courtyard, a church and a bell tower with a spiky tip. A huge mosaic covers the front wall, rimmed with gold: three flying angels, a woman riding a horse, her arms crossed against her chest. The place is breezy and graveyard-quiet, the kind of quiet that hums, that clings to you the way humidity does in the city. I think I'm alone but then I notice a monk—his face warmly lit by the setting sun—sitting on a bench in what I realize is an actual cemetery: a few graves laid between trees and bushes. He's looking over the valley; doesn't move, doesn't see me, like a statue.

I walk up a few more stairs, drawn to the sound of voices singing in some language I can't make out. The visitors spill out just
as I reach the door to the chapel and I lower my gaze, afraid they
can see through me, know I don't belong. Once they are gone I
peer in. The high ceilings are covered in murals, depicting scenes I
don't recognize from stories I don't know. The setting sun tints the
paintings a rich orange, drawing long shadows on the tiled floor. I
sit in a pew and try to feel something that isn't discomfort. I shift
in my seat and the wood creaks, then echoes, amplified. Maybe
God is here. Maybe I've never felt him because I've looked in all
the wrong places. I close my eyes and try to concentrate, breathe,
meditate. I try. I really fucking try. I feel nothing.

My phone rings. A priest I haven't noticed before glares at me.
I apologize and hurry outside to answer, surprised to hear Natalie
on the other end.

"Lior." Her voice is choked. "Have you heard?"

The pigua. "Where?"

"Café Rimon. Seven dead."

"Oh my God." I skitter down the stairs to the courtyard, past
the cemetery, through the gate. "When?"

"About twenty minutes after we left. I just found out."

Shelly. I glance at her handwriting on my wrist. Did she make it
out in time?

"There are no names yet," Natalie says as if she can read my
mind.

"I can't believe it. Twenty minutes?"

"I'm in Ein Kerem," she says. "I got in the car and drove here,
then I realized I don't even know where you're staying."

"Park by the spring," I say. "I'll be there in a minute."

I race down the path. The sky over the valley has grown darker, bruised blue, red and purple. The setting sun has sucked the warmth out of the air, and the mountain breeze feels cool on my skin, billowing out the back of my T-shirt as I run down the stairs to Hama'ayan Street.

Natalie is washing her hands in the drizzle of the spring, and then turns and sees me. "Oh, Lior." She grabs my hand—touches me—squeezes it with wet, cold fingers. Her eyes are pink. "We were just there."

"I know."

"I keep thinking, what if we'd stayed a bit longer?"

Street lights click on along the street, their warm beams offsetting the fading daylight's bluish tones. I look around. The neighbourhood appears new, sharper and clearer somehow, as if it had just rained.

"It was weird, like I suddenly felt I had to go," she says. "I just felt like it was time."

"I wanted to stay," I say. "I wanted to talk more."

"It was weird," she repeats.

"You saved me," I say, the words strange in my mouth, my hand—still in hers—breaking into a sweat.

"I didn't do anything," she says.

A car drives down the hill, its headlights blinding us, and Natalie squints and pulls her hand away. She has that swimming look in her eyes, before tears. I cross the street, stop and turn to Natalie. She hesitates but then follows. We walk down the path to the house, where we are hidden from the road, lower than the asphalt. We stand by the pomegranate tree. I don't invite her in.

"I'm sorry I came here." Her voice shakes; her shoulders quiver. "I didn't know where else to go."

"I'm glad you did," I say. I picture the patio in my head; summon up the faces I memorized. "Remember the couple that was sitting next to us?"

"They spoke French," she says. "I was admiring her head scarf. I remember thinking it looked expensive. And there was that old guy . . ."

"With the fedora. By the door. He was writing."

"Oh no." She puts her hand over her mouth. "The mother with the stroller."

"She left right after you did."

"Thank God." Her eyes fill with tears. "It was so close today. One more coffee and we'd be dead. And instead of thinking how dangerous it would be to have a child in this place, like you said, it just makes me want one more." She cups her face with her palms and breaks into sobs.

I watch Natalie with my hands tightly curled inside my pockets, going against my instincts, which tell me to hold her, touch her, console her. But then she bows forward, as though she may fall, so I open my arms and catch her, and she buries her face in my chest, her tears soaking through my shirt. I stand there, stiff, my hands like slabs of dough on her shoulder blades, my head pulled back, looking up at the stars blinking between the clouds, at the valley, now dotted with flickering lights, and I'm not breathing her in, not wiping away her tears, not saying a word, just being a rock she can lean against. After a long while, her trembles subside and she sniffles into my chest, and we remain still, breathing. Her body hardens against me, so slowly that at first I think I must be imagining it, then her arms tighten around me, and she's clinging to me as though we're suspended over a cliff and I'm the one at the end of the rope. I can feel her breasts through her shirt, the heat from her body. My heart starts going double time;

my erection presses against the fabric of my jeans. "Natalie," I breathe out.

She pulls me down onto her and we fall, knees buckling, onto the earth, which smells sharp, warm, moist, like blood. She has a determined, focused look in her eyes as she scrambles to open the zipper of my pants, lifts her skirt and leads me inside her, her wetness and warmth, and it's like our bodies have memory, like they have never been apart. I try to kiss her but she moves her face and I kiss her neck, drink in her scent—body lotion and coffee and milk—and I remember: this is how love feels. So many times over the years I've pictured this, fantasized about it: her body beneath mine, her breath tangled in my breath. She clutches my shirt with her fists, whispers, "Deeper, deeper," and I move up and in, the way I know she likes, and she arches her back, and cries out when she comes, a quick sharp yelp, and I come too, collapsing onto her in tremors, and she's closing on me, holding me in, and it's a moment without doubt or question. There's a reason we didn't die in the pigua. Natalie is smiling, her cheeks glistening with tears. "Don't pull out yet," she whispers. "Stay." She squeezes me in. I feel her heartbeat against my chest, soft and fast like a fluttering bird.

When I finally pull out, I roll over and stretch out on the ground next to her. Through the pomegranate tree branches, the moon swims in and out of clouds. Natalie tilts her hips up and raises her legs, folds her knees into her arms like a fist. I turn on my side, lean on my palm and take all of her in, the curve of her hips, the line of her neck disappearing into her blouse. I'm feeling greedy. I want to follow that line; I want to touch her hair, those black ringlets starting to break free from her head scarf. I want to feel the skin of her breasts, take them in my mouth one last time. I want to at least glimpse them. I slide my hand under her shirt, stroke her warm belly.

She puts a firm hand on mine and shakes her head no.

"I love you," I say.

She smiles like she's sad. "Aw, Lillosh," she says, using the nickname she'd given me. She gets up, buttons the top of her shirt, glides a hand over her skirt, tucks in strands of hair into her head scarf. I memorize her, etching her image into my brain. I know it's the last time I will see her. She bends down beside me and caresses the stubble on my cheek, tipping her head to look at me. "Thank you," she says.

I stay on the ground after she leaves, listening to the roar of her car fading away. I don't remember when the last time was that I lay on the earth, felt its pulse, the heat of the day emanating into my core. I dig into the soil with my nails, let the gritty roughness sift between my fingers. The night air is crisp and still, but my body is vibrating: warm, alive, as if I've been turned inside out. A long time passes and I feel I am becoming a part of this earth, this tree, this night. It feels a little bit like prayer.

SAY IT AGAIN, SAY SOMETHING ELSE

The day Lily meets Lana is her two-week anniversary in Israel. She's lying on her belly in the dried grass outside the apartment building she now calls home, watching insects through her macro lens. She's sweating in her faded blue jeans and Converse high-tops. Then a shadow eclipses her sun.

"You're new here," the girl says. "Where did you come from?"

Lily squints up. Ripped black stockings underneath an acid-washed jean miniskirt. A white sleeveless tank top. Blonde hair in a high ponytail. "Canada," Lily says.

"Cool. We moved here from Belarus two years ago. I'm Lana."

Lily looks up again, this time intrigued. She doesn't know where Belarus is.

"I live at entrance C. You live at B?"

Lily nods. She wonders if the girl is her age. If she'll be starting grade nine in the fall too, if she goes to the same school.

"Aren't you hot in those jeans?" Lana says.

Lily shrugs.

"You should cut them. Make them into shorts."

"I don't wear shorts." Lily presses her eye against the viewfinder. A ladybug navigates her way through giant leaves.

"Can you take photos of me?" Lana says. "I need some portfolio shots, for this modelling agency in Tel Aviv."

Lily clicks the shutter. "I'm not that kind of photographer."

"We can barter," Lana says. "I can cut your hair for you. I'm good at it."

"Why do I need to cut my hair?"

"You can't even see your face like that." She watches Lily. "Do you have a boyfriend in Canada?"

Lily shakes her head.

Lana shifts her balance from one foot to the other. Silvery strappy sandals. Chipped blue nail polish. "Hey, a bunch of us are going to the beach tomorrow. Do you want to come?"

Lily raises herself onto her elbows. "Really? I mean, sure."

"Cool." Lana turns and walks away, into the dark stairway that leads to entrance C.

Up the stairwell to entrance B, Lily lives in a small apartment with her aunt Ruthie and her cousin Talia, who is a soldier in the army and only comes home on weekends. The apartment building—a long, tawny three-storey with three entrances and rows of laundry strung between windows—is opposite a falafel stand that reeks of oil and chickpeas and garlic and cigarette smoke. At night, when the air is juicy and the street lamps paint everything a warm, forgiving colour, men with beer bellies and women with hennaed hair sit on their small balconies, cracking sunflower seeds and spitting the shells into the hibiscus bushes with their red trumpet flowers. Through the open windows of the buildings on the block, Lily can hear TVs blaring and dishes clanking, kids crying and couples fighting and having sex. Teenagers hang out on the metal barricades in front of the building, smoking cigarettes and laughing. Some evenings they bring down narghile pipes and set them on the sidewalk, and the smell of apple tobacco sweetens the night air.

At the end of the street, on the edge of Petah Tikva, a narrow highway leads to Ben Gurion airport. Teardrop-shaped cypress trees line both sides of the road, their tips piercing the sky. All day long, Lily watches planes circle over the neighbourhood of Sha'ariya before landing and wonders if they carry newcomers like her, immigrants like her grandparents once were, having been airlifted from Yemen on a secret operation when Israel was founded. It was the first time they had ever seen an aircraft. Lily imagines them—her grandmother Saida, whom she remembers from previous visits, and her grandfather Salim, whom she's only seen in pictures—holding hands and mouthing prayers as the plane descends toward the Holy Land.

Back when her grandparents arrived, her mom told her, the whole neighbourhood was Yemeni, and even now, with all the new immigrants—Russians and Ethiopians—when Lily walks down certain streets, she still sees old Yemeni ladies just like her grandma sitting on their front porches in large dresses and flowery head scarves. These streets are fragrant with fenugreek and turmeric and coriander, and from the synagogue she can hear men singing prayers in an undulating Yemeni accent she doesn't understand. This is where her mother was born, where she grew up and lived before she moved to Canada. Lily even looks the part. But she feels like a stranger, a tourist.

The next day, Lily wakes up disoriented again, thinking she's still in Vancouver, then is jolted into remembering as her eyes adjust to the white light that floods through the plastic shutters.

She wriggles into a sports bra and steps into her swimming trunks. Ruthie is at work, Talia is back at the base. Lily prepares pita sandwiches with hummus and pickles, washes grapes and stuffs them into a Tupperware container, grabs a water bottle she placed in the freezer the night before. She waits in her room—a small converted balcony with sliding doors that lead to the living room, the glass covered with sheets for privacy. It's small, but Lily likes having three walls of shutters. When she first arrived, she opened the shutters during the day until Ruthie pointed out that the heat is better left outside. Then in the evenings, cockroaches swarmed in and mosquitoes swirled around the lone bulb hanging from the ceiling. She couldn't sleep, hearing them crashing into the walls, buzzing in her ears. Outside, late-night buses growled, crickets chirped, people huddled by the falafel stand, talking and laughing, and the light of the street lamp streamed in, drawing lines of orange on her sheets.

She cried every night for the first week. Missing Vancouver. Missing her life. Missing her mom. It almost felt as if Ima was still alive, just back home in Vancouver. It reminded her of the only time she had been apart from her mother for an extended period, the one time she had visited her dad in Montreal. She only cries when she's alone in bed because she has promised herself she won't cry in front of people. If she's going to make friends in a new school, then she can't be known as the crybaby, the sad girl. In her first year of junior high in Vancouver, she'd been picked on for her boyish clothing and her hair, for hiding behind a camera. She doesn't want to give bullies more reasons to torment her.

By noon Lily thinks: Lana isn't coming. Of course. It was too good to be true. She hooks her camera to her laptop and starts uploading images to her photography blog. She titles them as she goes along. "Splattered oil. Falafel stand." "Friday night. Men on way to synagogue." "Baby chicks behind chain-link fence." "Lemons under tree." "Old Yemeni women on park bench." She scrolls down and looks at older photos. There is a four-month gap where she took no photos at all. After Ima died. And then from the two weeks before she left for Israel there is a flurry of photos, things she wanted to remember from her East Vancouver neighbourhood. "Mountain view from back deck." "Dreadlocked drummers outside Co-op." "My Vancouver aunties"—Ima's four best friends, who took Lily in, rented out the house, arranged her trip to Israel. Lily scrolls back to seven, eight months ago. There's Ima with a shaved head, smiling, hands around a cup of tea, covered in a colourful blanket on their back deck. And even farther back. Biking on Salt Spring Island. The peace rally on Granville Street, Ima holding a big sign that says "Jews for Peace!" The last Thanksgiving at their house. A few years back, Ima had wanted to cook a turkey but didn't know how. "I didn't grow up making it," she cried, and in the end she drove to Hastings Street and donated the uncooked bird to an outreach place, and made enchiladas instead, which had since become tradition. The photo was titled "Thanking the Mexicans."

Lily thinks of the photos she didn't post from that evening. The ones her mother took of her in an A-line, knee-length black skirt she had bought for Lily on a previous visit to Israel. They had gotten into a huge fight in the store. "Just this once," Ima had pleaded with her. "When do I ever ask you for anything?" They had been invited to a Rosh Hashanah dinner with all their relatives; she wanted to make a good impression. When Lily emerged from the change room, her mother beamed. "You look so beautiful," she said and asked Lily to twirl, ignoring her sulking. It was Lily's idea to wear the skirt for Thanksgiving. She knew how happy it would make her mom. A small price to pay.

At 3:00 p.m. Lily turns on the TV and flips channels, fighting tears of frustration. She ignores the honking in the street below, and when it persists, goes to the balcony-turned-bedroom and tilts the slats down to look out. On the parched asphalt Lana stands next to a dusty Fiat, wearing a sheer white dress and a wide-brimmed hat. She's waving.

Lily slides the shutters open along their tracks. "It's late," she yells.

Lana cups her hand over her large sunglasses. "Oh, you haven't been waiting, have you? It's too hot in the day. We always go after four, stay for sunset."

Lily closes the shutters and jogs downstairs. Lana introduces her to Tzion and Igor. Tzion is dark-skinned, Yemeni, with a shaved head and a chunky gold necklace. Igor has longish blond hair and his gangly legs are stuffed into the small space behind the passenger seat. They both smile. Lily hesitates. They seem old, much older than her. "They don't bite," Lana says, pushing the front seat forward.

Lily wiggles into the back seat next to Igor, who cocks his head and ogles her. Lily jerks her head so that her long bangs fall over her eyes. "So how do you like Israel?" Igor says, his Russian accent heavy.

"It's okay." Lily wipes her clammy hands on her swimming trunks and pulls her camera out of her bag. She starts taking photos through the window even though the sun is in the middle of the sky. Rows of buildings with eyes shut, grey, brown and yellow, streaked with black lines like runny ink. The sky is white. Everything is faded by sunlight. Even the trees and the pink bougainvillea seem tired at this time of the day. In Vancouver, the colours were so much brighter, everything cleaner, freshly rained upon.

The beach is crowded and speckled with blue and red umbrellas. Lana pulls her dress over her head, revealing a purple bikini, four triangles tied by strings on her hips and her back. Her hips and collarbones stick out, but her breasts and belly are softly curved. Her skin is white and freckled. She hands Tzion a tube of sunblock and he begins rubbing it on her back in long strokes.

Lily takes off her T-shirt, flings it on the sand and heads toward the water. The white sand is burning her feet, so she starts to run. The beach has always been her favourite thing about Israel. She used to spend long afternoons here with her mother, eating watermelon slices out of a Tupperware container, building elaborate sandcastles with moats and tunnels, decorating them with shells and seaweed. "Wait, I'll come with you," Lana calls after her. They run into large waves that slap their bellies and spray their faces with salt, the white foam hissing as it settles. They turn around and walk backwards, against the waves, until they are past the break. Around them a few couples are kissing, their bodies shiny, their limbs entangled. The water rises with the waves, gently lifting Lily off her feet and setting her back down, the sea floor spiralling around her feet. Lily loves the waves; Vancouver beaches were always so calm. She loves feeling weightless, carried away, tossed around.

"So Igor likes you." Lana rearranges her bikini top.

"He doesn't even know me," Lily says. "Besides, he's too old."

"He's sixteen," Lana says. "I invited him here for you."

"I just wanted to come to the beach," Lily says.

Lana looks at Lily intently, beads of water hanging on her eyelashes. "What, you don't like boys?"

"I didn't say that." Lily starts swimming toward the wave breakers. She feels a current pulling her south, toward Jaffa. She hears the lifeguard's megaphone, instructing bathers to move north, and starts swimming diagonally to compensate for the pull. "Don't go too far," Lana says, trying to catch up.

"I'm going to swim to the wave breakers," Lily says. "You want to come?"

Lana eyes the string of rocks. "Okay," she says. "But if something happens, you'll have to save me."

When they make it to the wave breakers, Lily climbs up first and gives Lana a hand. "Wow, cool," Lana says. "I've never been here before." They stand and watch the Tel Aviv shoreline: the scalloped bays, the row of palm trees along the seawall, the beach cafés with their clumps of blue and green umbrellas, hotels with mirrored windows winking sunlight, and skyscrapers dipped in haze. Then the city descends into the smaller, amber houses of old Jaffa—easily concealed by a thumb—with a spire marking the city's southern edge. To the north, a line of boats clings to the marina. The sounds of the beach—paddle balls hitting rackets, children squealing, the ice cream men yelling—are muffled by the waves and the breeze. On the other side of the wave breakers, the sea is choppy and dark blue, and silhouettes of tiny boats are poised on the thin line between water and sky.

"I can't wait to be old enough to move here," Lana says. "Petah Tikva is a shithole. Wait till you start school."

Lily looks at Lana. "You go to Brenner?"

Lana nods. "The girls were so snobby when I first moved here." She bends down, digging out a handful of seashells and wet sand from between the rocks. "Now I just don't care anymore. Fuck them."

"Yeah," Lily says. "Fuck them." Their eyes meet and both girls smile.

"It's hard, starting in a new place." Lana throws a shell far into the sea, then another. "In Belarus my mother used to be a pharmacist. My father was an engineer. Now he works in security and my mom cleans houses. It's pretty bad here. It's hard to find jobs."

Lily looks down at the glistening rocks, the salt stinging her eyes.

Lana stretches her arm back, then she hurls the remaining shells toward the beach. "What about your parents?"

Lily feels a wet stone sliding down her throat. "My mom is dead," she says. She'll never get used to saying that. "She died six months ago."

Lana puts her hand over her mouth. "Oh my God, I'm sorry. And your dad?"

"He has a new family," Lily says. "I live with my aunt."

Lana stares at Lily, then she leans over and hugs her. Wet skin on wet skin. Lily almost loses her balance.

When they get back to shore, Igor and Tzion are playing paddle ball. "We thought you drowned," Tzion chortles.

"So you just went on playing?" Lana rolls her eyes at Lily. Tzion picks Lana up from behind and threatens to throw her back in the water. She squeals and laughs, kicking her legs in the air. When he puts her down they kiss. Lily notices Igor is watching them too.

Lana wrings out her hair and sits on her towel. She pulls the sunscreen out of her bag, but this time hands it to Lily. Lily coats Lana's warm back with it, mimicking Tzion's motions. When she's done, she grabs her camera and snaps a shot: Lana's back, studded with golden sand, her eyes closed, her blonde hair wet and glued to her cheek. The sun hovers like a red Chinese lantern over the wave breakers. She titles it in her head: "My first Israeli friend."

Lily lets Lana cut her jeans at the knees, but not her hair. In return, she takes photos of Lana one evening before sunset; it's the best time for portraits, she tells her, a time photographers call "sweet light." They hike to the end of Sha'ariya, where the streets abruptly end and yellow fields unfurl until the highway. Lana is comfortable in front of the lens. And she's beautiful. But Lily thinks her poses are too flat, not artsy enough. Lana always looks down at the camera, eyelids heavy, lips moist and slightly open. Still, Lily enjoys playing fashion photographer, enjoys watching Lana through the lens. Sometimes she pretends the flirty gaze is intended for her and she feels a quick, hot, confusing rush.

They hang out at Lily's place because it's always empty. Most days they just watch TV. When they watch American shows, Lana asks Lily to repeat some of the lines in English and then laughs. "You sound just like them."

"Actually," Lily says, "our accents are different."

But Lana just says, "Say it again, say something else."

One afternoon Lana asks to see Talia's room, and Lily opens the door and lets her in. The room is painted lavender and smells vaguely of stale perfume. Posters of Israeli TV stars hang on the walls. Lily cracks the slats open, letting in air and light. Lana passes her hand over Talia's clothes, pulls a green minidress off the rack, holds it to her body in front of the mirror. She picks lipsticks from a wicker basket, testing them on the back of her hand. "What does she do in the army?" she asks.

"She's an instructor in the armoured corps."

Lana looks at Lily through the mirror, eyes lit up. "Does she have a gun?"

Lily nods.

"Cool." Lana applies pink lipstick to her lips, smacking them together.

"Check this out." Lily digs out a shoebox full of photos from the closet, hidden under some winter clothes. Lily found them in her first week while snooping in her cousin's room. Most of the pictures were from childhood, class shots, family vacations, but in the bottom of the box she found a few photos in an unmarked envelope: Talia in lacy red lingerie, holding a rifle between her breasts, looking at the camera seductively. In one of them, she's wearing her cap and saluting. In another, her eyes are closed and she's sending a kiss to the camera, her lips blood-red.

Lana sits on the double bed, which bounces under her weight. She snatches the photos from Lily's hand and flips through them, eyes wide. "Wow, hot."

"You think so?" Lily reaches for the photos but Lana lifts her arm up and away from her.

"You don't think it's sexy?" Lana says. "Not even a little bit?"

"I hate guns," Lily says.

"So what are you going to do if they give you one in the army?"

"I'm not going to go to the army. I'm going to go back to Canada before then." She knows better than to tell Lana that she's a pacifist, or that she doesn't support the Israeli army, or that her mom promised her she'd never have to join. When she first arrived she had said these things to Talia and Talia had stared at her in shock. She's been calling her "Little Arafat" ever since.

"When I first moved here I wanted to go back so badly," Lana says. "I cried every day. But you get used to it. Then you start to love it and you don't want to leave."

But I don't want to get used to it, Lily wants to say. "Whatever," she says instead, stretching her arm to grab the photos, but Lana moves her hand again. She waves the photos over her head, while Lily watches her, waiting. Finally, Lily gets hold of Lana's wrists and pins her down to the bed, kneeling, hovering over Lana's body. "Gotcha," she says.

Lana laughs, letting her hand unclench, and the photos scatter on the bed. Lily releases Lana's wrists, and Lana reaches over and moves Lily's hair from her face. "You're like a boy," she says. "With this hair."

Lily laughs shortly. "No, I'm not."

Lana tucks a strand of Lily's hair behind an ear. "A pretty boy," she says.

Lily doesn't know where she's supposed to look. In her search she meets Lana's eyes briefly and sees in them something like curiosity.

"Have you ever even kissed someone?" Lana says.

"No."

It all happens fast. Lana perches herself on her elbows and plants a kiss on Lily's lips. Lily feels like a wave has just lifted her off her feet and dropped her back to the ground. Lana leans back on the mattress. "Well, now you have."

Lily collects the photos, jumps off the bed and puts them back in the box, hides the box back in the closet. Her fingers are shaking. Her lips taste like lipstick: cherry gum and wax.

"Don't look so shocked." Lana laughs. "It's no big deal."

Lily doesn't see Lana for the next few days, and she wonders if something has changed. She tries calling Lana from downstairs but Lana doesn't answer. Lana has never invited her in.

The days are getting hotter, stickier. Lily didn't think it was possible. She starts taking two or three short cold showers a day, grateful for the tile floors, which Ruthie washes with a bucket of ice water twice a week. Ruthie has bought her a standing fan that she sleeps with now; its whooshing sound reminds Lily of rain. Every evening when Lily sits with her aunt after dinner and watches the tail end of the evening news, the weather forecast is the same. The long country, shaped like a wonky ice cream cone— blue dots like beads on a string on its east side—is littered with smiley suns. Her favourite part of the weather forecast is when the newscaster lists the height of the waves.

On the weekend, Lily sees Lana talking to Tzion on the sidewalk. Tzion has one flip-flopped foot against the barricade. Lily walks over and says hi, and Lana looks up tiredly. She's smoking a cigarette.

"I didn't know you smoked," Lily says.

"So what?" Lana hands Tzion the cigarette.

"Lana," he says, pleading. "Wait."

"Can we go to your place?" Lana says to Lily, sliding her arm through Lily's. "Watch a movie or something?"

"You shouldn't be hanging out with that girl so much," Talia says to Lily later that day as the two of them share watermelon slices in the kitchen. "Her family is fucked."

Lily looks up. "What do you mean?"

"They're messed up." Talia spits a seed onto the plate. "Her dad is a drunk and her mom . . . People saw her walking around with Eli from the grocery store."

"So?"

"These Russian chicks, they come here and take all the men. Israeli men love blondes. The couple next door divorced and two weeks later he moves in with some Natasha."

"She's a pharmacist," Lily says. "And they're not Russians, they're from Belarus."

"What?"

"She's a pharmacist and he's an engineer. It's hard in this country. They can't find jobs. And the language."

Talia stares at Lily for a while and breaks into a grin. "You looove her. Little Arafat is in love."

"No, I'm not." Lily blushes. She gets up and puts her plate in the sink, her face tingling.

The next day, a heat wave travels from Libya and Sudan, draping the city like a down blanket, painting the streets a desert yellow, the houses like sandcastles in the haze. Lana tells Lily that this is the time to hang out in the mall; you can die if you stay outside for too long. Neither of their homes is air-conditioned. While they wait for the bus, standing in the small square of shade behind the bus shelter, Lana says, "If you see someone looking suspicious, even if it seems silly or you're not sure, just tell me and we'll get off the bus. Better to be safe, you know?"

"How can you tell if someone looks suspicious?"

"Well, he has to look like an Arab."

"But how can you tell?"

"What do you mean?"

"In Canada people sometimes thought my mom was an Arab."

"Was she?"

"Well, no, but my grandparents came from Yemen, so we are Arabs in a way, Arab Jews."

Lana laughs. "No, that's impossible. You're either an Arab or a Jew."

"Yeah, but you're a Belarusian Jew. Why can't there be Arab Jews?"

"I'm Israeli now," Lana says. "And so are you."

The bus drops them on the side of a busy road, near a cream-coloured mall. They walk across a large parking lot full of cars, past a man pushing a snake of shopping carts. At the entrance people line up to get their bags checked. Lily flings her backpack forward and unzips it. "Don't bother," Lana says. There is something cold and hard in her voice.

"But . . ."

Lana grabs Lily's hand and leads her through. The security guard doesn't stop them. "Just keep walking," she orders.

Once inside the mall, Lily looks back and sees the security guard staring after them. His eyes look sad.

"What was that?"

"Nothing," Lana says.

"You know him?"

"That's my dad."

"You don't say hello to him?"

"I'm mad at him," she says. "Can we go into the jewellery store?
I want to get some earrings."

They spend a couple of hours wandering through the concourses,
up and down the escalators, and Lily's skin dries and cools, fresh-
ened by the artificial draft. They meander into stores: Lana holds
earrings to her ear, poses in front of the mirror wearing different
hats, Lily tries on sunglasses, browses through magazines. They
stop for frozen yogurt and eat it leaning against the railing, looking over a busy food court surrounding a small fountain.

When they step outside the mall, squinting against the sun, Lana
turns to Lily and says, "Close your eyes."

"Why?"

"Just do it."

She lifts Lily's hair and Lily's skin breaks into goosebumps. She
feels something cool dangling against her chest and Lana's hands
fiddling at the back of her neck. "Okay," she says.

Lily opens her eyes and touches her chest. A silver pendant of a
hand with a blue eye in its centre is hanging from a leather string.
Lily remembers seeing the necklace in the jewellery store. But they
left without buying anything.

"It's a hamsa," Lana says. "It protects you against the evil eye.
Do you like it?"

Lily looks at herself in a store window.

"It's not too girly, is it?" Lana frowns.

"It's perfect," Lily says. "I love it."

Lana pushes down Lily's baseball hat and laughs. She glances
at the entrance to the mall, scans the parking lot and says, "Go
ahead, kiss me."

"Here? People can see us."

"Fuck them." Lana smirks.

Lily leans forward; she has to angle her head so her cap won't get in the way. She touches her lips to Lana's, feels Lana's tongue pushing into her mouth. It tastes like strawberry frozen yogurt. When they part, Lana says, "That was good. You're getting better at it." She walks toward the bus stop, swinging her ponytail from side to side. Lily feels her feet carried up by a wave, but this time she stays suspended, rocking on the surface of the water. She can't believe she just kissed that girl, in the blue dress and the high ponytail, in the middle of this parking lot.

For the next couple of days Lily tastes strawberry frozen yogurt in everything. "Lily and Lana," she mouths to the orange striped sheets at night. "Lana and Lily," she whispers to the bugs crashing against her walls. But after three days of not seeing Lana, her feet hit the ground with a thump. Lily starts to wonder why Lana never comes to the window, why she never invites her over. Why she acts as if nothing has happened.

One afternoon, when Lily goes for a walk with her camera, she sees Lana sitting on a street bench in the park with Igor. They're laughing. Lily is about to wave, but then Igor leans forward and kisses Lana, and Lana wraps her hand around his neck. Lily freezes; she stands and watches them. She wants her feet to move, to take her away, but they're stuck.

At night Lily wakes up to yelling outside her window, a bottle smashing. She slides the shutters open. A man is standing in the ring cast by a street light, wobbling, yelling in Russian toward entrance C. Shards of glass glitter on the asphalt around him. Talia comes to the balcony to look, sits on Lily's bed and leans on the bars. "Not again." She yawns. Lily squints and recognizes the man from the mall. Lana's dad. A few windows rattle open, lights turn on in buildings across the street. A woman's head pokes out of a window above entrance C. She yells back.

Lana steps out in shorts and a T-shirt. Her hair is down. She talks to her dad quietly, tries to touch his hand, but he flings it away from her. Her mom calls to her, but Lana ignores her. Her father continues yelling at the window, and then he swipes his hand across Lana's face. She falls to the ground, palms down. Lily gasps. "Lana," her mother cries. From a balcony across the street a man shouts, "Leave the girl alone!" Lana looks at her hands, bleeding from the shattered glass, and then up at the spectators. She sees Lily and Talia. They both duck.

When Lily looks out again, Lana is gone. A neighbour is talking to her father, a police siren in the background.

The next day Lily calls Lana from downstairs, but Lana doesn't come to the window. In the evening, she sees her from the balcony and quickly opens the shutters and calls her name. Lana hurries inside.

It's the last Friday of August and school is just about to start. Earlier in the day Ruthie took Lily to see her new school and walked her through the empty hallways. There were no lockers; students carry their books from home, stay in the same class-room for the entire day.

Ruthie and Lily walk back from the bus stop, carrying bags of books and school supplies, when they see Lana leaning on a car across the street, chewing gum. She's wearing her blue strapless dress and silvery sandals. She looks like she may be going to the beach, without Lily. Lily pauses at the entrance. "Go." Ruthie waves her on, taking the bags from Lily's hands, and disappears into the dark stairwell. Lily crosses the street. Lana's mom heaves suitcases into the trunk of a car. "Where are you going?" Lily says.

"To stay with my aunt in Rishon for a while," Lana says. She doesn't look Lily in the eye.

"For how long?"

"I don't know."

"What about school?"

Lana shrugs.

"Are you okay?" Lily says. "I've been worried about you."

For the first time, Lana looks up at her.

Lana's mom turns and says something in Russian, and Lana answers without looking at her, sounding annoyed. Her mom sighs and walks across the street and into the building. Lily pushes her hands into the pockets of her jeans and kicks the curb. "I saw you," she says. "The other day. With Igor in the park."

"So?" Lana says.

Lily looks down at her shoes. "So nothing."

"Oh my God," Lana says slowly. "You're jealous." She starts laughing. "That's so cute."

Lily doesn't remember walking away. She has to move fast because her tears are coming. She bumps into Lana's mom on the way, mumbles sorry in English, runs up the stairs but doesn't enter the apartment. She sits on a cool tiled stair in the dim stairwell and cries. The door opens and the sensor light above her turns on. "Lily," Ruthie says. "There you are. I was just going to get milk."

Lily nods at the floor, wiping her tears with her forearm.

Ruthie sits down beside her and searches her face. "Are you okay?"

Despite herself, Lily bursts into tears again.

"Oh, sweetie." Ruthie pulls Lily to her and pats her head, rocking her lightly. "She's no good," she says. "That girl."

Lily says nothing. She's heard it all from Talia. She doesn't need to hear it again.

"You can do a lot better," Ruthie says quietly, and this time Lily looks up. In her aunt's eyes she sees warmth, recognition. Blood rushes to her cheeks. She buries her face in Ruthie's shirt, breathing in the scent of coffee and spices.

They sit on the step for a while without talking. Sometimes the light turns on and then clicks off, leaving them in darkness. Sometimes people squeeze past them, going up or down the stairs. They hear muffled laughter behind closed doors, a scooter speeding off down the street. Evening shadows sneak into the stairway, the smells of dinners and cigarette smoke. Lily doesn't move.

"It's okay," Ruthie says. "It's okay."

BRIT MILAH

At the passport check, Reuma Hamami pulled out a folded piece of paper from her purse and handed it to the woman behind the counter. The woman was young, with narrow eyes, Chinese perhaps, and her black, shiny hair was rolled into a neat bun. Her face was caked with dusty powder and her eyebrows were pencilled on. She looked up and eyed Reuma. "English?"

"Little," Reuma said. She reached and pointed at the paper. "My daughter."

"Your daughter lives in Toronto?"

"Yes." Reuma nodded.

The woman flipped through the pages in Reuma's passport, filled with stamps from the organized trips Reuma had been taking over the past three years with a group of women from her neighbourhood of Sha'ariya, many of them widowed like her, all of them Yemeni.

"First time in Canada?"

Reuma nodded again. Ofra had been living here for seven years, but she had been visiting Israel regularly. There had never been a reason for Reuma to come before. In fact, Ofra had been home just a few months ago, in her second trimester, and Reuma proudly showed her off around the neighbourhood, walked with her down Petah Tikva's main street. In the evenings they had sat in the yard and drunk tea, and Reuma finally got a chance to pass on some of her knowledge. She had raised four children after all. When her daughters-in-law had given birth, Reuma had learned to be quiet, keep her advice to herself, especially after Rami, her eldest, accused her of being overbearing. They had their own mothers to consult. But Ofra listened to her, didn't dismiss her advice as she had in the past, seemed softened by the pregnancy, more forgiving toward her mother.

"Born in Yemen?" The woman looked at Reuma. Reuma noticed a small golden cross dangling against her chest.

"Yes."

The woman's lips tightened, she tilted her head to read some of the stamps. She thinks I'm an Arab, Reuma thought and hurried to add, "Jewish." She looked around for something that would help her explain. "Me . . . baby." She lowered her hand to indicate her height. "Go to Israel with Mother and Father."

The woman flipped another page.

Reuma wanted to make conversation, to tell her that she rented the shed in the back to people from China, but she didn't know the words. Growing up she'd never seen Chinese or blacks in Israel, but now they were everywhere, migrant workers who were fill-ing positions Israelis were too lazy for, jobs Palestinians used to have before the intifada, and Yemenis before them, in Israel's early days, when she and her parents first arrived in Sha'ariya: cleaning homes, washing dishes, picking oranges.

The woman stamped her passport, and Reuma thanked her and continued through tunnels and up escalators to the conveyor belt.

As Reuma waited for her suitcase, she imagined meeting Yonatan, her new grandson. For years she had waited anxiously for Ofra to get pregnant, but had been careful not to pressure her, since any attempt at broaching the subject had led to arguments. Speaking with Ofra had never been easy for Reuma; she used to envy Shaul: with her father Ofra was loving, warm, receptive.

But things had been better between the two of them since Ofra had gotten married, and better still with her pregnancy. Reuma remembered how much closer she had become with her own mother after she had Rami. She was thrilled when Ofra and Matthew asked her if she would come and stay with them for the first little while after the baby was born, glad to be of help, to be needed. She could picture it: once it was time for Reuma to leave, Ofra would realize just how much she needed her mother, and she would beg Matthew to move back to Israel. Reuma had seen it happen. Recently her niece—her sister, Shoshi's daughter— moved back from Miami following childbirth, giving up a good- paying job and a big house, just so that she could be near her mother. Reuma had it all planned: Ofra and Matthew could have the house, the three-bedroom bungalow where she and Shaul had raised Ofra and her three brothers, and which recently had been repainted, the fifties-style tiles in the bathroom replaced with new cream-coloured ones, and Reuma would move to the rental unit in the back, where the Chinese workers now lived. She could help babysit, cook and clean. Matthew was a naturopath; Reuma knew there was a demand for his line of work in high places in

Tel Aviv, where people might not even mind him speaking English.

Finally, she recognized her suitcase, the pink ribbon she had fastened on its handle, and she dragged it onto a cart and followed the exit signs. When she made it out of the arrivals gate, she was disappointed to see Matthew standing alone, his coat open to reveal a plaid shirt, his beard now grown, but his hair starting to recede. In his arm he held a puffy coat he handed Reuma. "Ofra was busy," he said, rocking an imaginary baby in front of his chest. She beamed and nodded. Matthew leaned over and kissed her on both cheeks, his glasses colliding with hers. "Good to have you," he said, and Reuma smiled, unsure of the meaning of this phrase. She was frustrated by her inability to speak to Matthew, whom she liked from the moment Ofra had first brought him home for Rosh Hashanah three years ago. From the way he looked at her daughter, tended to her, Reuma could tell that he was a good man, and strong enough to deal with Ofra's temperament. She had always worried for her daughter: she was an opinionated woman, too smart for her own good and a complete failure in the kitchen. Reuma had tried to teach her how to make her spicy schug, bake jichnoon for Shabbat, cook Yemeni soup, but Ofra wasn't interested. Reuma envied her sister, Shoshi, whose daughters borrowed recipes from their mother and even confided in her about their marital problems. Ofra never spoke to her about such things, had waited until she was thirty-eight to have a child, and had finally married Matthew at city hall a few months ago, already visibly pregnant in a white, shapeless dress, her hair loose and curly and her lips carelessly drawn in red, matching a pair of red high-heeled shoes. "At least they're married." Shoshi threw her hand up in dismissal when Reuma showed her the photo and sighed. "Today, some young people don't even bother. Look at Tsila's daughter. Even had children. God help us."

They paused before the glass doors, the mass of blinding whiteness outside, and Matthew waited as Reuma put on the large, puffy coat that went down to her knees, arranging the furry hood over her head. She tightened her scarf, put on gloves. She had only ever seen snow in Jerusalem, when she and Shaul had been on vacation, and there—crowning the ancient stone buildings, the tips of cypress trees, the surrounding hilltops—it had seemed magnificent, romantic. Toronto was covered with patches of white, which from the air looked to Reuma as though erased, as though parts of the city were missing.

"Ready?" Matthew asked. "Ready," she repeated, ashamed of how clumsy the word sounded, her *r* flat, the stress placed on the wrong part of the word. The doors swished open and they were out, the cold assaulting her face, stabbing her exposed calves.

She followed Matthew to the car, squinting against the bright, thin light, the greyness of the sky. She sat in the front, smiling at the baby seat in the back. After a few minutes, warm air started blowing from the vents. Matthew didn't speak to her beyond asking if the flight was good and if she was tired. Reuma wondered if he intended on learning any Hebrew, now that he had an Israeli son. She wondered too if Matthew would agree to move to Israel. He often told her how much he loved Israel, and at least he had an Ashkenazi name, Levin, even if he wasn't completely Jewish. Out of her four children, not a single one of them had married a Yemeni. When she looked at her grandchildren she was sometimes surprised. Itay's daughter, Lilach, had golden curls and grey eyes. Elad's son, Itamar, had skin even fairer than his mother's. She was delighted when Ofra said, "Yonatan's a real Yemeni," and when Reuma saw photos she began to tear up. Her grandchild reminded her of her dead husband.

They drove on a multi-lane highway through a graceless

monochrome landscape, the view dirtied by slush, spat on their windshield by passing cars, then wiped clean, the wiper blades squeaking rhythmically over the glass. The road curved, hugging the shore of a silvery lake, and the city skyline emerged, jutting out of the earth and moving rapidly toward them. Matthew took an exit, and they were on a busy street with two-storey buildings coloured reds and blues, small quaint stores and cafés, their windows painted over with snowflakes and Santa Clauses, chains of blinking lights framing their edges.

Their house was just off the main street, long and narrow and wedged between two other houses, with snow on its turret roof, like something out of a fairy tale. The trees that lined the street were stripped naked, their branches bowed over, weighed down by a thick layer of snow. Reuma stepped out of the car and her boots squeaked on the sidewalk. "Careful," Matthew said, and mimicked losing his balance. "Very slippery." He carried her bags as she walked up the stairs, holding on to the cold railing. Ofra swung the door open with her arms wide and Reuma fell into them, inhaling the baby and breast milk smell of her.

"You look good," Reuma said, though Ofra was clearly tired, her curly hair unwashed and gathered into a messy bun, her complexion faded by winter.

"I'm so happy you're here," Ofra said. "Matthew's mom just left yesterday but . . . it's not the same."

"Matthew's mom?" Reuma felt a stab of jealousy. "I thought she didn't live in Toronto."

"She doesn't," Ofra said. "She came from Winnipeg for two weeks."

"Where is he?" Reuma looked around.

"Come." Ofra smiled as if holding a secret. Reuma followed her up the narrow carpeted stairs to their bedroom, where Yonatan slept in his crib. "My God." Reuma's eyes filled with tears.

"Isn't he handsome?" Matthew whispered, poking his head in between mother and daughter.

"Bli ayin hara," Reuma said. "Ugly, ugly. You shouldn't call a baby beautiful. It brings bad luck." She smiled, as if aware of how silly this might sound. "I also brought a hamsa you can hang over his bed."

"Okay," Ofra said. "Later."

Downstairs, her daughter made her tea with fresh mint, served with what Reuma suspected were store-bought cookies. Matthew had left to run errands. "I even bought you Nescafé," Ofra said proudly.

"I brought food too," Reuma said, bending down to unzip her suitcase, unleashing the sour smell of Yemeni spices.

"Ima," Ofra said. "You shouldn't have."

"Of course I should have." Reuma pulled out a jar of green, spicy schug, some jichnoons wrapped in foil, and a bag of savoury ka'adid cookies, dotted with black nigella seeds. "And some Hebrew magazines," Reuma said, handing Ofra women's and parenting magazines, "to read when you breastfeed."

"Thanks, Ima." Ofra leaned over to hug her, and took the food into the kitchen.

Snow had started to fall, soundless and slow, sticking to the glass and then sliding down. The fogged-up windows were decorated with a chain of flickering Christmas lights. A Hanukia covered with hardened wax drippings stood on the windowsill. Reuma could tell that someone had made an effort to tidy up, but there was still a layer of dust on the furniture, Ofra's hairs tangled in the carpet. She had her work cut out for her.

When Ofra returned, she told Reuma of Yonatan's sleep patterns, his eating habits, his rashes, his dandruff, his gas, and Reuma asked questions and made suggestions—olive oil for the dandruff, tomato juice for the gas—feeling like an authority, an expert.

"I forgot, I brought some baby clothes too." Reuma hurried to pull the clothes, wrapped in tissue paper, from her suitcase. "And this is from Shoshi, and wait, I have some from your sisters-in-law too."

"So how's everybody?" Ofra said. "How are you?"

"Getting old." Reuma sighed. "Soon you'll have to hire me a Filipina, or maybe put me in a home."

"Stop it," Ofra said. "You're only sixty-eight. Your mother lived to be a hundred."

"Or you can come back and live with me, because your brothers sure aren't going to."

Ofra just smiled.

Reuma told her about her brothers, how things hadn't been so good between Itay and his wife lately, how Rami hadn't been over for weeks, and Elad's daughter had been diagnosed with learning disabilities. She shared the neighbourhood news: Arnon the butcher had passed away, Shlomo, their neighbour, had already remarried and it hadn't even been a year. She was going to wait to tell her about Shoshi's daughter and her recent move home, but she got carried away, describing the new villa they were building on their grandparents' lot in Sha'ariya, how happy Shoshi had been since she came back. Petah Tikva was changing too, she said; it was no longer just a sleepy suburb. They even had sushi there now, a Japanese food young people raved about, and good cafés with the espresso drinks Ofra used to go to Tel Aviv to get.

Reuma paused, noticing her daughter yawning behind her hand. "You should sleep too," Reuma said. "If the baby is sleeping . . ."

"Yes," Ofra said. "Let me get you set up."

The guest room's walls were dark blue, the trim a glossy white. A desk with a computer was placed under the window, and a corkboard covered with photos hung on the wall next to it: Ofra and Matthew clinking wine glasses around a patio table with people Reuma didn't know; the two of them holding hands on some white-sand beach; a black-and-white photo of Ofra pregnant, wearing a sheer white dress that made Reuma uncomfortable. Outside, the snow was thickening, hiding bushes and fences under a soft blanket. Reuma stood by the window and tried to imagine what was underneath the snow, what the large shape in the corner of their backyard was, how deep the lawn was buried. She lay down on the sofa bed, just to rest her eyes, and fell into an easy sleep.

She woke up to the baby crying and lay in bed for a minute, adjusting to her surroundings. The room was dark. She glanced at the clock radio. She had napped for an hour and though it was only just after four, the daylight was already gone. She walked out of the room and saw that the door to her daughter's bedroom was ajar. The baby was lying in his crib, kicking and crying. She heard the shower running. "Hello, sweetheart." Reuma picked Yonatan up and placed him against her chest, rocking him and tapping him lightly on his back. "My eyes, my soul." She kissed his face, his neck, inhaling his smell, and then lifted him and smelled his diaper. "You made poo-poo?" she said, laying him on the chest of drawers.

Ofra rushed out of the shower, wrapping her body with a towel as she walked over, her hair dripping a wet trail along the floor.

"Finish your shower," Reuma said. "Why am I here? I can do this. He needs changing."

"He's hungry." Ofra extended her arms, and Reuma reluctantly handed her Yonatan. Ofra sat on the unmade bed and gave him a nipple. He latched on to it.

Reuma started collecting clothes from the floor.

"You don't have to do that," Ofra said.

"I want to help."

"You just got here."

"I can do things. At least I can help with the baby."

Ofra sighed.

"Something's wrong?" Reuma said, heart pounding.

"No."

"With the baby? With you?"

"No. Well, there is something we need to talk about, but we can do it later, over dinner. But nothing is wrong."

"Did you let Matthew's mom change him?" Tears welled up in Reuma's eyes.

"Fine." Ofra took Yonatan from her breast and handed him to her mom. "Change him." Yonatan started to fuss.

Reuma looked at her daughter with suspicion.

"Go ahead."

Reuma placed the crying Yonatan on her shoulder and soothed him, whispering words of comfort. Then she laid him on the chest of drawers, buried her face in his belly, cooed at him. Yonatan stopped crying and watched her, intrigued. She lifted his legs up with one hand and pulled the diaper off. She drew a wipe from a box on the chest and cleaned his bum. Then she saw it, a ring of foreskin around her grandchild's tiny penis, a shrivelled mushroom. She stared at it, counting days. It had been over four weeks.

"You haven't done brit milah yet?" She looked up.

Ofra shook her head no.

"Was there a problem? Did the doctor say to wait?"

Ofra tucked a wet curl behind her ear. "We decided not to do it."

Reuma stared at her, letting the boy's legs down. He started crying. "I don't understand."

"We don't think it's necessary."

"Not necessary," Reuma repeated.

"Ima—" Ofra started.

"He's Jewish," Reuma said. Yonatan's cries grew louder and she turned to him, raised his legs and slid the diaper underneath, working in urgent motions. "Of course it's necessary."

"Why?"

"Because . . . because this is what you do. You don't think about it. You just do it."

"That's not a reason. Why hurt him?"

"Because it's tradition. Because it's what Jews do. And it's also more hygienic and healthy . . ."

"That's not actually true." Ofra spoke quietly, calmly. "And I know other Jews who haven't circumcised. It's traumatic for the child. I won't put him through it."

"But you have to." Reuma raised her voice. "Who heard of such a thing? A Jewish boy, uncircumcised? Have you lost your mind?"

"Maybe we should talk about it later." Ofra stood up, tightening the towel over her chest. "I printed something for you to read."

"You think I wanted to hurt your brothers? I had to close my eyes to not see how they cried. No mother wants to do it. You just do." Reuma remembered how faint she had felt when Rami was screaming, his face turning dark red. She had run to the wash-room, sobbing until she heard the ululating sounds of the women and knew that it was done. It didn't become easier with the second or third. But did she ever question it?

"But Ima, I'm not religious . . ."

"Religious or not, it's tradition. Your brothers aren't religious." Ofra sighed.

"I won't allow it. You should be ashamed of yourself." She lifted Yonatan and planted him in her daughter's hands. He kicked his legs and smiled at her. She looked away. "I won't hold him," she said. "I won't."

Ofra stared at her in shock. "You can't be serious."

Reuma stormed out of the room and down the stairs.

"Ima," Ofra called after her. "Wait."

She put on the coat, slid her feet into her boots, wrapped a scarf around her face and walked out the front door. The cold felt like an icy slap. Where was she going? Street lights shone cone-shaped beams on the road, and Christmas lights—dangling from porches and draped over evergreen trees—warmed up the whites, blues and greys. The snow was piled high, blurring the borders of things, turning the sidewalks into narrow tunnels. Her tears froze on her face.

Reuma had prided herself on moving with the times, unlike some Yemeni women from the neighbourhood who held on to the old ways, resisted modern appliances, still dressed as though they were in Yemen. Many years ago, when Shaul was still alive, Reuma had taken off the head scarf and learned how to drive; she even drove on Shabbat. She hadn't asked questions about Matthew's other half, the non-Jewish part, and she had always been proud of her daughter, saw it as a sign of her own progress and success, that despite Reuma growing up with illiterate parents and never earning a high school diploma, she'd raised a daughter so smart, so successful. Shoshi's daughters may have married young, but her own daughter had a Ph.D., which she had acquired in Canada, in English.

But this was too much.

She pulled the scarf up to cover her stinging nose. She saw the lights of a café on the corner. She just had to make it there.

She missed Shaul now, grief gnawing at her as though she'd just lost him yesterday. What would he have done? Shaul, who went to synagogue every Friday, out of habit more than religious duty, his time with the men a reprieve from her and the kids. He watched TV on Shabbat, turned on appliances. He would have been able to talk some sense into Ofra. Perhaps she would have circumcised Yonatan had Shaul been alive; she had always wanted to please him. And when Shaul and Reuma fought—and they had fought endlessly when they were younger—Ofra had always taken his side, always blamed her mother. "You and Shaul are fire and fire," Reuma's mother used to say. "You have to give up every now and then, let him be a man. You're pushing him away." Later, in their older days—both mellowed and tired of conflict—they had become best friends again. But Ofra was living away by then, in Tel Aviv and then Toronto. She only remembered the bad times.

Reuma finally made it to the café, her coat speckled with white and her glasses steamed up. She stood at the entrance, blind, then found a seat by the window and heaved herself onto it. Thinking of Shaul here, in this faraway, cold place, made her feel lonely. Perhaps she *had* pushed him away. Maybe she had pushed Ofra away too. Across the world. Maybe it had all been her fault. When Ofra was thirteen, she had accused Reuma of treating the boys differently. "Why do I have to help with the dishes after dinner? Why do they just get to sit and watch TV?" Reuma's mother, still alive, smiled at Reuma and said in Yemeni, "This one is like hot pepper. Worse than you." Years later, she had overheard her daughters-in-law complaining that their husbands didn't raise a finger at home, didn't know how, that it was Reuma's fault, she had done everything for her boys. "Poor Ofra," one had said. "Can you imagine?" It was true: Reuma had been harder on Ofra, but she'd done it for her own good. She had thought she was preparing Ofra for marriage, the same way her own mother had done for her.

A streetcar rumbled outside, and then stopped across the street, letting passengers off onto the slushy road. The same year that Ofra had accused Reuma of favouring her sons, she had invited her aunt Miri, Shaul's younger sister, to Mother's Day in junior high—a school on the other side of town, where kids from an affluent neighbourhood, most of them Ashkenazi, were integrated with Yemeni kids from Sha'ariya. The teacher had called to inquire about Reuma's health because Ofra had said that she was ill. Soon after that, Ofra stopped eating Reuma's food—Reuma found the sandwiches she had prepared for her in the garbage. "It smells funny," Ofra said. "Kids make fun of me." It wasn't just Reuma she had rejected: she despised anything Yemeni, even her curls, which she began straightening every morning. She even changed the way she spoke; as a little kid she spoke like her parents, with guttural hets and ayins. Reuma lost her daughter over and over again: first she became Ashkenazi, then Canadian; it was in her melody of speaking, the polite words she'd started peppering her sentences with, the way she smiled at passersby on the street. Reuma had heard her speaking on the phone to her friends, and then to Matthew, in English, laughing in English. A stranger. And now she was no longer Jewish.

Ofra burst into the café, her cheeks flushed. "My God, Ima, you scared me half to death. Let's go home."

"No." Reuma crossed her arms against her chest, not looking at her daughter.

"We planned a special dinner for you," Ofra pleaded. "And I need you here. Please."

Reuma stared out the window.

"Let's at least talk about it," Ofra said.

Reuma watched a woman decorating a Christmas tree at a store across the street, hanging sparkly ornaments on its branches. She looked around the café, the young people hunched over their blue laptop screens, the steam rising from the coffee machine behind the bar. She got up and put her coat on.

They walked the two blocks silently, the wind whistling between them, their faces buried in their scarves. Everyone they passed was bundled up, faceless, anonymous figures. What a lonely place to live, Reuma thought.

The warmth of the house enveloped them. Matthew peeked out from the kitchen and smiled. Reuma hurried in, scowling in his direction, and climbed up the stairs to her room.

Ofra followed her. "Don't be mad at Matthew. We made this decision together."

Reuma scoffed. "He's not even Jewish."

"Who? Yonatan? Of course he is."

Reuma jerked her chin toward Matthew in the kitchen. "What's half-Jewish? You and I both know there's no such thing."

Ofra gave her a hard look. "He was raised Jewish. He feels Jewish."

"Doesn't matter. According to the Halacha he's not Jewish."

"Since when did you become a rabbi?"

"Is that why you married in city hall? Like the goyim?" Reuma felt as if she couldn't stop. "You'd never think not to do brit on your own."

"That's not true," Ofra said. "I've been thinking about it for years. I've done a lot of research. You know, I prayed for a daughter just so I wouldn't have to deal with this."

"It's not right." Reuma sat on the bed, inconsolable. "Your father would have never accepted it."

Ofra looked down. "I know."

"He would have been furious at you."

"Ima, you're acting like it's the end of the world. If you just took some time . . ."

"It is." Reuma shook her head. "It is."

"But we're happy, I'm happy. I have a son, a family, a home. How can you not see that?"

"What am I going to say to people?" Reuma started crying again.

Ofra sighed at the ceiling. "Who cares?"

Reuma glared at her.

"Fine, then lie."

Reuma looked at the photos on the corkboard, the strangers hugging her daughter, the photo of Ofra in the sheer dress. It was as though she didn't know her daughter at all. What a fool she had been to think this trip would bring them closer.

From the kitchen she heard water running, dishes clattering. The smell of cooking permeated the room, growing familiar: turmeric and chilies, cumin and garlic. "What are you making?" Reuma said, her hunger awakening.

Ofra smiled. "Matthew wanted to surprise you."

"Matthew?"

"He's been making Yemeni soup every Friday. He even learned to make jichnoon. We have a whole Yemeni dinner planned."

"Matthew cooked?"

Ofra nodded. "He got some recipes from Shoshi—"

"From Shoshi?" Reuma cried. "You should have gotten them from me."

"Then it wouldn't have been a surprise, would it?" She looked at Reuma. "Are you okay?"

Reuma didn't answer. She looked at her lap, twirling her wedding ring on her finger. Ofra hesitated, then placed her hand on Reuma's shoulder and squeezed. She left, her footsteps tapping on the stairs.

Reuma remained seated a moment longer, then went to the washroom to wash her face. She looked at herself in the mirror; her eyes were red, her skin blotched from crying. She threw water on her face, then pinched and patted her cheeks.

Downstairs, Ofra was setting the table with Yonatan strapped to her chest. Matthew poured salt into the soup and smiled at her over his shoulder. Any other time she would have been pleased by the pungent tang of Yemeni spices in her daughter's kitchen, by the familiar spread on the table: a finely chopped vegetable salad, a bowl of schug, the cilantro in it smelling fresh, as though it had just been prepared, and even a bowl of hilbe, a spicy fenugreek paste none of her daughters-in-law had ever learned to make. But now Reuma slid into a chair, not offering to help, her hands resting in her lap. She couldn't help it; knowing it hadn't been her daughter who prepared the meal soured it for Reuma. These recipes had been passed down through the women of their family for generations.

"Thank you, honey." Ofra walked by and kissed Matthew on the cheek. "It looks amazing." She turned to her mother and said in Hebrew, "Can you believe how lucky I am? And wait till you taste his jichnoon."

"You know," Reuma couldn't resist. "My mother always said that women's hands are better for kneading dough."

Ofra raised an eyebrow.

"It's true," Reuma continued. "Our hands are naturally colder. Men's hands are too warm."

Ofra smiled, saying nothing.

Finally Matthew placed a bowl of steaming yellow soup in front of her, his face open and expectant. Reuma examined the soup. It looked right: a shiny film on top, a yellow chicken drumstick, a carrot, half a potato, wilted stems of cilantro. She raised a spoonful of it to her mouth, feeling the urge to criticize—it could have used more garlic, less turmeric—but holding herself back. It tasted different, but it was fresh and spicy.

"So?" Ofra said.

"It's good." She nodded, reluctantly, and Matthew grinned, recognizing the word.

Reuma said nothing until she finished the soup. Then she pushed away her bowl and leaned back, letting the heat settle in her stomach. Her daughter sat across the table, nursing Yonatan. Reuma knew she had to give it one last try. She owed it to Shaul, at least. "So what's going to happen if you come back?" she said.

Ofra looked up. "Come back?"

"Did you ever think about what's going to happen to Yonatan then? And in the army? He'll always be different than the other boys. Everyone will make fun of him."

Matthew glanced up from his plate quickly, tensely. Ofra looked at her as if she was studying her. "I'm not coming back, Ima."

"Not now, but maybe later."

"No, Ima."

"How can you be so sure?"

"I'm sure. We're sure. This is my home now."

"But you're alone here."

"We have good friends," she said. "We have Shabbat dinners with them."

"You have Shabbat dinners?"

Ofra nodded. "Every week."

Reuma felt more confused than ever. "It's not like having a mom here. To help you."

"Then come here, stay with us. Live with us."

Reuma stared at her daughter in disbelief.

"You can stay in the guest room," Ofra said and Matthew nodded. Perhaps he understood Hebrew more than she thought.

"And leave my sister and my friends? And your brothers?"

"It's up to you," Ofra hurried to say. "Even just for a while. I could really use your help."

The snow was falling heavily now. Every time Reuma looked outside she was taken aback. She tried imagining herself living here but could not picture it. She wondered how the city looked in the summer, couldn't fathom how this bleak landscape could possibly come to life again, though she knew that the trees would turn green and the flowers would bloom. Ofra had told her the summers were hot, sometimes as hot as they were in Israel.

"Beautiful, isn't it?" Ofra followed her gaze. "I just love this time of the year. It's magic. I can't wait for Yonatan to grow up, so we can make snowmen and snow angels . . ." She looked at Yonatan and her face softened, her tone changed. "Buy you a tiny little snowsuit."

Reuma looked at her, surprised: Ofra was smitten with the

weather, with the naked trees, with the season; she felt at home in this cold, strange country. Reuma felt a sharp, quick pinch in her heart. Her daughter wasn't coming home.

Matthew cleared the table and Reuma watched as he began loading the dishwasher, wiping the counters, a towel thrown over his shoulder as Reuma always did. Sleep was tugging at her. "You said you know other Jews who . . . didn't," Reuma said. "How did their families react?"

Ofra glanced at Matthew. "In different ways. Some didn't mind. One friend's family didn't speak to him for two years."

"You see?" Reuma said.

"What do I see? Is that what you want, Ima? They're talking to him now, and they missed two years of their grandson's life."

Reuma leaned on the table, picking at a hardened turmeric stain on the white tablecloth. "I just . . . I don't even know what to think. I can't accept this."

Ofra levelled a tired look at her mother. "So what do you want, Ima?"

"I want you to circumcise him," Reuma said, taken aback by the question. What she wanted was off the table; she wanted to rewrite everything, she wanted the story she had told herself when she was younger, growing old with Shaul, with her family around her, sharing recipes with her only daughter, watching her grandson being circumcised in an event hall by the same Yemeni mohel who had circumcised her children, celebrating the birth at their local synagogue, among friends and family.

"Well, that's not going to happen," Ofra said sharply. "Now what?"

Reuma thought of Shaul. Though he had always been quicker to lose his temper, he was also first between the two of them to calm down. It was Reuma who held a grudge, who struggled to forgive. She wondered if she had it all wrong. Yes, Shaul would have been furious, disappointed, heartbroken, for weeks, maybe months. He would have yelled, slammed doors, and Reuma would have had to beg him to take it easy. "Your heart," she would have said. "Your health." But then it would have been him who would have forgiven his daughter first, his baby girl. He would never have been able to keep it up.

"I don't know," Reuma finally said. She looked up, stunned into silence when she saw that her daughter's face was wet.

Yonatan let go of his mother's nipple, hanging off her arm while Ofra wiped her tears with the back of her hand. She had hardly touched her soup. "Here." Reuma stood up and stretched her arms out to her daughter. "You eat." Ofra looked up and her face brightened. She handed her Yonatan over the table. "Hello, my soul." Reuma looked at Yonatan's face and saw her husband, the dimple in his chin, the wide nose, the dark complexion. "You look just like your granddad," she said, her eyes watering. Yonatan flapped his arms. "Who's Grandma's little angel?" she whispered. She placed him on her shoulder, the weight of his little body against her familiar and comforting.

THE POETS IN THE KITCHEN WINDOW

The missiles started falling on Tel Aviv on the night of January 17, a few hours after Operation Desert Storm began in Iraq. They had been prepared, carrying their gas masks with them everywhere for weeks: cardboard boxes with dangling straps, like purses, which some girls in Uri's class had decked out with stickers and collages. At school they had run drills, with everyone sitting in a row on the floor, leaning against the wall, elbowing each other and giggling. None of them had ever sat in shelters, had ever even heard a siren. The only war in their lifetime had been the Lebanon War, which erupted in 1982, when Uri was four, and had never really ended. From images he saw on the news, Uri knew that people up north had sat in shelters, knew soldiers had died, even a classmate's brother, but in Ramat Gan, the suburban town where he lived, hours away from the border, it was sometimes easy to forget.

When the first siren sounded, Uri thought it was a part of a dream. He had been dreaming about wars a lot lately; dreams where he was taller and braver and Ashkenazi, his skin lighter, his eyes blue, like one of those black-and-white pictures of soldiers he had seen in history books, tears glistening in their eyes after they'd liberated Jerusalem. Uri knew the exact day those pictures were taken: June 7, 1967. He had memorized those dates for his school exam, mapping the history of the country through a string of military operations, neatly spaced, one for every decade: the War of Independence in '48, Operation Kadesh in '56, the Six Day War in '67, the Yom Kippur in '73.

As Uri watched the sepia movies his teacher had screened in history class, the stiff, clownish, fast-moving soldiers waving from tanks and marching in the streets, he wished he had been born earlier, back before independence, when the pioneers had built kibbutzim and paved roads and hid weapons and rebelled against the British, when soldiers cried at the Wailing Wall and there was a purpose, a greater meaning, a larger battle. It seemed like everything of significance had happened before he was born. In his last year of elementary school, he had written a poem about it, titled "Other Wars," which had won his school poetry contest, earning him publication in the school paper and a month of mockery from the boys in his grade, who recited parts of it with a lisp and substituted the word *fag* every time *war* appeared in the poem.

That first night, Uri sat on his parents' bed with his dad, their gas masks pressing red marks around their faces. Uri had fastened the straps so tight that his chin ached. They had sealed the room a few days earlier: covering the windows with heavy-duty plastic sheeting and duct tape like the IDF spokesman had instructed on TV, storing food, water and board games in the closet. Now they stared at the screen, where a blonde, smiling woman demonstrated strapping on a gas mask, placed a mild-mannered baby in a plastic crib, soothing him through a transparent sleeve. The mask smelled of rubber, like a new toy, and Uri could hear his breathing as though he were underwater. He thought of his mother, wondering if they had sealed her room at the hospital, if the nurses made sure she wore her gas mask. He hoped that her room was high up, where the gas was unlikely to reach. When she was first admitted, his father had told him that she was on a retreat. When Uri figured it out—overhearing hushed phone conversations—his father said that his mother couldn't have any visitors, but he knew his father visited and his aunt once asked him if he'd been yet. Secretly, he was relieved not to have to visit his mother. It had been hard enough to be around her those few weeks before she left.

When the first missile hit, Uri's heart lurched in his chest like a jerked knee. His father—looking like a frightened giant ant—wrapped his arm around him and pulled him closer. Five or six more explosions echoed in the distance, sounding like fireworks on Independence Day, or a fighter jet that had broken the sound barrier. And then one more, closer this time; the seventh-floor apartment walls shuddered with the reverberation. Uri's body was tense, his jaw clenched, but it was the kind of fear that put things into proportion, making every other fear he'd ever felt—of failing a test in school, of jumping headfirst into the swimming pool, of embarrassing himself in front of Avital Ginsberg (back when he used to like her, which he no longer did)—seem trivial. It was the kind of fear that made him stronger, a man.

The following day, Yasmin called. It was a cool, sunny January morning, the air as crisp as broken glass, and Uri and his father sat on the couch in their living room, watching the IDF spokesman on TV. The missiles had fallen in and around Tel Aviv, the spokesman said, pushing his squared glasses over the bridge of his nose. None of the missile heads was chemical, and there were no casualties. He urged everyone to stay at home and keep calm. Then they cut to shots of panicked crowds lining up at Ben Gurion airport.

"I'm coming home," Yasmin said. The line crackled and her words echoed faintly.

Uri's heart gave a little start: surprise, delight, anticipation. Then he remembered that he was still mad at her. "When?" he said coolly, turning away from his father's outstretched arm.

His dad reached over and pried the phone out of his hand. "Don't come," he said. "Everyone is leaving. If we had a place to go we'd be leaving too."

"I'm coming." Uri could hear his sister's voice on the other line. "And that's that."

Yasmin knocked on their door two days later, clad in an Indian outfit: silky blue pants and a matching tunic studded with white and silver rhinestones, and a long, sheer scarf wrapped around her neck, its one end trailing behind her, brushing the floor. Her hair was short and sprouted small curls, and she had a teardrop-shaped sticker in the middle of her forehead. Even with the tattoos crawling up her arm and the ring threaded through her lip, Uri was startled by how much she had grown to resemble their mother: her smile, her eyes, the fair skin, which Uri had always envied. Yasmin screamed, dropped her bag and swallowed him into a hug: incense, cigarette smoke and foreign spices. "You're gigantic." She ruffled his hair, felt his arms. "And what's this? Muscles? What have you done with my little brother?"

"I'm still the shortest in my class." He looked into her eyes briefly.

"Well, you're bigger than I remember." She flounced in, taking over the space, dropping her bags, tossing her scarf over the couch, removing her earrings and placing them on the table. "Oh my God." She grabbed him again and hugged him hard. "I missed you so much. Tell me everything. Wait, where's my gas mask? I'm dying to try it on."

Uri led her to the safe room and she nodded in appreciation. She pressed the plastic sheet stretched over the window with her palm, as if testing its durability. "Weird," she said. She threw herself on their parents' bed, flinging off her flip-flops. "So strange, being here. I was just in India, like, a few hours ago." She turned and sniffed the bed covers. Uri looked away. "I can't even smell her anymore," she said.

"She's been gone a few weeks," Uri said.

Yasmin tapped the space beside her and Uri sat down next to her, ankles crossed. He studied the pattern on the wooden door leading to his parents' washroom. "I'm sorry I didn't come sooner," she said. "It just seemed like it was best. Seeing me might have driven her over the edge."

Uri chewed on his bottom lip as if to stop the things he wanted to say from spewing out, things like, "What about Dad and me?" and "Spare me the excuses," which was his mother's phrase, one she had often used when speaking to Yasmin.

He had been little when Yasmin was a teenager, but he still remembered the fights she and their mother used to have, spectacular displays of passion and melodrama that left Uri and his dad—

the gentle, collected portion of the family—in awe. In high school, Yasmin ran away several times, hitchhiking to Sinai and the Galilee, staying God-knows-where, doing God-knows-what. Even when she was home, she got herself into all kinds of trouble: there was an affair with a substitute teacher, there were nights when she stumbled home late and then passed out on their bathroom floor, drunk.

Uri concentrated on his socks, curling and uncurling his toes. Their father walked into the room then and Yasmin jumped off the bed to hug him. Uri took the opportunity to slip out. He grabbed his skateboard and his gas mask and rode the elevator down to the parking lot behind their building, where his dad allowed him to play, close enough that he could make it back if a siren sounded.

It had always been an adjustment, letting Yasmin back into their lives. She had taken off to Sinai right after army service, then Amsterdam, then India, and had come home sporting a new haircut, a new tattoo, a nose ring, a pierced eyebrow. She stayed with them until she found somewhere else to crash, worked and saved money for a few weeks or months, then left again. There was no reason to believe that this time would be any different.

It had been over a year and a half since he'd last seen her—the longest she'd ever been gone—and so much had happened since. Uri wasn't sure where to start catching up. They had always been close, despite her long absences and the eleven-year gap between them. She was the only fun person in Uri's family, a group of serious people with stern faces and tight lips, whose gatherings resembled political conferences he had seen on the news. His father had a permanent groove wedged between his eyebrows and his shoulders were stooped in surrender, as though the whole world weighed upon his small, wiry frame. His mother was fun sometimes; on a good day she was shiny and beautiful and charming, she sang, she put on funny accents, she was the life of every party. But her bad days were so bad that it never quite seemed worth it.

Yasmin was the one who took him to movies and to the beach, made him hot chocolate with melted scoops of ice cream. And she was the only one in his family who knew about his poetry. In fact, she had gotten him into it. A few years ago, when she still lived at home, they started a game: sitting at the table over lunch or breakfast or hot chocolate, they gazed through the kitchen window, finding metaphors or stories in the world out there. They watched people on the sidewalk, or falling leaves, or cars in traffic, or shapes in the clouds, or faces in the moon. Yasmin would get excited by the things he said and yell, "Amazing! A poet is born!" She'd slap the table, or let her mouth hang open in awe or pretend to swoon. "Seriously," she used to say. "If you don't write it down I'm going to have to kick your ass." And once she was gone and he had no one to play with, he did.

That night, when the siren cried, Uri and Yasmin hurried to their parents' bedroom. By then, Uri and his father had developed a routine. There was no talking as they put on their gas masks. Uri turned on the TV, his dad wetted the same towel—the one his mother had taken from a hotel in Eilat during a family vacation—and stuffed it in the gap under the door. Uri wondered how a single wet towel was going to protect them from nerve gas. In his head he started to compose his next poem. *This is my generation's war. A war fought with plastic sheets and duct tape, a wet towel stolen from a hotel room in Eilat, a picture of a sandy beach on a sunny day.* After the poetry contest—the bullying that followed— he had conceded that poetry was nothing short of social suicide and resolved to quit writing at once. Being the shortest, youngest boy in class was challenging enough. And what was the point anyway? There was no future or fame in poetry.

Last year, he had found a notebook in his father's nightstand filled with scribbled verse, dated decades ago. He struggled to decipher the handwriting; he couldn't even tell how good the poetry was. When he asked his mother, she told him that his father had given up writing when they met because he thought it was impractical for someone like him, and went on to become an accountant instead. Uri understood. The poetry they taught at school, the books he found in the school library, were mostly written by old Ashkenazi men. He had never heard of a Yemeni or Iraqi poet, or any Mizrahi poet for that matter. His father had come from a poor Yemeni family, had grown up with no electricity in a tiny two-room bungalow in the Yemeni Grove in Tel Aviv; had worked since he was a kid to help his parents, who arrived in Israel with nothing and hardly spoke Hebrew.

His mother, who was born in Baghdad to a family of scholars, had told Uri that her parents disapproved at first of the frail, dark-skinned Yemeni boy with whom she had fallen in love, but that his father had walked to their home in Ramat Gan and pleaded with them, promising to work hard, give their daughter the life she deserved. "He was always a romantic," his mother had said, smiling as though reliving the moment.

Uri never told his father he wrote poetry, but he ended up finding the school paper in Uri's room. "It's just this stupid thing I had to do for school," Uri said, and his father eyed him strangely but said nothing. Later, Uri saw that his father kept the paper on his bedside table, tucked between books.

Last summer, in preparation for junior high, Uri started an

exercise routine. He didn't want to wait, like his father, until he was older. Junior high was his chance for a new start; half the kids there didn't know him as the "nerdy poet boy." It was time to change direction, find a more manly vocation. Inspired by his history textbooks, the heroic men in uniform, he'd decided he'd like to become an officer in some elite unit when he grew up, maybe even a pilot. He knew there weren't many Mizrahi pilots out there—he wasn't sure why—but this was something he could work at. He had five years before he'd be called up, five years to build the kind of stamina and character and strength heroes are made of. Plenty of time.

He took up jogging, did daily sets of sit-ups and push-ups. He asked his father to install a chin-up bar in his room. He saved the money given to him on his birthday and bought himself a skateboard, and every day between two and four, when the streets were siesta-quiet and the sun placed its hot, sweaty palm on his forehead, he practised jumps and new tricks. He found the sound of the skateboard crunching gravel, hitting pavement—like cracking branches—oddly satisfying. But it was during these times, skating or running up the stairs to Monkey Park, that some of his best poems were born.

Yasmin posed in front of the mirror in her gas mask while Uri and his father sat on the bed and waited, trained for the faded echo of the missiles, which Uri always felt as an amplified heartbeat in his chest. She turned to them. "I have to go get my camera."

"It's too late," their dad said.

"It's not even thirty seconds away."

"Just wait, will you?"

Yasmin rolled her eyes at Uri. Then they heard the missiles hit their targets, and Yasmin froze, her eyes widening behind the mask. She joined them on the bed and clutched Uri's hand. "Wow, you can really hear them."

"Did you think they weren't really shooting them?" their father said. "It's not a joke. It's a war. People get hurt."

"I thought no one had died," Yasmin said.

"Yet," their father said.

Yasmin glanced at Uri and mimicked their father's stern face, whispering, "It's a war, people get hurt." Uri smiled and looked away, grateful to the war for bringing his sister back. She made being stuck in the safe room with his father a little less lonely.

Within days, Yasmin's touch transformed their house, wiping away months of neglect and disregard. Even before his mother's hospitalization, the house had been in bad shape. First, his mother stopped tidying, then it was the laundry, piled up high on the floor by the washing machine, and finally she gave up showering, her hair growing an oily film, smelling sickly sweet, like wilted flowers. After she was gone his father hired a house cleaner who came every two weeks, but the rest of the time the apartment reeked of socks and sleep and ripe bananas. Uri didn't mind. There was something about living with his dad that prepared him for later, for the army, where guys shared rooms and tents and bodily odours, bonding without ever talking about their feelings. He loved watching soccer with his dad: the living room TV-blue, the coffee table littered with glasses and dirty plates, the two of them rising from their seats, pounding the table, yelling at the screen, grateful for the chance to be angry at something.

Now, with Yasmin back, rugs were shaken and windows were flung open, allowing in skies, suns and moons, flickering stars

and distant city lights. The deep-fried stench that had clung to
the kitchen cabinets was overtaken by the aroma of Indian spices,
brewed chai and incense. In the washroom, Yasmin arranged candles with an earthy scent around the tub and lined little jars of
coconut and lavender oil on the shelves, the foreign labels darkened with oil and smeared with fingerprints. A poster now hung
on one wall of her bedroom: an old man who reminded Uri of
his Yemeni grandfather, with brown skin, a long white beard and
smiling eyes that followed Uri everywhere. His name was Osho,
Yasmin said without elaborating. Even the soundtrack to their
lives had been replaced. Before it was the hum of the fridge, the
fake laughter on TV, the lonely echo of a phone ringing in an
empty apartment. Now there was music and singing, the clinking
bangles on Yasmin's wrists, the bells on her anklets, which accom-
panied her footsteps as though she were a lost sheep.

Uri noticed that his father had changed too. He seemed lighter
with Yasmin around, the crease on his forehead smoothed, relaxed.
Uri knew that he was pleased to be relieved of kitchen duty as well;
his father approached cooking as if it were a battle where he was
bound to be defeated—by ants on the kitchen counter, the smoke
of burning lasagna, the piles of unwashed dishes, the memories of
better meals.

One afternoon, after missiles had fallen not far from their home the
night before, Yasmin rapped on Uri's door. "Want to go see where
the missiles hit?" His father was visiting their mother at the hospital. Uri hopped off the bed and grabbed a sweatshirt.

Ramat Gan was quiet, sedated, washed with the warm, sticky
light of an early Shabbat morning. They walked to Monkey Park,

the highest part of town, from where they could see the entire city unfold, brightly coloured after a rainy night, and even a blue hint of the sea, seeping into the sky. The park was abandoned, people still afraid to leave their homes for long periods, the swing set swaying in the breeze. They walked down the stone stairs and then a few more blocks until they reached Aba Hillel Street.

They could see the spot from afar; it had been one of the worst hits so far, many injured and two dead. The road was blocked and emergency teams were picking through the rubble, their vehicles blinking red. All along the street, apartment windows yawned, shutters were scattered on the ground, car windows were smashed and doors ripped open. They walked all the way to the cordons. Two burnt cars were parked in front and a plucked tree lay blackened, its roots pointing up like fingers. Yasmin and Uri stood and watched without speaking. The missile had destroyed an aging apartment building, now a pile of concrete next to a deep crater. The front wall of another building had collapsed, offering the interior views of the three front suites like a dollhouse: a corduroy couch facing the street, a skewed frame on the wall. The sun shone into the houses, illuminating the dust that rose from the wreckage. Uri felt like an intruder, staring into these people's homes. He looked at the debris at his feet, things people had once owned, written notes and coins and shattered china and broken glass, legs of furniture, a computer keyboard, a pizza box. The smell of gas and bonfire smoke stung his nostrils. "Can you imagine if it was our apartment? On the seventh floor?" Yasmin said. "We'd be toast." Uri pictured the missile hitting their building, the impact, in slow motion, the blinding cloud of dust, the walls of their safe room bursting like they were made of Styrofoam.

That day the family decided to forgo the safe room in favour of the bleak concrete bomb shelter in the basement of their building. They weren't the only ones. The issue was debated in the papers, discussed at length on TV and on the radio, military experts invited to weigh in. Saddam may have threatened to use chemical warfare, but so far the missile heads were all conventional, people argued, so while being in the sealed room was safer against chemical attack, it clearly didn't protect those whose homes were reduced to rubble. Now, whenever the siren wailed, the family ran down seven floors to the shelter, where many other tenants had already gathered, more joining them every day. For an hour or two they sat in their pyjamas and gas masks (just in case, the IDF spokesman advised), speaking in soft voices, listening to the sound of falling missiles and sirens, and the announcements on someone's transistor radio.

As time passed, Uri grew accustomed to the war, his initial fear giving way to uneasiness. Ramat Gan had been hit the hardest, making people joke that Saddam was targeting the city because it was where most Iraqi Jews lived, that the missiles must have been drawn to the pungent smell of amba, that tangy mango pickle condiment Iraqis were so fond of. The war had settled into a rhythm, the sirens becoming an inconvenience, hijacking their dreams. People gradually began going back to work, getting on with their lives. Patriot missiles were imported from the States to intercept the Scuds; American soldiers in funny-looking camouflage uniforms smiled next to them in newspaper photos. At night, when the sirens woke them up, Uri had to shake Yasmin from her sleep, get her to shuffle to the shelter, where she would often fall asleep again, sprawled on a blanket in the corner, not bothering to put on her mask. She already seemed bored by the war. Uri started to wonder why his sister had really come home, if she was there for the experience, seeking thrills, the same way she had travelled from country to country, jumped out of airplanes and went scuba diving, as though she was checking off a list. From her restless energy and dimmed eyes, he could sense that she was ready to leave again.

One evening the phone rang and a polite man on the other end asked to speak to Tanmayo. "Tanmayo?" Uri repeated in wonder, marvelling at the exotic blend of syllables in his mouth, and Yasmin burst out of her room and grabbed the phone, dragging the cord and closing the door behind her. Uri could hear shreds of conversation, sweet words whispered like a song, I miss you. When Yasmin came out, her face was glowing.

"Who was that?" he asked.

"Tatagat," she said. It sounded like a stutter, but lovely in her mouth.

"Why does he call you Tanmayo?"

"It's my sannyasi name," she said, clarifying nothing.

A few days later Yasmin disappeared for two days to visit the mysterious Tatagat. When she returned she announced she'd found a job as a waitress in a bar on Sheinkin Street. "People in Tel Aviv are partying like it's the end of the world," she said. "You should come visit me at work," she told Uri. "You must be bored to death."

And he was. His father was back at work; his only real friend, Nadav, was out of town. Nadav's parents had packed up on the very first day and moved to a hotel in Jerusalem, away from Tel Aviv and its suburbs—Saddam's primary targets. Theirs was just one of many vacant apartments in the city, the lit buildings checkered with dark holes. He was sick of the shelter, too: most people were old and his father was busy talking to a widow from the fifth floor, who would bring down sweet rogalach in Tupperware to share with them. Under her housecoat she wore a short, silky nightgown, trimmed with lace, and whenever she crossed her legs Uri could see a bit of her thigh, vanilla-white and smooth and young looking. Uri was embarrassed by the swelling in his pyjama pants. He didn't even find her pretty, thought it was odd that she always came down already made-up, her face encrusted with powder, her lips pink, as if she had fallen asleep with her makeup on.

While his father was out late at a business meeting one evening, Uri found Yasmin in the kitchen, pulling a tray of sesame cookies— his mother's recipe—out of the oven. The house was immaculate, the tiles freshly washed, and wild flowers stood in a vase on the counter. Tatagat was coming over. "He'd like to meet my little brother, who I've been talking about so much," Yasmin said. She boiled water in a kettle and made them both Nescafé, brought over a plate of warm cookies, and the two of them sat by the kitchen window, which framed a rectangle of the city. The heavy blanket of clouds lifted to allow the last rays of sunlight to shine through, flooding the room, painting Yasmin's face a ripe peach. In the west, feathery clouds in gelato colours travelled across the narrow strip of clear sky.

"Tell me stuff," Yasmin said, rolling a cigarette. "You never talk to me anymore. Do you have a girlfriend?"

"Nah," he said.

"Come on, you used to tell me everything."

"Nothing to tell." Nadav, like almost all the other boys in his class, was into Avital Ginsberg, who was tall and blonde and looked like a Barbie or someone on American TV, and had family in America who sent her new Reeboks and Nikes before they came to Israel. Uri used to like her too, until he overheard her telling her friends that she would never date anybody Mizrahi.

"How's your writing?" Yasmin licked the side of the cigarette. "How's school?"

"It's okay." He didn't want to talk about his poetry, and there wasn't much he could say about school. He was bullied less now than he had been in elementary school, but he still didn't have many friends.

"I can't wait to read your new poetry."

He took a sip of his milky Nescafé. "Actually, I'm not doing that anymore."

"What? Why?"

He shrugged. "It's not like there's a future in poetry. Especially not for someone like me."

"What do you mean?"

"Mizrahi," he said.

Yasmin coughed out smoke. "You've got to be kidding."

Uri placed his mug on the table and crossed his arms. "Name one Mizrahi poet."

Yasmin took a long drag from her cigarette, wrinkled her forehead in concentration.

"See."

"Maybe that's exactly why you should write. Ever think about that?"

"I guess," Uri said, hoping to end the conversation. Outside, a pregnant rain cloud sagged over the neighbourhood.

Yasmin leaned back in her chair, closed her eyes and sniffed the air deeply. "Do you smell it?" she asked. Uri inhaled the rich scent of baking emanating from a neighbour's kitchen. Apples and cinnamon. "It smells like . . ." Yasmin squinted, staring into the sky. "An old lover who has come back to mess with your head."

"I don't feel like playing," Uri said.

"Sure you do," Yasmin said. "It's your favourite."

He sighed. "Fine. Like a . . . disease."

"A disease?"

"Yeah, contagious, infectious," Uri said. "Or . . . how about chemical weapons?"

Yasmin narrowed her eyes. "And the sun?"

Uri looked at the sunset for only a moment. That was easy. He had some lined up. "An open wound bleeding onto the skyscrapers. An egg yolk stabbed with a fork leaking into the sea. Planes cutting through the clouds like sharp blades slashing through flesh."

"Whoa. Fantastic." Yasmin stubbed out her cigarette in the glass ashtray, examining him. "Kind of dark." Uri picked up a newspaper from the end of the table and stared blankly at a half-filled crossword puzzle.

"You've changed," she said.

"You've been gone for like two years."

She looked at him. "Are you mad that I wasn't here?"

"No," he said.

"Because I couldn't help her," she said. "No one can. Besides, she hates me."

"She doesn't hate you."

"Actually, she kind of does." Yasmin's voice hardened. "You don't know. You were too young to understand. Do you have any idea how it feels to know that your own mother doesn't love you?

I've spent the last two years trying to come to terms with . . . all of this. To heal from this."

Uri drew moustaches on the faces of a young couple on the back page of the newspaper, both blond and wearing flared jeans. The sun had sunk between the buildings and the room turned instantly darker. Rain tapped hesitantly on the roofs. He wanted to tell Yasmin that she too didn't know how bad it had become after she left. She wasn't there when their grandmother—their mother's mother—died (she was honouring her spirit in a meditation retreat in northern Thailand, she said, grieving in a more holistic way). And she wasn't there when their mother lost her job soon after, spending days on the couch watching TV in her sweatpants, swallowing pills, drinking cough syrup even though she didn't have a cough. Some days she cried loudly in her bedroom, the door locked, and neither Uri nor his dad could get her to open it. His father became a ghost, slowly shrinking until he disappeared, like a coin tossed into a gaping void.

After their mother was admitted, his dad began looking for Yasmin, sitting by the kitchen table stained with crescent shapes left by endless coffee mugs, dialing long numbers with nervous fingers, stuttering impossible sentences in English. When Yasmin finally called, and Uri told her what had happened, she took a deep breath before saying, "I'm so glad she's getting help. She's in my heart and I'll be praying for her every day. But I'm doing a lot of work on myself right now. I can't come home." For the first time, Uri had felt anger rising up in him toward his sister, who up until then had been his favourite person. He wanted to slap her, shake her by the shoulders.

Yasmin looked at him, searching for his eyes. "Sorry I got upset." She smiled. "You hungry?"

Uri took the elevator down to the falafel stand on the corner, the twenty-shekel bill Yasmin had given him clutched in his palm. Brief rain had come and gone, and the city was washed clean, suffused in the pink glow after sunset, traffic lights bouncing off the shiny asphalt like a strobe on a club floor. He got three orders of falafel, including one for Tatagat, and had just finished filling each pita pocket with pickles and salad and fries and amba when he heard the music on the radio abruptly stop, followed by a high-pitched sound and the familiar military code, nachas tsefa—*viper*—which preceded the siren. His heart leapt. He froze, tahini ladle in hand. The siren followed seconds later, the announcement on the radio: "Due to a missile attack on Israel, Israeli residents are requested to put on their gas masks . . ."

"There's a community shelter across the street." The falafel guy nodded toward it while grabbing his gas mask, shooing Uri out so that he could pull down the metal shutters. Uri dropped the ladle, spraying himself with tahini, stuffed the last pita pocket in the plastic bag and sprinted, his heart beating faster than his footsteps, the plastic bag banging against his thigh. He'd never been outside when the siren sounded, without a gas mask, alone. Why did he leave the kit behind? He always took it everywhere with him. On the roads a few cars were abandoned in a hurry, double-parked, their passengers scrambling to seek shelter. When he made it to their building, he dashed upstairs and stormed into the apartment to find Yasmin sitting at the kitchen table with a man he didn't know, playing cards. Indian music poured from the tape recorder. Uri panted. "The siren," he said between gasps. "Didn't you guys hear?"

Yasmin looked up at him. "Uri, this is Tatagat." Her face had that glow again. Tatagat smiled. "Nice to meet you, Uri." His voice was deep.

"Why didn't you go to the shelter?" Uri said, barely glancing at Tatagat. He placed the plastic bag on the table and fumbled with his gas mask with numb fingers.

Yasmin waved her hand in dismissal. "It will be over in a minute."

Uri removed the cap and tightened the straps, then folded his knees and lowered himself to the ground, where he sat, leaning against the door, staring at Yasmin and Tatagat through the two holes in the mask. Tatagat got up to fetch plates. He was much older than Yasmin, Uri observed, with deep lines carved into his cheeks and around his eyes. He was dressed in white, the crotch of his pants hanging low, like a diaper, and Uri could see the traces of him dangling freely. His head was bald but he had a long, pointy black beard, embroidered with silver.

The echoes of the fallen missiles sounded far away this time. After each one fell, the sky above the kitchen table flared up. "Done," Yasmin said. "Now, can we eat?"

"You go ahead," Uri said. "I'm going to wait for the announcement."

Yasmin shut off the tape recorder and turned on the radio for him. She raised the clear plastic bag to eye level and examined it, laughing. Tahini pooled in the corner of the bag and some vegetables had fallen out. She gingerly pulled out the pitas, wiping them off with a napkin before placing them on a plate. Tatagat's pager beeped and he picked it up, looked at the screen and asked to use the phone. Uri watched him, surprised to hear him speaking Arabic. When Tatagat hung up he said, "My mother making sure I'm still alive."

"You speak Arabic with your mom?" Uri frowned.

"Sure." Tatagat shoved the fallen vegetables back into his pita.

Uri studied Tatagat. He wondered what his real name was. He

had never really met an Arab before, except for the construction workers in the new building on the corner, who listened to loud Arabic music while they worked, but Uri always quickened his pace when he walked by them.

Yasmin took a bite of falafel and gave Uri an oblique glance. "Mom and Dad spoke Arabic with their parents."

"That's different."

"How?"

Uri wasn't sure why it was different but he knew that it was. And he didn't want to talk about it in front of Tatagat, who was smiling at him with such warmth that Uri had to look away. He was relieved to be wearing a mask.

"So is Tatagat Christian or Muslim?" Uri asked later. They were watching TV on the couch, the cold light illuminating the dark apartment. Their father had come back and gone to sleep. The night was warm so they had left the doors to the balcony open, and every now and then a cool gust would slither in, brush over their faces, ruffle their hair.

Yasmin sighed loudly. "Why are you so fixated on that?"

Uri hunched his shoulders. "I just think it's weird."

At school, everybody said Sima Landau fucked Arabs, which Uri supposed was another way of saying she was a whore who'd sleep with anybody. Uri laughed along with everyone else but felt awful afterwards because she was the only girl who had ever kissed him. It was at a house party at the beginning of the year. They were playing Seven Minutes in Paradise, and as soon as he and Sima were inside the closet, she had leaned over and kissed him on the mouth, her tongue poking between his lips. Then she said, "You can touch my tits if you want," and he placed an awkward hand on her shirt, feeling the rough material of her bra underneath, a lacy tablecloth. Now Uri placed a cushion on his lap, mortified by the hint of an erection that the memory brought him. He closed his eyes, imagining his mother in the psych ward, her oily hair, her saggy arms.

"Not that it matters," Yasmin said, fiddling with the ring on her lip. "But he did go to the army."

"He did?"

"You know what, it doesn't even matter, because he wouldn't go now and neither would I."

"Why not?"

"Because we don't believe in the occupation, and we don't believe in war."

"But the war is happening. Like right now."

"You can choose to be a part of war or a part of peace. I want to spread positive stuff in the world. I want to do good."

"I can't wait to go to the army," he said.

"Why? So you can 'defend our country from the enemies who want to throw us into the sea'?" she mocked.

He stared at her. "What, you don't think we need defending?"

"From what?"

"From this." He pointed at the sky outside.

"You think this is a threat?" She snorted. "This is nothing. People in Iraq are dying."

"Then why did you come back? If it's nothing?"

"Because I worried about you. I didn't want you to be alone. With Dad."

"I'm fine. You don't have to worry about me."

"I know you're fine," Yasmin said. "You're the bravest kid I've ever known."

Uri looked away, down at the darkened trees swaying in the wind, their branches blindly grasping, the foggy beams of the street lamps, the silhouettes of people in faraway windows, turning off lights in children's bedrooms, the erratic flickers of TVs in other living rooms.

"Listen, I was going to talk to you about something," Yasmin said. "Tatagat and I are thinking of opening a shop and staying here."

"A shop?" he said.

"Yeah, we want to import things from India."

"Oh." Uri looked at the TV. "Cool."

"I thought you'd be more enthusiastic." Yasmin searched his eyes. "We'll hang out more. You can be my little helper. You can sit at the store and write as much poetry as you like."

"Once school starts I'll be busy. Junior high is harder than elementary."

"There are more important things than school," Yasmin said.

Uri squeezed his hands into fists. "Just because you didn't like school . . ."

"What's wrong?" she said.

"Nothing." He stood up and forced a yawn. "I'm going to bed. I'm tired."

He saw less of Yasmin over the next few days. Nadav was back from Jerusalem with a new girlfriend—he had met her in the hotel shelter—and Uri spent his days skateboarding with him and listening to his stories. He showed Uri pictures of a curly-haired girl with lip gloss and hoop earrings, a shirt with a Madonna print, a bandana wrapped around her wrist and her hair tied in a side ponytail.

He told Uri they'd had sex, and although Uri didn't believe him, he enjoyed his detailed descriptions all the same. "It's the war," Nadav said. "It drives chicks crazy. Why do you think there were so many babies born after the Yom Kippur or Six Day War? It's genetic programming. People want to procreate when their survival is threatened, so they start having sex and shit. It's the best time to get laid."

Uri thought of his father and how he seemed to be in a better mood these past couple of weeks. Twice the widow had dropped by with cookies and lasagna, dressed in revealing blouses, her hair blow-dried in waves, her pink lips puckered like a closed tulip.

One evening, he came home to find a book of poetry from the library on his desk. A poet by the name of Roni Someck. Uri flipped through it: the pages were worn out and dog-eared, some darkened with oily stains. That night, he lay in bed, mouthing the poems to himself. He had never read poetry like that, hadn't known it existed: the verse written in an easy, fluid language, sometimes even slang, and often about everyday things. Yet it was beautiful, haunting, filled with such passion that Uri felt seized by it himself, unable to put the book down, too wired to fall asleep. The back of the book said that Someck was born in Baghdad—an Iraqi poet!—and lived in Ramat Gan, which both pleased and stunned Uri, the idea that a real poet lived and walked and found inspiration in these dull suburban streets. He studied his picture on the back, a young man with a broad forehead and dark olive-pit eyes, and wondered if maybe he'd seen him somewhere, in the supermarket, on the number 61 bus, if his house was visible from Uri's apartment, if his was one of the windows that stayed lit late at night.

At first, Uri only wrote in the shelter, sitting in the corner with a school notebook, filling pages upon pages with new poems while

Yasmin slept, snoring lightly, and his dad and the widow laughed inside their gas masks, her hand on his knee. Then he bought a small spiral-bound notebook that fit in his back pocket for when he went skateboarding in the afternoons, and when poems tugged at him—sometimes just fleeting images, other times words, full sentences—he pulled the notebook from his pocket, sat down on a park bench, a curb, a stone fence, and wrote.

On Purim morning, six weeks after the war had started, Uri's father woke him up to tell him it was over. Saddam had withdrawn from Kuwait; a ceasefire was being negotiated. Just in time for the holiday. His dad took photos as Uri and Yasmin ripped the duct tape off the glass, flung the plastic sheets into a heap on the floor, slid open the windows to clear the room of its stale air of anxiety.

Outside, the sky was the rich, promising blue of spring. The streets were teeming with children in costumes, hundreds of Saddam Husseins competing with the usual cowboys and Supermen, Queen Esthers and Disney princesses. Uri and Nadav skateboarded through town, feeling free without their gas masks. They checked out the girls parading by in their costumes, some wearing sandals and short skirts, revealing secret winter skin. The wind tasted sweet on Uri's tongue, and as he skated down the steep, windy Arlozorov Street, he opened his mouth and drank it in, feeling invincible, more mature somehow.

When he came home that evening—legs achy from skating, eyes and throat irritated from the wind, dust and car exhaust—he found Yasmin bundled in a blanket by the kitchen window, a dark silhouette against the silvery moonlit sky, smoking into an overflowing ashtray. Her eyes were swollen and her face drawn. She kept biting her lip ring, rolling it forward and backward. "Tatagat left," she said. "He went back to India."

Uri joined her by the window. His father was working late again. The city was abuzz with party preparations. The smell of meals rose from apartments below, mixing with the sharp, fresh scent of night. Yasmin shuffled to the fridge and grabbed a bottle of beer. She threw herself back on the chair, folded her knees up, tightened the blanket over her shoulders. "Every time I think I know where I'm going and what I'm doing, something shitty happens that makes me question everything." She glanced at him. "I'm such a bad sister. I'm so sorry."

"You're not."

"I exhaust people. I exhaust you. An energy sucker, that's what Tatagat says. No wonder Mom couldn't stand me."

"That's not true."

"I'm just like her," Yasmin said. "I'm going to end up in the psych ward." She hesitated, tilting her head to wind a short curl around her finger. "You know, I went to see her."

He swallowed. "When?"

"Well, I've been a few times actually." She looked at him. "Don't be mad. I wanted to tell you, but Dad thought maybe we shouldn't."

He could taste the tears at the back of his throat. He looked out; the city lay flat and grey, the roofs bejewelled with sparkling solar panels. He drew invisible arcs from one roof to another, all the way to the sea.

"She asked about you," Yasmin said. "You know she misses you, right? She just doesn't want you to see her like this."

"Yeah, I know." Uri fixed his gaze on a woman who was taking laundry down outside her window. The laundry line screeched as she pulled it toward her, the clothes bouncing along.

"It was strange." Yasmin sipped from her beer. "She was . . . calm. Too calm. Like she wasn't mad at me at all." Tears leapt out of her eyes. "Which was worse. And I looked at her, and I kept thinking: this is where you're going to end up."

"You're not," Uri said. "And Tatagat is an asshole. A good boyfriend would have stayed and helped you, if you needed help."

"Oh, sweetie." For some reason this made Yasmin burst out sobbing. Uri placed a hand on her bony shoulder and rubbed it, then pulled away. Yasmin quickly composed herself, shaking her head as if to dry off the tears. She looked up at him, then out with a distant gaze. "Sometimes people have to help themselves before they can help others," she said.

It was then that Uri knew that his sister was leaving. Panic dug its fingernails into his heart; he had to stop her. Maybe she'd stay if he thanked her for the book, if he told her that he'd been writing again, that he understood now that poetry was everywhere, even outside their kitchen window, that it was more than just a game. He had always thought real poetry had to be about grand and important things, like the land and the people who died for it. He never knew he could write about the number 61 bus to Tel Aviv, the toddlers' fingerprints on the windows, the whiff of sea salt and cigarette smoke it had brought from the big city. He wrote about Sima Landau, the taste of mint and chocolate on her lips, the warmth of her breath, the pink smell in her hair. He wrote about skateboarding: on the board he was the captain of a ship, a pilot, a fierce explorer of sleepy suburban streets.

But he knew there was nothing he, or anybody, could do to make her stay. Trying to keep her was as futile as trying to hold water in a tight fist. His sister was going to leave and come back and then leave again. She would become a handwritten note on postcards, a distant voice on the phone, a line in a poem. All he'd have is a series of recycled moments, like this moment in the kitchen, and he could feel it slipping away, seeping into memory, fading into the past, already tinged with nostalgia and longing. Already gone.

He looked at Yasmin, curled into a ball with her knees against her chest, and then at the darkening patch of sky outside the window, the clouds that swirled and eddied, filling up the spaces between the stars, and he said, "The sky looks liquid today." And Yasmin gazed up at him, her eyes red and brimming, and a smile skirted across her lips. "Like a stirred dirty martini," she said.

"The moon is drunk," Uri said. "A lemon wedge floating on top."

Yasmin's smile grew. Uri placed his hand over hers and gave it a light squeeze. Neither of them moved or talked for a while.

CASUALTIES

Around our third shot of tequila, I know I'm going to have sex with the cute paratrooper who's been flirting with me all night. I raise my glass—the golden liquid ripples, seductive and warm—and I knock it back, twist my face and suck on a lime wedge. I'm glad my roommate, Vicky, stayed in tonight. If she were here, she would give me a hard time, not because of Oren, but because she thinks I should know better. It's an unhealthy pattern; I'm using sex to blah blah blah. She's been reading a lot of self-help books since finishing the army.

By the fifth round, the space between us is charged like the air before a thunderstorm. I'm stroking beer bottles and he keeps staring at my lips. The rest of the bar has been reduced to a blur, the people transformed into cut-outs. He starts touching my hand when he talks, removes a hair that's stuck to my lip. He's twenty-one, a pazamnik, got two years under his belt, so his uniform is worn out and fits him just right, and his red paratrooper's boots are faded and caked with dried mud. His wrists are thick, and his forehead is large—a sign of a trustworthy man, my grandmother Fortuna used to say. As I walk to the washroom, the music and chatter and clinking of glasses blend into a soft, pleasant hum, the dimmed lights colour the room amber, making everyone more beautiful, and my high heels bounce as if I'm walking on a cushy playroom floor. I don't have to look back; I can feel him watching me.

In the washroom, I stand by the scratched-up mirror and reapply my eyeliner. The door swings open, letting in music and laughter, and he walks in and turns the lock behind him. He grabs me by the waist and kisses me between the mirror and the hand drier, which turns on automatically, blowing hot air. We laugh. "You're beautiful," he says. He smells of sweat and dust and cheap Noblesse cigarettes. I shimmy my panties down, undo his zipper; he pulls out a condom from his back pocket, rips the wrapper with his teeth and spits it to the side. He lifts me up easily, like I weigh nothing, his biceps bulging from underneath his folded khaki sleeves, and my skirt rides up to my waist. We fuck against the wall, sweat against sweat. Our rhythms sync, our bodies fit, our tongues interlace. The sounds from the outside are muffled, but I can feel the bass reverberating through the wall, pulsating against my spine. It's just what I need: eyes closed, mind shut, no strings attached. Then he says, "I'm coming," and I say, "Wait," but it's too late. He freezes, disengages, lets my legs down and leans against me, heavy. "Sorry," he says into my nape. "It's okay," I say, even though my body is buzzing like a power line on a hot day. He traces my mouth with his finger, then gently pushes against it until I part my lips, let his finger in. I suck on it, twirling my tongue around the rough skin, the ashy taste of cigarettes. He pulls it out and brings it down to my clit. When I come, I forget to be quiet and go, "Oh God oh God oh God," until he laughs and puts his hand over my mouth.

Someone knocks on the door and the paratrooper yells, "Go away." He zips up his pants and I pull down my skirt, pick up my underwear from the floor and stuff it in my purse. We stand side by side, fixing our hair, rearranging our clothes, washing our hands. He looks at me in the mirror as I retouch my lipstick and shakes his head. "This was so unbelievably hot."

I smile, lean forward and smack my lips together.

He wipes off a lipstick stain on his neck, straining to see in the mirror. "I wish I didn't have to go back to the base tomorrow." He puffs out his cheeks and sighs. "I'm so sick of the army."

For some reason—maybe it's the alcohol, maybe it's the way he looks at me, maybe it's that post-orgasm high—I reach into my purse and hand him a gimel form, already signed and stamped by the clinic, for two days off.

He stares at the paper and starts laughing. "Where did you get this?"

"Shhh." I put my finger on his lips.

"You're amazing," he says, kissing me one more time before walking out.

I lean against the wall and stare at the graffiti: girls' telephone numbers, lines from bad poems, lipstick kisses. I can't believe I just handed a stranger a forged gimel form. Stupid. I'm usually a lot more careful.

I wake up to the phone ringing. The shutters are closed but the window vibrates with the drone of rush hour traffic. I've dreamt

of swimming again. The water tequila golden. I glance at the
clock and gasp, jump out of bed, still in my black miniskirt and
push-up bra, a dangly earring caught in my hair. I grab my uniform from the floor, a khaki pile I'd kicked off last night before
I went out. The house is empty, Vicky already gone to work. In
the bathroom I pop two ibuprofens and wash my face with cold
water. My olive skin looks yellow this morning, and my straightened hair is starting to curl. I quickly apply some mascara, eyeliner and lipstick. I pick through the heap of clothes on the floor,
looking for my cap. Finally, I find it in the laundry basket, all
squished, and stuff it in the loop on the shoulder of my uniform.

Outside, Tel Aviv slaps me across the face. It's hot, summer hot,
too hot for May. The city breathes with the fixed rhythm of traffic
lights: pause, anticipate, resume; pause, anticipate, resume. Across
the street, cars wedged in traffic blow their horns at a minivan that
is parked on the curb, blinking yellow. I squint and rifle through
my purse for my sunglasses, when I remember the call from this
morning and dig out my cellphone. I listen to the message. It's
Oren. I haven't spoken to him since he was posted to Gaza about
a week ago. His voice is shaking. "I really have to talk to you. Can
you call me as soon as you get this?"

A bus heavy with commuters waddles to the stop and I squeeze
on, grateful for the air conditioning. I dial Oren's number but it
goes straight to voice mail. I'm almost relieved. Our relationship—
if you can even call it that, considering how rarely we see each
other—has been dying slowly for weeks now. Oren must know it
too, but then whenever we talk, he tells me I'm the one thing that
keeps him going. I can't possibly break up with him now.

Oren and I met the summer between high school and the army
in my hometown in the south. Oren was visiting family who lived

in the new townhouses by the dunes. He was from Haifa, and I liked that about him. Everyone else I'd ever been with had known me since childhood. To Oren I was new; he didn't know what had happened with Tomer and Lital, hadn't heard the rumours that were going around about me. I didn't even mind the long-distance thing. It was romantic: the longing, the anticipation, the reunions. Every Friday afternoon, I picked him up from the central bus station on my bike. Once, I took the bus to visit him in Haifa. He lived with his mother and brother in a big house on Mount Carmel with panoramic views of Haifa Bay. It was beautiful there, the air fresh and cool, the colours brighter—back home everything seemed to be tinted yellow, covered in a layer of sand, marked by the desert—but his mother was cold and asked too many questions, so I never went back. In my house, my mom was working two jobs and didn't care what I was doing or who I was hanging out with.

Oren treated me like a princess, which was a nice change: where I come from most guys are pricks who know nothing about how to treat a woman. He listened to me—really listened—and after sex he would stroke me in bed for hours, or bring me coffee in the morning, dark and sweet, the way I like it, or surprise me with a pair of earrings for no reason. He made me want to be different, the kind of girl who would date someone like him.

I make it to the clinic just in time. Buzaglo, Lieutenant-Colonel Mizrahi's driver, is smoking his Marlboro Reds on the front steps. He slides his sunglasses up to his forehead, looks me up and down, and releases a sound like a deflating balloon. "Damn, Yael," he says. "What do you say I take you out tonight? Somewhere nice?"

Buzaglo has that rough quality I've been missing lately. Oren is so fragile that sometimes I almost don't feel his weight. I used to like how gentle he was, but once on the seawall some creep was trying to pick me up right in front of him and Oren just kept walking. Buzaglo would have kicked the shit out of that guy.

"I have a boyfriend." I wave a finger at Buzaglo. "You know that."

"That Ashkenazi boy? He can't handle a Moroccan firecracker like you. You need a good Moroccan man."

I laugh. "He can handle me just fine."

"Where is he, anyway?" Buzaglo looks around. "I don't see him anywhere."

"He's in Gaza, watching over your lazy ass." I shove his shoulder when I pass by.

"Hey, I was injured in Gaza," Buzaglo yells after me. "I've done my part."

When I walk laughing into the clinic, Officer Sagit glares at me. "Yael, do you think you could iron your uniform from time to time? You look like you just fell out of bed." She flips back her blonde ponytail and walks into her office.

Sagit hates me. Jealous, Vicky says. My grandmother, who had one glass eye, used to warn me of jealous girls. She always said beauty was a curse, not a blessing. I used to love hanging out in her front yard, watching her crushing chilies, grinding spices or threading her eyebrows, and listening to her stories: how beautiful she used to be, how many suitors she'd had back in Casablanca, how the envy of other women had caused her to lose her eye. Sagit and I are both nineteen, but she thinks she's better than me because she has a stupid rank on her shoulder and her father is some big-shot Tel Aviv lawyer, who gave her a brand new car for

her eighteenth birthday. So it drives her crazy that the cute lieutenant from the intelligence unit next door—whom she's totally
obsessed with—has been hitting on me for weeks.

I put a white coat over my uniform and sit at a table, stacking
papers, uncoiling and re-coiling the blood pressure belt, filling a
glass with hot water and placing a thermometer in it. I smile at
Shuli, the new girl. Her uniform is stiff and too green.

Within minutes I fall in sync with the rhythm of the clinic. This
is an administrative base, so I mostly have to deal with soldiers
who feign flu symptoms to get sick leave. No battle injuries, no
training accidents. Soldiers come and go, I ask routine questions,
check for temperature, heart rate and blood pressure.

I always wanted to be a medic. When I started the medic course,
I hoped I'd be posted somewhere exciting, serve in a combat unit
and see some action. Oren and I had talked a lot about the army in
the months before we were called up. He wanted to do something
meaningful, he said. I thought I did too. I figured I'd be a good
medic. I've seen some nasty stuff in my life. When I was thirteen,
a rocket fell in my neighbourhood and a girl I went to school
with got hit. She was playing outside, listening to her Walkman
and didn't hear the siren. Her parents were both at work. When
I came out of the shelter, she was walking down the street covered in blood, like someone in a zombie movie, and there were
pieces of glass stuck in her arm and lodged in her forehead. People
screamed when they saw her, but I just went to her and talked to
her, calming her down until the ambulance came. And then there
was the way my parents used to fight before they split up. My
mom would punch my dad in the face or scratch him until she
drew blood, and my dad once threw a glass at her and she needed
stitches in her shoulder. I was good at giving first aid.

I was beaten up pretty bad myself after Lital found out I was sleeping with her boyfriend Tomer the summer before twelfth grade. One night, three older girls I had never met waited for me after my shift at the shish-kebab restaurant and grabbed me by the hair, knocked me off my bike and roughed me up. When I came home that night with two black eyes, my mother—absorbed in her telenovela reruns—didn't even notice.

After that, I started hanging out with the guys in front of the pizzeria, drinking too much and sleeping around. By the end of twelfth grade, I hated our town so much that I wished for rockets to fall and wipe everything out, and then a sandstorm to come and cover the ruins with fresh dunes.

I was ecstatic when I was finally called up to the army—anything to get me out of that shithole. On the first day of the medic course I opened my locker and saw that inside some girl had written in marker, "Welcome to the medic course! This is going to be the best part of your service. P.S. Don't forget to clean underneath the locker. The sergeant always looks there." Somehow, that note made me hopeful.

But during my first week there, I recognized a girl from my high school, a good friend of Lital's, and she went and told all the other girls that I was a slut who slept with other girls' boyfriends. That had only happened with Tomer, and he and I had a real connection. He'd been there for me through my parents' divorce, having experienced the same thing the year before. I didn't know how else to show my gratitude. After the girls found out, the course was like high school all over again. Once, when we practised inserting IVs, Lital's friend jabbed my vein so many times that I still have scars. Another time I lost my hat, which meant staying extra hours on Friday. Usually, if a girl couldn't find her hat, all the other girls helped look for it, but this time, only two girls helped me, and I'm pretty sure Lital's friend hid it, because she smirked at me while I was searching. I watched the entire class leave for the weekend, laughing and talking on their way to the bus stop. Then the base was empty and quiet, and all I could hear was the wind in the eucalyptus trees. I sat outside my room, and for the first time in months, I broke down and cried.

One good thing that came out of this course was Vicky. I've never really had a girlfriend before. She worked in the canteen and was two years older, almost done her service. On her way to the bus stop that Friday, she saw me sitting alone in the yard, and she came over and sat beside me. "You can't let those bitches get to you," she said. "I know the army seems like everything right now, but these two years will pass in a flash. Just don't think too much. Follow orders, keep your head down. It will be over before you know it."

I check my messages over lunch outside the canteen. Another one from Oren. His voice has a nervous edge to it. "This place is hell. I need to get out of here. I feel like I'm going crazy." He sounds like he's been crying. I sigh and press delete. I worry about him, sure, but a part of me just wants to tell him to suck it up. I mean, I know things are hard in Gaza, but the army isn't supposed to be fun. Things are hard for everybody. I snap my phone shut. The irony isn't lost on me: I have just the thing to help him out, but he's there and I'm here.

I started selling gimel forms a couple of months ago. The money from the army wasn't enough and trying to hold a waitressing job on the side had me sleep deprived and distracted. I fucked up so many times that eventually I was held back from getting my rank and spent three days in detention. One day at the canteen, I ran into Yafit, who I knew from junior high. Her family had moved to Tel Aviv after ninth grade. She was working in the maintenance department. When she heard I was a medic, she asked if there was any way that I could score her a couple of gimelim. She said she used to have another contact, but he had finished his service. It made me think. I saw soldiers come to the clinic every day with pretend limps, carrying a Thermos of hot tea they drank a minute before I checked their temperature, eyes swollen with creams and drops.

I stole empty forms over the next couple of months, a few each day until I'd amassed a decent stack. I photocopied the doctors' signatures and practised forging them. One day I took home the doctors' stamps and sat up all night stamping the forms. I brought them back early the next morning so the officers didn't even notice they were missing. I never sell in the clinic, even though it's tempting. Yafit hooks me up for a small commission. I just hand her the forms as she requests them. Fifty bucks a gimel. Clean.

I've never told Oren. I don't think he'd approve. He's changed a lot since he started the army, become distant and depressed. When we see each other he mostly wants to catch up on his sleep.

I come back from lunch and see two army police officers sitting in Sagit's office. Sagit looks up at me through the glass and keeps talking. My heart jumps. "What's going on?" I ask Shuli. She shrugs.

I sit down at my station, go through the motions, but I can't concentrate. I keep glancing in the direction of Sagit's office.

Just before the officers leave, they stand and scan the room. I look down at the file on my desk and then ask the soldier sitting in front of me to roll up her sleeve.

As soon as the soldier is gone, I get up and peek into Sagit's office. "Everything okay?"

She writes something down on a notepad, doesn't look at me. "What do you mean?"

"The army police."

"Wouldn't you love to know?" She leans over, opens the filing cabinet on the floor beside her and browses through folders. I stand there a bit longer. Eventually she raises her gaze. "Anything else?"

I walk out. Buzaglo winks at me from the swivelling chair outside Mizrahi's office and nods toward the door. I step out and he follows.

He lights a cigarette and offers me one. I take it. "I heard Mizrahi talking about it in the car this morning," he says. "They suspect a gimelim operation at the base."

I cough on the smoke. "Gimelim operation?"

"Some guys at human resources gave their officer fake gimelim. I guess he suspected something because he checked them against other gimelim from the same doctor and the signatures didn't match."

I cough some more. "Like they weren't forged well enough?"

He gives me a narrow look. "No, like way off. Just a scribble or something. You okay?"

I nod, tap the cigarette on the railing until it's out. Good. Not my work. My forged signatures are works of art. "How can you smoke this shit?" I hand it back to him.

He shrugs.

"So how did they get the forms?"

"They think they broke into the supply room, stole them straight from the printer."

I exhale. Not related to the clinic. Not related to me.

I pretend to get a call and walk away, texting Yafit: Need to talk. We should probably lay low for a while. I remember the paratrooper at the bar and my face flushes. Shit.

Oren finally gets a hold of me while I'm out grabbing coffee. "Thank God," he says. "It's so good to hear your voice."

"Are you okay?" I sit on the front step and blow on my coffee.

His voice is distant and the line is choppy. "I don't know."

"Oren, I only have a minute. What's going on?"

He's breathing into the phone. "It's just shitty here . . . Everything. My sergeant is an asshole. The entire unit is going out this weekend, but I'm staying behind because my weapon wasn't clean enough."

"Oren, you have to be strong."

"It's not just the sergeant. Yesterday we had to go into a house, the sergeant kicks the door open, and it's the middle of the night and we scare the shit out of this family. They all sit in the corner, Mom, Dad, three kids, looking at me with these eyes. The two young kids are scared, but the older one—he looks at me like he hates my guts. I mean, can you blame him? I'm in his house, in the middle of the night, with my gun. And the sergeant is opening doors and drawers and throwing everything everywhere. Food. Underwear. Books. It was fucked up. When we got back to the base he was making fun of me in front of the whole platoon, calling me a pussy. I couldn't trash their house. I froze."

Sagit opens the door and taps her foot. I lower my voice to a whisper. "Oren. I have to go. Tell them you need to see an army shrink, okay? And call me after five. Everything will be okay." I hang up.

Sagit purses her lips. "I thought we had a discussion about personal phone calls."

"I'm sorry," I say. "It was an emergency."

For the rest of the day, every time I catch her gaze, she's looking at me funny. I have an awful feeling in my gut.

When I get home, Vicky is sprawled in her underwear on our faded corduroy couch, watching a telenovela. Her legs are on the coffee table in front of the TV, and the spaces between her toes are stuffed with cotton balls. She's blowing on her long red fingernails. I sit next to her, stretch my legs on the table, nudging an overflowing ashtray and an empty coffee mug. The shutters are closed to block out the heat and noise, but you can still hear the city. We live right on Allenby Street, opposite the market, and the street never stops: buses and people and cars and sirens and vendors and street cats and taxis and car alarms. In the evenings, when it cools down, we open the windows and the city barges into our home.

"I'm meeting Dan at the bar tonight," she says. "Remember Dan? I met him there last week."

I yawn.

"Come with me." She curls up to me. "A drink will do you good."

Vicky and I strut in our strappy sandals down Allenby Street, arm in arm. She has let me borrow her silver minidress for the evening, to cheer me up. A Subaru blasting Middle Eastern pop slows down to a crawl beside us and two guys look out the passenger window.

"Where are you going, pretty ladies?" asks the one in the passenger seat.

"We already have dates, honey." Vicky exhales cigarette smoke. Behind them a taxi honks its horn. "Okay, okay." The driver waves his hand and takes off. The sidewalk is littered with cigarette butts and plastic wrappers. A gang of emaciated street cats are fighting for scraps by the garbage bin. Before I moved here I used to think Tel Aviv was all long beaches and white houses with rounded balconies, but Allenby is lined with crumbling buildings in grey and yellow, leaning against each other like a row of crooked teeth. Sometimes I miss the silence and open spaces of the desert.

Dan is already at the bar, and he's brought a friend. His name is Gabi and he's got a pretty cute face, though his chest is broad and bulky, a bit too big for his height. He tells me he just finished his service, he works in security now. I let him buy me drinks and feed me lines I've heard a thousand times. When he goes to the washroom I check my phone and see I've missed a call from Oren. I bum a smoke from Vicky and step outside to call him, but the phone just rings. Gabi walks out. He has a bit of a swagger, and his chin is tilted up, as if he's trying to gain a few extra centimetres. "What are you doing out here all alone?"

In the bright light of the street lamp, he doesn't look so cute anymore, a little Neanderthal, his face too boxy, dumb-looking. "I had to make a call."

"You want to get out of here?"

"I think I'm just going to go in, finish my beer." I drop my cigarette and stub it out with my heel.

Once we're back inside, Gabi turns me toward him for a dance, his hands a little too low on my back. I laugh. It's Tom Petty's "Learning to Fly"—not the most danceable song. Gabi leans over and kisses me. He smells like Johnnie Walker. I move my face.

"Come on, don't be a tease."

"I'm not," I say sweetly, moving away from him. "I'm just not feeling too good."

"Come on." He breathes in my ear.

I glance at Vicky but she's laughing with Dan, leaning forward, her hand on his wrist. "I tell you what." I feign a smile. "Why don't I give you my phone number and we'll get together another time." He weaves his fingers through my hair, pulls me closer and sticks his fat tongue down my throat. I push him away and this time I say loudly, "I said no."

Shai, the bartender, steps from behind the bar. "Is there a problem?"

"No problem." Gabi smiles like a hyena.

"There's definitely a problem," I say.

"Whore," Gabi hisses.

"Out." Shai places his hand on his shoulder. "You're done here."

Gabi shakes Shai's hand off and raises both hands. He walks out slowly, shooting a cold look at me.

"You okay?" Shai puts his arm around me and looks at me with concern. He smells like laundry soap. I put my face in his chest and start to cry.

Back at the apartment, I sit on the couch, staring at the streaks of light from passing cars crawling up the cracked white walls, across the dog-eared poster of Bob Marley. The window is open, and the night sky is black and foggy. You can hardly see stars.

"Are you okay?" Vicky asks, stepping into the apartment, tossing her purse on the chair. "What the hell happened?"

"I should have just stayed home," I say.

Vicky sits next to me and hands me a Marlboro Light. "What's going on?"

I lean my head back against the couch and inhale deeply. "Things are stressful at the clinic. And Oren is freaking out on me. I don't know what to do with him."

Vicky stares at me like she's about to say something, then shakes her head.

"What?"

"You know exactly what you have to do with him," she says.

By the time I get to bed it's three in the morning and I can't sleep. Cats in heat are yowling and moaning outside my window. I hear a car door slamming, girls laughing. An alarm goes off, causing a choir of dogs to howl. I press my hands over my ears. I moved to Tel Aviv to start fresh, and now everything is going to shit again. I tell myself I'm going to stop selling gimelim, quit drinking, break up with Oren. Maybe I can take up swimming. I've been living in this city for six months, two blocks from the beach, and I've never gone in the water. I can see it from our living room windows, peeking blue between the buildings.

When I fall asleep I dream I'm swimming all the way to the string of rocks that break the waves, taking long, well-formed strokes, immersing my head in the water. Everything goes silent and peaceful, the city finally muted.

Outside the office, Buzaglo singsongs, "Yael, Yael, Yael. Why must you be so cruel?" I smile tightly. I'm not in the mood today. Before

I open the door, Shuli steps outside. "Heads up, there are officers here to see you."

I pause. "To see me?"

"What have you done?" She grins.

"I keep telling you." Buzaglo shakes his head with mock gravity. "This girl is trouble."

As soon as I walk into the office, Sagit corners me. I don't even get to drop my bag. "Can I see you in my office?" She gives me a fake, saccharine smile. I glance at her office and see three officers standing behind the glass, looking at me grimly. My heart beats inside mouth. I take two steps backwards. "I forgot something," I say. "I'll be right back." I turn around and walk out, colliding with Buzaglo at the door. He steps aside.

"Yael?" Sagit calls after me. I pick up my pace and make it through the gate. I hear Sagit calling, "Stop her," in a high-pitched voice, but I'm already off the base. I bump into a soldier and he grabs me by the elbow. I look up at him and whisper, "Please." He lets me go.

I start running. Across four lanes of traffic on Ibn Gabirol and up Dizengoff. I take a left on King George. My phone rings non-stop, vibrating against my thigh. King George is crowded and people are staring at me, parting as I run through. "Soldier," some call after me. "You okay?" I turn onto a narrow street, pass Meir Park on my left: mothers pushing strollers, people walking their dogs, lovers kissing on a bench. When I reach Trumpeldor Street, I slow down and catch my breath. At the end of the street I see a shimmering patch of blue. The sea. I can smell it, the salty, fishy breeze. For the first time since I started running, I look back. The street is empty, the windswept buildings seem deserted, their windows shut, everything momentarily still. I can hear birds chirping, leaves rustling, the whisper of waves crashing on the beach.

I check my phone. I have seven missed calls. But they're not all from the clinic. Vicky, my mother, a friend of Oren's from Haifa. I close my eyes and picture the officers in Sagit's office. I realize they weren't wearing army police caps but purple caps. Purple. Oren's unit. Their grim faces, Sagit's pleading tone. I can't breathe. My heart becomes heavy, full of water, sinking slowly like a punctured boat. The ring of my phone startles me. I look at it, surprised, as if I don't know what I'm supposed to do with it. And then I place it carefully on a stone fence and carry on running. Toward the blue.

INVISIBLE

A rental van was parked in front of Savta's house early Saturday morning. Rosalynn had tilted the shutters in the living room to let in air, and watched as a young, lanky man climbed out of the front seat of the van, opened the back doors and started piling boxes on the unpaved road.

Savta called from the washroom and Rosalynn hurried over, placing two hands under her employer's armpits and shifting her into her wheelchair. It was easier to lift her now; over the past few months Savta had become smaller, lighter than she had been a year ago, when Rosalynn had first started working here. Then, she had called her employer Mrs. Hadad. Now she was Savta: Hebrew for *grandmother*. It was what her family called her. It was the name Savta preferred.

Rosalynn wheeled the old woman into the living room and set her by the window, where a beam of sunlight filled with dust particles fell into her lap. The sound of men singing at the synagogue down the street crept into the room, and Savta closed her eyes, humming along. Rosalynn wiped Savta's watery eyes with a handkerchief. "Someone moving into the back?" she asked.

Savta nodded. "Ilan's friend. Good boy."

Rosalynn slipped her fingers through the plastic slats, peeking out. The young man slammed the van's back doors. There was no furniture to speak of, just one queen-size mattress leaning against the chain-link fence. He hoisted a few boxes and walked past the house to the small shed in the back, which had been empty since the young Ethiopian couple had moved out months ago. On his way back to the van, he glanced at Rosalynn, his eyes startling blue behind black, thin-framed glasses, and she quickly stepped away from the window.

"Why you hiding?" Savta said. "Boy don't bite."

Blushing, Rosalynn retreated into the kitchen. She boiled water for tea and watched as the man balanced the mattress on his head. He jerked his head to get a loose strand of his auburn hair out of his eyes, and Rosalynn admired the warm, rich colour of it, like autumn leaves, and the dramatic lines of his jaw and cheeks. She poured Savta a cup of black tea with mint and steered her outside, to her barren front yard, the old concrete cracked and strewn with weeds. The morning was fresh, the first after many hot, stuffy fall mornings to offer a bit of breeze. Rosalynn loved when the weather cooled like this, which it almost never did back home in the Philippines. There, the air often felt saturated, as though it could be wrung into a bucket.

At the synagogue down the street, the morning service had come to an end, and a steady stream of men in white-buttoned shirts tucked into dress pants, white kippahs on their heads, wrists crossed behind their backs, strolled past the house. Savta nodded at two elderly Yemeni women who walked by, both in loose dresses with colourful prints and head scarves, just like the ones Savta wore. The women slowed down, exchanged a few words in Arabic, clucked their tongues at something Savta had said and went on their way. The street fell silent again.

Rosalynn pulled a lip gloss from her pocket and quickly applied it, and then brushed her hair with her fingers, contemplating tying it up. Savta watched her. "You know," Savta said. "I was beautiful once, like you."

"You're still beautiful," Rosalynn said.

"I'm old." Savta sighed, her shoulders rising, then dropping.

"You're not that old." Rosalynn dabbed Savta's puffy eyes. "You want me to paint your nails today?"

"Too old." Savta waved her hand, fingers heavy with silver rings. "I wish God take me away."

"Shush." Rosalynn frowned. "Don't speak like that."

"Then I can be with my husband, may he rest in heaven." Savta looked up. "My husband, he save me. In Yemen the government"— she spat, cursing in Arabic—"they take all the Jewish orphans."

This was Savta's favourite story, one she never tired of relating. Years of working for elderly people had turned Rosalynn into a patient, engaged listener. Her first employer in Israel had been a frail holocaust survivor with a faded number on her wrinkly arm. Even though Rosalynn understood little at first, she nodded when her employer spoke, patted her shoulder when she cried. It was easier now, even with Savta's heavily accented Hebrew. Savta had told Rosalynn about her parents, who had died when she was a little girl in Yemen, about how the authorities had threatened to convert her to Islam. She told her how she had walked for weeks through the desert, from San'a to Aden, with a group of Jews on their way to Israel. How she too had worked in people's homes when she arrived, cleaning and doing laundry for the rich Ashkenazi.

A rickety scooter pulled up to the front of the house and shuddered to a halt, a cloud of dust trailing behind it. Ilan hopped off, removing his helmet with jerky, fast movements, shaking loose the black, curly 'fro he'd been growing ever since his release from the army. "Savta." He bounced into the yard, arms open for a hug. He kissed his grandmother's cheeks noisily. "How are you?"

Savta didn't reply, suddenly hard of hearing. Rosalynn knew she was angry at her grandchildren for not visiting more often. "In Yemen," she had told her, "the grandmother was queen."

"Savta," Rosalynn said loudly. "Ilan came to see you. He asks how are you."

"Hara," Savta muttered—*shit* in Arabic. "That's how I am."

Ilan burst into a short laugh and turned to Rosalynn. "You met Yaniv yet?"

Rosalynn shook her head no.

"Yaniv, my man," Ilan hollered.

Yaniv stepped cautiously from the back, his shoulders hunched. He towered over Ilan, who—like many Yemenis Rosalynn knew—was small and wiry. Up close, he looked younger than she had first guessed; his narrow, freckled face had an unfinished quality, yet to settle into itself. His longish hair, tucked behind his ears, suggested he was also recently out of the army. He pushed his glasses up the bridge of his nose, his deep-set eyes seeming sad, the blue speckled with black. When he shook her hand, it disappeared into his large, warm palm.

Over the following week, Rosalynn watched Yaniv settling into the shed. He woke up early and was often gone by the time Rosalynn and Savta came outside to drink their morning tea. He returned in the evenings, his clothes smeared with paint. As Rosalynn removed laundry from the lines in the front yard, she peeked down the grassy trail that led to the shed. She could hear him hammering nails into the walls, dragging things across the floor. One day, he hauled a dusty, worn-out couch off the street, leaving it under the plastic awning outside his door, where it sagged into the broken paving stones. He often sat there in the evenings, quietly strumming his guitar.

Rosalynn welcomed the sound of his music; by then she had almost grown accustomed to the quiet evenings here in Rosh HaAyin. In the beginning, she had been unnerved by the lack of traffic, the abundance of stars, the insistent chirping of crickets. She had moved to this small town, inhabited mostly by elderly Yemenis, almost a year ago, after her visa had expired with her employer's passing. She had thought about going home then, to her young daughter, Carmen, but her husband—a good-for-nothing drunk she had married at twenty-one—was long gone, and her family was relying on her to provide: not just for her daughter, but for her mother, her siblings, their families. "Maybe stay a little longer," her mother had pleaded on the phone. Her friend Beatrice, who had been living in Israel for fifteen years now, married to an Israeli, recommended her to the Hadad family, who had hired her under the table, paying her in cash.

The old neighbourhood in which Savta lived was pressed against the borders of town, edged by a narrow highway and open, yellow fields spread out against a big sky. To the east, the ruins of an ancient fortress stood atop a softly curved hill. It felt like a world away, not just from Manila, but from the rich neighbourhood where she had lived with her previous employer in Tel Aviv, where she had had her own ensuite bathroom in the basement of a large villa, and where the murmur of the city—like a pulse—was always present. She looked forward to her days off, when she travelled back to Tel Aviv for a night out with her girlfriends, all of them Filipina caregivers like her.

At nights, after Savta went to bed, the neighbourhood swallowed up by darkness, Rosalynn missed home, missed Carmen, who was now almost thirteen. It had been eight years since she'd last seen her: Carmen was just a pigtailed little girl then, playing with her rag dolls in the mud outside their shed. Now, thanks to the money Rosalynn had been sending every month, Carmen was living with Rosalynn's mom and extended family in a house Rosalynn had paid for, sleeping on a firm mattress, dressed in nice clothes, playing with Barbie dolls. Rosalynn called her mother twice a week, and her mother answered Rosalynn's questions—how were Carmen's grades? How tall was she now? Had her breasts grown yet? Had she gotten her period? Did she eat her vegetables?—before passing her on to Carmen, when Rosalynn would feel tears flooding her throat. She became good at speaking through them, forcing herself to smile.

From her room at the back of Savta's house, Rosalynn could spy on Yaniv through the lemon tree branches, trace his silhouette—not more than seven steps away—through the open shutters, hear him play guitar, smell the coffee he brewed in the mornings. He spent most evenings alone, except when Ilan showed up unannounced, sometimes alone, sometimes with friends, dressed in dark jeans and a tight T-shirt and smelling of too much aftershave. Ilan tried to get Yaniv to come out with him to a bar or a club in Tel Aviv, but Yaniv always said no. His friends would stay for a beer or a joint, and she could hear their chatter and laughter. Rosalynn envied their freedom: at their age she was already a mother, was already struggling with marital problems and money.

A couple of times she was woken up at night by Yaniv yelling in his sleep; a short, sharp cry, the words incoherent. She lay in bed with her eyes open, hearing nothing after that but the drone of crickets, a rooster calling, the murmur of a faraway car on the highway. In the mornings, she wondered if she had imagined it.

One Friday morning, after she had heard him coughing through the night, Rosalynn noticed Yaniv's shutters were still closed. Through her daily chores, the door to the shed remained closed, the coughing persisted. During Savta's afternoon nap, as the neighbourhood began closing up for the Shabbat—last buses speeding up on the emptying streets, shopkeepers pulling down metal shutters, men heaving bags of groceries onto kitchen counters—Rosalynn walked to Yaniv's shed and stood outside his door. She looked at the chipped wood, leaned in to listen, turned to gaze at the street behind her. Then she heard him cough inside and rapped lightly on the door. When he opened it, he was wrapped in a blanket, squinting against the bright daylight. The room smelled of sleep and moisture. His nose was red. "You're sick," she said.

"It's nothing," he said. "Just a cold."

"Okay," she said. "First, let's open your windows. You need air. Go sit outside."

He obeyed, slouching on the couch. She went to Savta's and came back with a cup of steaming tea, lemon slices and grated ginger floating on top, and a pill, which he leaned his head back to swallow. "Thank you," he said, hands around the cup, glasses steaming. "You're an angel."

"Just a mother," she said, and immediately regretted it.

"You have kids?" His eyes widened.

"A girl. She's almost thirteen."

"Thirteen!" he exclaimed. "What, you were fifteen when you had her?"

She laughed, bashful.

"No, really, how old are you?"

"Not polite," she reprimanded him.

She came back after dinner, carrying a bowl of turmeric-yellow chicken soup. It was already dark out and cool enough that she needed a sweater. The neighbourhood had settled into its Friday night lull: Shabbat candles flickered in windows; families gathered around dinner tables for kiddush; children, reluctant to eat, played in the quiet streets. Yaniv was sitting on the couch, covered in a blanket and playing his guitar, his long legs spread on either side of the milk crate he used as a coffee table. He straightened up in his seat when he saw her.

"Feeling better?" Rosalynn said, her Hebrew sounding awkward to her all of a sudden.

"Much better." He nodded. "And what's this? You brought me soup? You are too nice to me." He went inside to fetch a spoon, and she caught a glimpse of a hot plate on the counter, a lidded pot. It occurred to her that he may already have made himself dinner. Embarrassed, she placed the soup on the milk crate. "You can keep for later," she called to him, half turning to leave.

"No way." He came out with two glasses of water, handing her one. "I love Yemeni soup. Ilan's mom used to make it all the time when I lived with them."

She looked at him. "You lived at Aviva's house?"

He sat down on the couch. "When I was a kid. My mom . . . she was going through some stuff, so Ilan's mother took me in for a couple of years. Why are you standing? Sit."

She sat at the other end of the couch. It was the first time she had heard of an Israeli mother who had left her child with someone else. There were many mothers like Rosalynn among the migrant workers—her friend Jemma had three kids back in the Philippines—and she knew that Israelis judged them, pitied them. She didn't know how to explain that she did what was best for her daughter, that leaving her behind was the biggest sacrifice she could have made for her.

She watched Yaniv: he ate ravenously, uttering sounds of pleasure. She felt sad for the abandoned kid he'd been, and then a fleeting stab of guilt.

The following evening, as Rosalynn was spooning rice and vegetables onto dinner plates, Savta said, "So now you take care of Yaniv too, ha? Maybe you don't have time for me anymore?"

"What? No," Rosalynn hurried to say, but Savta winked and waved her hand. "Yaniv is a good boy. Hard life. No money. His father died in the war when he's only a baby. His mother, she put him different places every time."

Rosalynn set a plate in front of Savta, tucked a napkin into her collar.

"No woman to feed him. Maybe you call him for dinner?"

Rosalynn, who had just sat down, got up too fast, pushed her chair back. She eyed her reflection in the mirror by the door, moistened her lips, fluffed up her long black hair.

When Yaniv opened the door, his hair wet and brushed behind his ears, he seemed to brighten at the sight of her. "Savta invites you for dinner," she said. "I mean, if you're not busy."

After dinner, Savta and Yaniv sat at either end of the Formica table, sipping tea while Rosalynn washed the dishes. Savta grabbed Yaniv's hand, holding it between hers. "We take care of you now."

Yaniv laughed. "I can take care of myself. I've been doing that all my life."

"We take care of you," Savta repeated, tapping on his hand. "You know, I was an orphan. My parents they die in Yemen." She blinked her eyes, tears pooling at the edges.

"I didn't know," Yaniv said.

"In Yemen they take the Jewish orphans, the government. Make them Muslims. I was hiding when they came. I go downstairs." She lowered her voice. "Hide where the donkeys lived, in the corner. I hear them walk in the house, I hear my aunt yelling, and then they come and they open the door and they look."

Yaniv set down his cup. "What did you do?"

"I pray to God, please make me disappear. And then I close my eyes and make myself very small, like you can't see me, like I'm not there."

"Invisible."

"Yes. They open the door, look around." Savta paused for effect. "They close the door. They don't find me."

"But how?" Yaniv asked.

"Magic. God makes me invisible." Savta raised her palms to the ceiling.

"Wow." Yaniv leaned back in his seat.

"Also, inside it was dark. Outside very sunny. So they can't see good." Savta clutched Yaniv's hand. "Tomorrow you come? Rosalynn makes good food. But not enough salt."

"Savta." Rosalynn turned to her, waving a finger. "The doctor said no salt."

Yaniv held back a smile. "I'd love to," he said.

Over the next few weeks, Yaniv volunteered to catch the mice, replace light bulbs, fix a leak in the bathroom sink, plant a row of herbs in the small patch of earth by the gate: mint and basil and cilantro. Once, he insisted on making Savta and Rosalynn spaghetti and meatballs for dinner, took over Savta's kitchen, refused to let Rosalynn help. Savta liked having him around, was delighted to find someone new to tell her stories to, relished the male company. Some evenings, he joined them on their walks, taking turns pushing Savta's wheelchair through the narrow streets, lined by small, plain one-storey houses, and steeped in the smells of spices, guava and citrus. As they passed by the elderly Yemenis, sitting in their wheelchairs with their Filipina caretakers in a parallel row on a park bench, Rosalynn felt their stabbing stares, the questions in their eyes. Yaniv was clearly not Savta's grandson, too tall and big and fair to be Yemeni. The three of them made a peculiar trio.

Other times, when Yaniv came home late, Rosalynn would deliver a plate to his shed and watch him eat. She felt small sitting next to him: his large folded legs, his long torso bent over the milk crate. They didn't talk much, though he always asked about her daughter. On rainy evenings they sat inside: his shed was not much bigger than her room, just enough space to fit a mattress, a table with two wobbly chairs, a small fridge that would jolt into bouts of noisy humming. A faded rug covered the cracked tiles and a lone bulb dangled in the middle of the ceiling. Over the bed, a shelf supported a few books. A photo was held by a magnet on the fridge, its edges curled by moisture: Yaniv as a young soldier against eucalyptus trees, arms wrapped around another soldier's shoulder, their caps angled over their foreheads, their rifles dangling behind them, facing opposite directions.

"My friend Yotam." Yaniv nodded. "He died," he added between bites, as if it was no big deal. "In the army."

She put her hand over her mouth. "I'm so sorry."

"It's not your fault." He looked up, smiling tightly.

When he finished eating she took his plate back to the house and washed it, placing it on the dish rack to dry, gazing through the window at the dark houses, the night sky black and shiny above their roofs. She went back to her room and lay in her bed, watched as his light—which drew yellow stripes across her ceiling—went off.

That night she was woken up by Yaniv's yelling again. She stared at the window, fighting an urge to go to his room.

"How come you never make Filipino food?" Yaniv said one evening as they sat on the couch outside his shed, the guitar cradled in his lap. They now spoke English when it was just the two of them, which she liked because in English they were equal, both hesitant, careful, like they were learning new dance steps.

"I make what Savta likes," Rosalynn said.

"A friend of mine spent some time in the Philippines after the army. He raved about the food."

"Where did you go after the army?"

"I didn't." He shook his head. "I've never been outside of the country. Except for Lebanon, I guess. But that doesn't count."

She looked at him.

"My friend said the Philippines were paradise, great surfing, beautiful beaches. Made me want to go."

She gazed into her tea. In the neighbourhood where she had grown up nobody cared about beaches or surfing. Rosalynn tried to imagine Yaniv in her hometown, pictured him walking with her on the dirt roads, saw through his eyes the patched-up shacks, the piles of trash, the streams of dark water, her extended family all living under one roof.

From the street, they heard car doors slamming, footsteps and voices, his friends' loud laughter. Yaniv looked up, the muscle in his cheek tensed.

"I better go," Rosalynn said. She rushed back to Savta's house just as Ilan and a couple other guys opened the metal gate, and she nodded vaguely in their direction, avoiding their eyes. One of them, a blond, stout guy she hadn't seen before, followed her with his gaze, lingering over her breasts. Back in her room she could hear Yaniv greeting them coldly. His guitar made a jarring sound as he put it down.

"She's cute," his friend said. "You get some of that yet?"

Rosalynn sat on her bed, heart pounding.

"You're a pig," Yaniv said.

"Dude, you need to get laid," the friend said. "I hear they're hot in the sack."

"Shut up," Yaniv said. "She can hear you."

"Get laid, go out, go see a therapist, just do something." She recognized Ilan's voice now. "All you do is hide in this dump."

"You hooked me up with this dump. You know this is all I can afford."

"I'm just saying maybe it's time you joined the living. Let go of the dead."

Yaniv burst into an unkind laugh. "That's deep."

"Hey, I'm just trying to help."

"I don't remember asking you."

"Fine, fuck it," Ilan said. "I don't need this shit." She heard him walking away, his friends calling after him, the clattering of the gate closing behind him.

Ilan showed up the following evening, as Rosalynn was applying her makeup in the hallway mirror. It was her night off and she was heading to Tel Aviv to see her friends. Savta was watching an Egyptian movie on TV and the replacement caregiver was on her way. "Hi, Savta." Ilan leaned in to kiss her on both cheeks.

"You're here for me or for your friend?" Savta said without taking her eyes off the screen.

"Both," Ilan said.

"Well, he's not here."

Ilan bit his lips. He looked out of the window, checked his phone, and then grabbed a chair and joined Savta in front of the old TV. He glanced at Rosalynn. "Do you know when he's coming home?"

"No," Rosalynn said, her face growing hot.

"Sorry, it's just . . . you probably see him more than anybody." He hesitated, kicking the floorboard with his sneaker. "I wanted to ask you . . . You think he's okay?"

She frowned. "What do you mean?"

"I worry about him. I don't know if you know, but when Yaniv was in the army, he saw half his unit die. In Lebanon."

She wasn't sure why Ilan was telling her this. She was relieved when Savta called her, asking to be taken to the bathroom.

Rosalynn was meeting her friends at a Filipino club near the old bus station, an aging, decrepit part of Tel Aviv that was now claimed by migrant workers as their own. The streets, bustling with discount shops, international phone booths, restaurants and street vendors, were suffused with a rich blend of aromas that didn't typically go together: coconut, cinnamon and cloves, smoked fish, fresh ginger, toasted green coffee beans, grilled skewers of meat, sweet narghile smoke. In sidewalk cafés men drank in front of TV screens blasting action movies, and in the side streets johns slipped into red-curtained massage parlours. Back when Rosalynn lived in Tel Aviv she had come here often. Whenever the immigration police raided the area, the party would come to a halt, everyone lining up to produce passports and visas. Rosalynn had seen friends who worked illegally, like her, escorted into vans, from which there was no coming back. Once, she had come close to being caught. The club owner had led them into the kitchen, unlocked the back door, and she and her friends had run outside, dispersing quickly. She had learned to be more vigilant.

Her best friend, Beatrice, was one of the fortunate ones who had been granted a permanent visa a few years ago, her Israeli-born kids speaking Hebrew with no accent and hardly knowing any Tagalog. Rosalynn thought about her own daughter and wished things could have been different. She imagined the two of them walking down the seawall eating ice cream, living in an apartment with appliances and hot water, her daughter riding a bike to her after-school activities and swimming lessons at the city pool.

She spotted her girlfriends seated around a table inside the club, Beatrice smoking her menthols, Jemma fluffing her hair, recently permed and dyed red, in front of a hand-held mirror. Vivian stretched her arm and waved at her. Vivian was the newest addition to their group; she was new in Israel, still legal—working with an elderly man in Holon—and young, with no kids or a husband back home. Jemma, like Rosalynn, worked illegally, raising a rich family's children in north Tel Aviv. For one night, they were away from the cleaning supplies, the crying babies, the dependent adults; dressed up in flashy outfits from Allenby Street, smelling of perfume and hairspray.

"Is Laura coming?" Rosalynn asked after she hugged and kissed her friends hello. Everybody looked at her, then glanced quickly at each other before dropping their gazes.

"You haven't heard," Jemma said.

"What?"

"She's gone. Deported last week."

"Not Laura." Rosalynn covered her mouth with her hand.

"Tina is leaving too," Jemma said. "Says she can't live like this anymore, always worrying."

"It's getting bad," Vivian said. "They're doing random searches in markets and bus stations now."

Jemma sighed. The women busied themselves with purses and cellphones and lipsticks. Beatrice waved at a waiter. A group of Filipino men approached their table, some of whom they knew, and they welcomed the distraction.

On the bus back to Rosh HaAyin, Rosalynn sat by an open window, deep in thought. The wind fluttered through her hair, silky soft on her face. A plastic bag on the bus floor flapped and trembled. She had left early, despite her friends' protest, after spending the entire night fighting off relentless advances by one of the men, a guy named Antonio who kept trying to drag her to the dance floor. She hadn't felt much like flirting: her mind was preoccupied with Yaniv, with what Ilan had told her, and with Laura, who was one of the first friends Rosalynn had made in Israel.

Before Rosalynn left, Beatrice had suggested they meet elsewhere next time, maybe at her home. Nowhere was safe anymore, she said, the new government was determined to catch and deport illegal workers: there were so many of them now. As Rosalynn breathed in the evening air, familiar and sweet, the thought of leaving filled her with an ache similar to the one she had felt when she left the Philippines.

She couldn't pinpoint when Israel had started to feel a bit like home, when she figured out the way of the seasons, when the conversations on the streets were no longer gibberish. And yet, she was still a stranger, probably always would be. Sometimes Israel and the Philippines would blend in her head, overlap, the smell of dusty concrete in August, the outpouring of orange after sunset, the musk of old, musty homes, the ripe stench of the vegetable market. Some nights, like tonight, delighting in the cool fall air, tipsy after an evening among friends, she felt guilty, wondering if really she was selfish, if by staying in Israel she had chosen her own life over her daughter's.

She was walking home from the bus stop, past a neon-lit falafel shop, Middle Eastern pop wailing from its speakers, when she heard her name. She turned, surprised to see Yaniv standing at the counter. "Yaniv." Her heart betrayed her, quickening its pace. She was pleased that he was seeing her all dressed up.

"Hungry?" Yaniv gestured. Though she had already eaten, she said yes.

She sat on the stool next to him at a long bar facing a smeared wall mirror. For the first time, she saw them together. She tipped her head. The age gap wasn't quite as evident as she'd imagined.

For a while they both ate without speaking. She could smell his scent: turpentine, beer and a strong, plain soap. She thought of things she could say, questions she could ask. When they sat on the couch the silence had never felt awkward. It was okay just being near him. But now, in public, she felt tongue-tied.

Yaniv threw his head back to take a swig from his Goldstar beer, caught her eyes in the mirror and smiled. She looked away, inserted a straw into her Diet Coke can with clammy fingers.

"You look nice," Yaniv said. "What's the occasion?"

She giggled, immediately wishing she hadn't. "Just a night with my girlfriends."

"And how's your daughter?"

"Good," she said, relieved. "I still don't know what to buy her for her birthday." The last set of clothes she had sent had been too small. The Barbie doll Carmen had passed on to a younger cousin. "I'm not a kid, Mom," she had said.

"What does she like?"

"I don't know," she said, her tone more sombre than she had intended. Carmen had been cold and irritable on the phone these past couple of weeks. She had stopped asking when Rosalynn was coming back a couple of years ago, which Rosalynn then saw as a sign of maturity and acceptance, but lately she couldn't help but feel as though her daughter had given up on her, was maybe even punishing her for leaving.

Two young women with straightened hair and short skirts walked into the joint, smelling of bubble gum and cigarettes and shampoo. Rosalynn watched in the mirror as they eyed Yaniv. She was pleased he didn't look back.

He downed the rest of his beer, hopped off the stool and gave her a hand. She stepped off, glancing at the girls with a tiny smile.

They strolled home down the quiet streets, past people's windows, the blue flicker of television sets, cats curled up on the hoods of parked cars. The asphalt sparkled under dim street lights.

"Ilan came looking for you today," she said.

"Oh yeah?" Yaniv tucked his hands in his pockets. "What did he want?"

"I think he's sorry," she said.

"Sorry for what?" He studied her, his face darkening. "Have you been listening to our conversations?"

"Of course not," she said too quickly. "I just heard fighting. You guys were loud." But it was too late; she had said too much.

"What exactly did you hear?" he said coldly.

"Nothing."

"Then stay out of it."

She looked at the ground, the words lodged in her throat, making it difficult to swallow.

When she reached the front door, she fumbled with the key, muttered, "Good night," without turning around. She released the replacement caregiver as fast as she could, eager to be alone, but Savta called out to her from the bedroom. "You come home with Yaniv?" she asked once Rosalynn entered the room.

"I ran into him." Rosalynn arranged the pillows behind Savta's head.

"So why you crying?"

Rosalynn said nothing, holding the blanket at one end and snapping it flat over Savta's body.

"I was in love once too, you know," Savta said. "My husband, he take me when I was twelve. He was eighteen. He married me so the government won't take me. He saved me."

Rosalynn sat on the bed. Savta laid a warm hand over Rosalynn's.

"He waited four years before he touched me. Four years he feeds me and takes care of me."

"I know, Savta."

"Here, you take this," the old woman said, wiggling one of her many rings—a thin filigree silver band—off her finger. "My husband, he made this. He was a silversmith in Yemen. For the king."

"No, Savta." Rosalynn pushed her hand away. "You keep this for Aviva."

"I give her enough rings." She shoved the ring toward Rosalynn. "I don't like to see you cry."

Rosalynn hesitated but Savta grabbed her wrist, planted the ring in her palm and folded Rosalynn's fingers over it.

"Thank you, Savta." Rosalynn leaned in to kiss the old woman's wrinkly cheek. She slid the ring on her finger and held her hand up, admiring it. The ring was loose, but to Savta she said, "It's perfect."

Yaniv didn't come for dinner the following evening, but after Savta went to sleep Rosalynn heard a knock on the door. She opened the door with her eyes lowered. Yaniv's body filled the door frame. "Can we talk?" he said.

"I made food for you," she said. She went to the kitchen, grabbed a plate covered in saran wrap and held it in front of him.

"Would you sit with me?" he said. "Please?"

She followed him to the couch outside his shed and sat at the edge, her hands on her knees.

"I'm sorry," he said. "I didn't mean to be so rude yesterday."

"It's okay." She stared at a row of ants walking across the paving stone.

"I can be an asshole sometimes."

She twirled Savta's ring on her finger.

"I just . . . I came to Rosh HaAyin thinking this was the one place I could . . . I don't know, disappear I guess. Here no one would bother me or get on my case. Sometimes it's better to just be, not to think so much about . . . the painful stuff. You know what I mean?"

She looked up at him. She had never heard him talk so much before. And she did understand. Every day she tried not to think too much, not to give in to guilt and regret. It was the only way she knew how to keep going.

"I have something for you." He dug inside his knapsack and handed her a metallic pink iPod. "For your daughter."

She held the gift in her palm. "For my daughter?"

"It's from the house I'm painting right now," he said. "The kid just got a new one, so she was going to throw this one out. It has music on it and everything."

She turned the device one way, then another, her eyes flooding with tears.

His face softened. "You're crying. Why are you crying?"

She shook her head, looking at the ground, trying to smile. He lifted her chin with two fingers and wiped a tear with his thumb. For a moment she held her breath, thinking he might kiss her, which was impossible, ludicrous, but then he leaned over, and he was.

"Is it okay?" he asked, pulling back for a moment.

She nodded and he kissed her again, or maybe she kissed him, their mouths uncertain and searching at first, as though forming unfamiliar words, a new language. But then something shifted and clicked and they were kissing, *really* kissing, and it was as she had imagined it, as she had wanted it to be. He rested his hand on the small of her back, and she wrapped her arm around his neck, feeling his pulse against her palm. Then she heard Savta's voice and they both froze, breathing. "I have to go," she said. She ran back inside without looking back at him, forgetting the iPod.

The next morning, as she made Savta's tea, helped her bathe and dress, Rosalynn caught a trace of the smell of him on her skin—sweat, soap, paint—and a warm, wonderful sick feeling churned in her stomach, coursed through her body, flushed her cheeks.

She dropped Savta at the elderly community centre and took the bus to the vegetable market in the next town. It was early in the morning on the market's quietest day, when it was the safest. She stood on the crowded bus, crammed with commuters and students, feeling anxious and excited about seeing Yaniv that evening. She had decided to make chicken curry, a Filipino dish, like he asked, and maybe bake cookies for dessert. Downtown, as the passengers shuffled on and off the bus, she felt a man's gaze upon her. It was one thing about Israel that she couldn't get used to, the way men stared at women, boldly and unapologetically. Some days she felt invisible in Israel: she had heard people speak about her—or people "like her"—in her presence before. Other times it was as though she was walking around with no clothes on: everyone stared.

The man hung onto the bar with one arm and leaned toward her. "You legal?" he asked. His face was unshaven and he reeked of cheap tobacco.

She stared hard out the window.

"I'm talking to you," he said. Now Rosalynn smelled alcohol on his breath. A woman standing on her other side glanced at Rosalynn, then at the man.

"You don't speak Hebrew?" he said.

"Leave her alone," the woman said. Other passengers turned to look.

"I'm just asking a question," the man raised his voice, slurring.

"I don't have to answer to you," Rosalynn said. "You're not police."

The man leered. His teeth were stained yellow. He waited a moment while some passengers got off the bus, and then he moved in closer and whispered, "Maybe I can help you." He winked. "We can help each other, if you know what I mean."

"I have visa." She levelled a bold look at him, speaking in loud, clear Hebrew. "My husband is Israeli. He was an officer in the army, so back off."

The man retreated, raising both hands, then shoved his way out. The woman beside her laughed, arching her eyebrows. "Good for you," she said. "You're one of us now, ha?"

Rosalynn stepped off the bus across from the market's main entrance, feeling proud of herself. Outside, it was one of those perfect winter days, blue-skied, the air warm enough for a light cardigan, the sun spilling all over the grey buildings, bouncing on the market stalls' tin roofs, glowing on the asphalt, still wet from an early morning hosing. She walked with a light step, almost believing her own lie, that she was legal, married to Yaniv, one of them.

Maybe that's why she wasn't immediately alarmed when she saw the white van stopping in front of the market, its doors slapping open, cops swarming out of it and spreading like bees released from a jar. Maybe that's why it took her a moment to remember that she should be running. The cops approached a group of men hanging out by the barricades. Two female officers crossed the street toward her, one entering a building where Rosalynn knew migrant workers lived, the other walking in her direction.

Rosalynn took a step back and leaned flat against a cool brick wall. She scanned the surroundings, shops were just beginning to open, their metal shutters rattling as they rolled up, a few people carried baskets filled with produce, a shopkeeper sat smoking on a milk crate, his radio playing a cheery jingle. She glanced across the street, her eyes meeting those of another Filipina woman, who then turned and ran into the market. Two men were being cuffed and escorted into the van. A narrow stairway was a step away, a dark cavity between two stores, and Rosalynn slid against the wall and turned into it, blinking to adjust her eyes, debating for one moment if she should run upstairs, before deciding it would be safer under the stairs.

The alcove was filled with junk, littered with cigarette butts and stinking of urine and mould. She crouched next to an old, broken stroller, hidden by a piece of plywood, breathing fast and shallow, her body vibrating. She wasn't ready to leave Israel. She needed more time. Savta needed her. Her daughter's future relied on the money she sent. And there was Yaniv. From where she was hiding, she could only see a fragment of the street: a sliver of sunny pavement, black army boots marching past. She heard a woman crying on the street in a foreign language, running footsteps growing louder, then fading away. A female officer stopped on the front step, speaking on her walkie-talkie, her broad back to Rosalynn. Rosalynn's heart beat heavily, like a metal bell clapper punching her chest from the inside. She fiddled with Savta's ring, swirling it back and forth, and it slipped down to her bony knuckle, then over it and off her finger. She reached to grab it but it was too late. The ring bounced on the tile with a high-pitched chime, rolling before it came to a stop against the plywood. Rosalynn froze. The police officer turned around, and Rosalynn could see her eyes squinting in the dark.

Rosalynn took a long, steady breath in, and as she did, caught a quick, startling whiff of Yaniv's scent still on her, out of place and comforting. At her feet, Savta's ring glinted. Clarity washed over Rosalynn like a bucket of cold water. She closed her eyes and willed herself to disappear. She heard the officer shifting, her army boots crunching pebbles, a voice urgently speaking on the walkie-talkie, and felt her body shut down, become small and quiet and limp, her breath soft and light, her clothes a vacant, bodiless heap on the dusty floor. On the street a car alarm went off—a loud, piercing whine—but Rosalynn could not hear it. She was no longer there.

BELOW SEA LEVEL

When the time for their trip came, the streets of Montreal were already snowy, the sidewalks outside their Mile End apartment heaped with grey slush. David and Josie flew first to Amsterdam, spent a night in a hotel overlooking a canal, then to Tel Aviv, where they strolled along the seawall in jackets and boots, wrapped in wool scarves, watching the Mediterranean in all its wintry fury, a lone surfer battling large silver waves that dashed to shore.

Now, driving down the desert roads to Inbal, they were shedding layers, uncoiling scarves, rolling down windows, until it was hot enough to turn on the air conditioning, all in the course of two hours. The view through the windows turned yellower, sparser as they drove down a narrow winding road into the Jordan valley. David clutched the wheel, foot hovering above the brake pedal.

With every turn he pictured the car continuing over the abyss or crashing into trucks coming up the road.

"There it is," Josie gasped, pointing straight ahead. The Dead Sea glistened blue and long in the crease of the earth, inviting, deceptive. "200 Metres Below Sea Level," a sign on the side of the road announced. David imagined the seas he knew, the Pacific, the Mediterranean. Two hundred metres below their surfaces there must be no colour, no life. The thought made him shudder. Once, in grade six, he had nearly drowned at a Tel Aviv beach. He remembered the murky green-white, the silence penetrated by a thin hum, like a computer buzz. He'd been terrified of the sea ever since.

"You don't seem excited." Josie looked at him evenly.

"Sure I'm excited."

"You're worried. Why are you worried?"

He forced a smile. "Hello. Have you met me?"

She undid her seat belt and leaned over, kissing his cheek and neck.

"That's not helping." He tensed up.

She slumped back in her seat. "I'm the one who should be nervous."

"Don't worry," he said. "My dad is going to love you."

Josie cocked her head and looked at him. "Yeah?"

"He's not going to care that you're not Jewish. He's not like that. He used to rant about how Orthodox Jews don't go into the army and we have to serve for them, how our boys get killed so the Orthodox can live here, and they don't even acknowledge us."

"So let me get this straight." She held up her fingers and ticked them off. "No talk about Palestine, wars, terrorism or Orthodox Jews. Anything I'm forgetting?"

"No talk about me not going into the army." He glanced at her. "Ever."

It may have been eight years since he'd dodged service, but he didn't expect his father to ever really forgive him. As a child, David used to count the days until his dad came back from the army, envious of his classmates who had their fathers around to help them with homework, teach them how to ride bikes, be there for their birthdays and graduations. When his dad finally returned, dressed in uniform, smelling of metal and sweat, he took David out to play soccer, shoot hoops or watch a game, bought him gifts David had no use for, signed him up for activities he hated. At first, David played along, even though he was miserable, terrible at sports. He was into arts, a theatre buff, a Dungeons and Dragons enthusiast, a comics fan. Later, he started protesting, but his dad would hear nothing of it. "It's what men do. What are you? A little girl?" It got worse after the near-drowning incident. His father had taken him swimming on a red-flag day. We won't go far, he promised. But David swallowed water and when he came up for air, a huge wave filled his open mouth, his nostrils, tossed him violently, his knees scraping the bottom of the sea. When his father pulled him out, he seemed more annoyed than concerned. The water was only waist-high. "Why are you crying?" he snapped. "You're alive." David started dreading his dad's visits, shut down when his dad was home, felt relieved when he returned to the base. He looked forward to summers, when he and his mother would fly to Vancouver for two months, staying with his grandparents in Burnaby.

David and his mother moved to Canada soon after his eighteenth birthday. He was happy to leave; his friends had all started their service, coming home on weekends with their khaki uniforms and Uzis and steel boots, telling stories about basic training, using abbreviated lingo he didn't understand. Soon, they were calling less often, too busy to visit when they were on leave.

David gazed over at Josie, who was taking in the view, snapping shots with her cellphone: the long line of her neck, her strawberry mouth, her pale, rice-paper skin. There was another reason why David didn't want to talk about army service in front of her. He had been meaning to tell her the truth, but he had waited for the right moment, and now it was too late. They'd been dating for a year and a half. He felt the heat from the outside creeping in, sweat gathering on his forehead. He cranked up the air conditioning.

Josie put her hand on top of his, over the gearshift. "Relax, baby," she said. "It's all going to be fine."

He exhaled a breath he didn't know he had been holding. He worried still, of course. He always worried. "You're like an old woman," his father used to sigh. David couldn't help it. His mind saw potential catastrophes everywhere. Not just in Israel, where there were all the more reasons to worry, but in Canada too. The world was a death trap, and if it wasn't out to kill him, it was going to make things awkward and uncomfortable and unpleasant. He envied Josie, who lived life a day at a time. He envied all of those people he saw on the metro, on the bus, just walking the streets, listening to headphones, laughing with friends, not feeling like they were drowning.

It wasn't even his idea to come to Israel. He didn't talk to his dad much, only called on holidays and birthdays, kept their conversations short. Then one day David came out of the shower and found Josie standing by the window, laughing into the phone as if she was having a great conversation with a girlfriend. She covered the mouthpiece with her hand and whispered, "It's your dad."

David waved his hands in panic and mouthed, "I'm not here." But Josie was already handing him the phone.

"Three hundred metres." Josie pointed at a sign. They could see the shores of the lake now; hunks of salt floating in the water like misplaced ice floes. His ears popped. The lower they got the deeper his heart sank. Why would his dad choose to live here? At least in the city there was a crowd one could disappear into, streets and buildings in neat rows, the space organized and contained. The desert had always made David uncomfortable, how wide open and vast it was, its landscape hard and bony, like knuckles on a fist. And there was the silence, and the deadly heat—a monster ready to open its mouth and swallow him whole.

The village was lush with pink bougainvillea and groves of date palms. Small houses lined a narrow road, sprinklers rotating in the middle of green lawns. "This is so adorable," Josie said. The sun was setting over the Judaean Hills, colouring the shores of the Dead Sea mauve. The rental car crunched gravel as David inched his way along the main road, hunched over the wheel, squinting to read the house numbers. When he saw his father standing outside a small one-storey with a red tiled roof, watering flower beds, his heart flipped. After all these years, his dad still had this effect on him. "This is it," he said.

"That's your dad?" Josie's voice curled in surprise.

His dad grinned and waved. He was wearing faded jeans, a buttoned-up shirt and a cowboy hat. His Ray-Bans made him look like he was still in the army, though he'd retired a few years ago. He was fit and tanned. The Marlboro Man. David looked at his own skin, white from a Canadian winter, his thin arms.

He watched his dad through the glass as if there were still oceans
and continents between them. His father, sun-kissed in the warm
desert; David frozen in his chilled air-conditioned car.

His father walked toward the car and tried opening David's door,
which was locked. David smiled at him briefly, then unlocked the
door. "Open the trunk," his dad ordered in a thundering voice
that David hadn't inherited. "I'll get the suitcases."

Josie stepped out. "Mr. Sharabi," she said with a large, comfortable smile. "So good to finally meet you."

"Call me Eitan," his father said, opening his arms to hug her.
David watched her little frame in his father's giant arms and found
himself cringing. His father turned to him, grabbed him by the
shoulder and pulled him into an embrace. "Dudu," he said. "I'm
so glad you came."

Josie laughed.

"It's a common nickname in Israel," David said, cheeks turning
pink. "I knew you'd laugh."

"I'm not." She suppressed a smile.

Inside, the house was small with a dark tiled floor and arched windows. The living room was furnished with the black leather
couches and red Persian rug David remembered from his father's
previous apartment. In the guest room, a worn-out corduroy
armchair sagged next to a dusty chest of drawers. Books were
stacked on top of the chest: Israeli classics like Amos Oz and
A. B. Yehoshua, poems by Alterman and Bialik, a biography of
Ben-Gurion and a glossy book about the Jews of Yemen. The
futon was neatly made with striped sheets. David found it difficult to picture his father tucking in the sheets, meticulously

straightening the blanket on top. He heaved the suitcase onto the futon and unzipped it.

Josie threw herself on the mattress. The wood squeaked under her weight. She turned on her belly and shuffled toward him, looking up at him with a suggestive smile. "Now I know where you got your good looks from." She grabbed his sleeve and tried to drag him onto the bed.

"Don't," David said.

"We're on vacation."

He pulled out their toiletry bag and placed it on the chest. "Everybody says I look like my mom."

Josie cocked her head and looked at him. "You do have different skin tones, he's really dark. But you have the same eyes. And the smile."

"He has like four inches on me. And I have my mom's smile," David said. "Do you want to use the shower first?"

Josie looked at him a bit longer, then shrugged and hopped off the bed.

David was in seventh grade when he introduced Sharon Mizrahi to his dad. He'd met her in drama class and had had a devastating crush on her for the entire year. She'd been way out of his league, with long mocha legs, chocolate brown hair he could smell from where he sat in class, right behind her. She dated guys in the ninth grade. When they were assigned to do a dialogue together, he could not believe his luck. The afternoon Sharon came over to work on the assignment, his dad happened to be at home. Sharon giggled and blushed when his dad smiled in greeting. In David's bedroom Sharon whispered, "Wow, David, your dad is like a movie star."

When he was eighteen, after moving to Vancouver with his mom, he started dating Leah Rosen. She was his first serious girlfriend, his first everything. One day they were lying in his dorm room bed after making love, talking about marriage and babies. Leah's cheek was on his chest and she was playing with his belly hair when she said, "I know you'll age well, because I've seen photos of your father and he's smoking hot."

David pushed her off him.

He'd almost forgotten about all that. Living away from his dad, in Vancouver, and later in Montreal, had been good for him. He'd actually begun to develop some confidence. He was doing well at grad school, had published a few reviews in the local paper, and he had Josie, who found his neuroses endearing. She wasn't impressed by this macho stuff; she liked skinny boys, the artsy-nerdy type. She was the one who had asked him out, during his second year of university in Montreal. He'd seen her around; she was hard to miss, an art student with the kind of blonde curls you usually see on postcard angels. But she had a mouth on her that wasn't angelic at all: she swore, yelled, smoked and drank. David was intimidated and infatuated. She wore leg warmers when they weren't in style and a single feathery earring. She had a tattoo of a gecko on the back of her neck. She didn't wear a bra.

He stepped out of the room to find that his father had prepared dinner, set a table on the lawn with a white cloth over it, three place settings, a bowl of finely chopped salad and a bottle of red wine.

"Wow," David said. "You cooked?" His father grinned, inserting a corkscrew into the top of the bottle. David looked at the yard. The flowers, the mowed lawn, the fresh herbs: basil, cilantro, mint. His father was retired now. Perhaps he'd mellowed, become domesticated.

"You've got to love men who can cook." Josie emerged from the house dressed in a strapless blue summer dress and a grey cardigan, smelling clean, her curls shiny and wet. "David has a kitchen phobia."

"Mademoiselle." His father held the wine bottle in front of Josie and she nodded.

David leaned back in his seat, sipped wine and looked around while his dad brought over steaming plates piled with roasted chicken and mashed potatoes. The desert lurked at the back of the house, and David felt wary of its presence. A bright ribbon of left-over sunlight traced the tips of the Judaean Hills behind them, and the sea was marbled with pink and purple. Stars began to appear, spreading across the sky like a rash.

Josie sighed. "This is so magical. This is the calmest place I've ever been to."

David's father laughed. "And the West Bank is right there." He pointed vaguely south.

"What brought you here, Eitan?" Josie sipped her red wine.

His dad sliced a piece of his chicken and stabbed it with his fork. "I always wanted to live in the desert."

"You did?" David blurted out. He wiped his mouth with a napkin. "I always thought of you as a Tel Aviv kind of guy."

"I was barely there," his dad said. "I pretty much went wherever they sent me. But the desert—it's always been my dream. There's just so much space here. It's like you can really breathe."

"Must get lonely sometimes," Josie said. "No?"

"I found the city lonelier," he said. "All these people, and no one gives a shit."

David excused himself and went to the washroom. He washed
his face, wiped it with a towel and looked at himself in the mirror.
It had only been a few hours, but he already felt different, as if he'd
lost the little confidence he possessed, regressed to his younger self.
He didn't particularly enjoy small talk, had never been good at it.
The whole thing was awkward: the three of them, around the table.
It reminded him of all the times he had sat at dinners with his dad
and his dad's girlfriend of the week. David had been fifteen—his
limbs growing long and awkward, his forehead sprouting acne—
when his parents divorced, when he started spending weekends at
his dad's new apartment in the north end of Tel Aviv. Even when
his father wasn't dating, his apartment reeked of bachelor: empty
bottles of wine lined up on the balcony, dimmer switches on the
walls, a bedroom with dark silky sheets and melted remnants of
candles on the bedside table. He'd been mortified when his father
tried to talk to him about sex, inquiring about girls in his school in
an attempt to bond. Some nights he could hear stifled breath, the
bed squeaking, the mumbled whispers and giggles that followed.
Now, his mind, which constantly produced images of car wrecks
and terrorist attacks and crashing planes, people jumping in front
of metro trains, was picturing his dad and Josie kissing over the
table. He had to close his eyes and shake his head to erase the
image. He threw some more cold water on his face before going
outside. When he returned, Josie was laughing, head back, her
bare shoulders gleaming in the moonlight.

He helped clear the table, wash the dishes, and then wiped his
hands with a kitchen towel and announced in Hebrew that he was
going to turn in.

"Oh," his father said, pausing. "Already?"

"I'm beat," David said.

"Oh come on." His father switched to English. "It's not even midnight. Is he always like this?" He turned to Josie, who shrugged. "I got some good Scotch. Would grow hair on your chest."

"How about tomorrow, Aba." David yawned.

Josie followed David into the guest room and sat down next to him. "Your dad wants to spend time with you."

"It's been a long day," David said. "I'm tired."

"We came all this way . . ."

"Let it go."

She sat on the edge of the bed a moment longer, and then walked out.

When he woke up, Josie wasn't in bed. The red numbers on the digital clock radio read 1:05. He threw the sheet off, got up and walked out of the room. The house was dark and the moon cast rectangular shapes on the tiled floor. He heard muffled voices from the yard. He stood by the screen door, next to a coat rack heaped with his father's jackets. He could smell cologne on the fabric and recoiled, surprised by his reaction. His father and Josie were still sitting around the table. Josie was wrapped in a blanket now, holding a cigarette and laughing, her body angled toward his father. His father sat with his back to the door. They seemed cozy together. Josie was describing David's mom's recent visit to Montreal. "—such a sweetheart," she said. "Of course she wouldn't let us cook a thing, which was a real treat."

His father sighed. "I used to dream about her roast when I was stuck with my unit for weeks."

"So what exactly did you do in the army?" Josie said, shaking ice in her Scotch glass. David tensed.

"I was commander of a troop," his father said. "You don't want to hear about that. It's boring."

"Oh my God, are you kidding?" Josie laughed. "I've never met an IDF officer before."

David stared in disbelief. Josie was the kind of girl who refused to watch violent movies, who marched in peace rallies, who judged men who joined the Canadian army. When they had first met and she found out he was from Israel, she looked him up and down and asked, "Did you have to go to the army?"

"I had to," he said, "but I didn't."

"Wow," she said. "A refusenik."

He hadn't corrected her then, or since. He liked that she was impressed. Nobody else had ever been. His mother had been relieved, of course, but even she thought that it would make his life difficult in Israel. The truth was, his not going to the army had nothing to do with ideology. He was terrified. In the first interview he told them he was severely depressed. He said he'd kill himself if they made him go. He even manufactured some tears, all those years of drama school finally paying off. His dad was furious. He told David he would have no future in Israel, this would be a stain on his record forever, nobody would ever hire him. He told him he was not a man, would never be a man, called him a coward, worse than those Orthodox yeshiva students. "At least they believe in something!" Soon after that, his mother decided to move back to Vancouver, and David joined her, eager to get away from the army, away from his dad's fury and disappointment.

Josie came to bed half an hour later, smelling of Scotch and cigarettes.

"Since when are you so fascinated by the Israeli army?" he said into the dark.

"Come on, who isn't?" She laughed.

He lifted his head to reposition his pillow, smacking it twice before lying back down.

Josie was quiet. "Are you mad at me?"

He didn't answer.

"Did it bother you that I was talking to him?"

David snorted a laugh. "My dad could never resist a beautiful woman."

"That's crazy," Josie said.

"I don't want to talk about it," he said and turned his back to her.

The smell of brewed coffee, rich and laced with cardamom, woke him. He sat up in bed and Josie squinted at him and put a pillow over her face. His dad was going to take them to the beach today. "I'm not going," she said.

"What? You have to come."

"No," she said, taking off the pillow. "I've decided. I'm going to hang out here and read a book."

"Josie . . ."

"Go." Josie shooed him, waving her hand.

His dad leaned against the counter in Bermuda shorts and a sleeveless shirt, reading the paper. The kitchen was immaculate, the cabinets streaked with sunlight. He smiled when David walked into the kitchen. "Coffee?"

David nodded.

His father poured thick muddy liquid into a cup from a small pot on the stove. "You guys ready to go?"

David blew on his coffee. "I am," he said. "Josie is staying here."

"Everything okay?"

He took a quick sip from his coffee, burning his lip. "She just wants some time alone."

David pointed his remote key at the rental car, which beeped open, flashing its lights. His dad was walking in the opposite direction. They both paused and looked at each other. "Oh," David said. "How far is it?"

"Not far. Maybe thirty minutes."

David glanced up. The sun was climbing up in the sky. "It's pretty hot already."

His father waved his hand. "You've been living in Canada too long. Toughen up."

"Aba, you know I'm not much of a hiker. I'm going to slow you down. You're going to get annoyed."

"It's just a little walk. It will be good for you." He could hear the irritation in his dad's voice.

David sighed, scratching his head.

"Fine." His father turned around. "Forget it."

"No, no, we'll walk," David heard himself say.

They walked in silence for a while, out of the village and down the road. The Dead Sea sparkled in the distance. His father walked one step ahead of him, the sound of his sandals against the stones hard and purposeful, his dark, muscular calves bulging. They made it to a T junction, where a rusty signpost pointed south, toward Eilat, and north, to Jerusalem and Tel Aviv. The highway was empty, a long black snake disappearing into wavering haze, the asphalt shimmering wet in the distance. They crossed the road and hiked across a desert plain strewn with shrubs. The sun, which had risen from behind the Jordanian mountains, was blasting hot on David's skin, washing out the landscape. David thought of the last time he'd walked in the desert, in sixth grade, on a school trip. He had become overheated, and eventually twisted his ankle and had to return with a chaperone to the bus. He was happy to sit alone in the air-conditioning, eating snacks and sweets his mom had packed for him. When he'd lived in Israel, the news would sometimes report lost, dehydrated hikers who had gotten stranded in canyons, lain broken-boned at the bottom of cliffs, been swallowed up by sinkholes that cracked open without notice. There were snakes and jackals and foxes roaming the area, even leopards. Now it made sense, he thought. Of course his father would choose to live out here, build a home in this harsh and hostile land.

"Josie is great," his father said, already three steps ahead. "I have to say I'm very impressed."

"What do you mean?"

His father laughed. "I'm happy for you. She's the real deal." He half turned to David. "Reminds me of your mom. Feisty."

David didn't answer. He could do without the small talk. They reached a small cliff overlooking the water. David watched the view: a cluster of luxury hotels dotted with palm trees on the far right, the salt-mining fields spread out beyond. His father began walking down the rocky trail to the beach, skipping downhill with quick steps, no hands. David followed more cautiously, holding on to the wall, sweat trickling down his face.

"So how is your mom?" His dad looked over his shoulder.

"She's fine."

"Is she seeing anybody?"

"Aba, please."

"What?"

"Why would you ask me that?"

"Can't I care about what happens to my ex-wife?"

David shook his head to himself.

They made it down to the beach, which was wider than David remembered from childhood trips; the waterline had receded. They were walking on a stretch that had once been underwater. David was out of breath, sweaty and irritated. They had four more days here, four more awkward evenings and dinners—his father and Josie laughing while he ate in silence. He resented Josie now, for finding his father charming. She was supposed to be on his side. And what was so charming about his dad anyway? He wasn't particularly smart or witty; his sense of humour was not very sophisticated. Once, in Vancouver, David had asked his mother what had drawn her to him. His mother had gazed up from the dishes she was washing, her eyes all dreamy. "There was something about Eitan," she said. "Everybody wanted to be around him. He made people feel special." She's still in love with him, David had thought in dismay.

"Actually, she is seeing someone," David said.

"Oh." His father stopped to catch his breath. "Good for her."

"I just don't understand why you care."

His father turned to him and David was startled by the wounded look in his eyes. His father quickly rearranged his face into a smile, but it was a faint one. "What can I say?" He shrugged and carried on walking. "She broke my heart when she left. Never quite got over it, I suppose."

David stared at his father's back, the sweat shining on his neck. He had always assumed it was the other way around: that his father had been unfaithful, that whatever happened between his parents had been his father's fault, that it was his mother's heart that had been broken.

His father stopped abruptly, hands on his waist, his shoulders rising and descending with his breath. He raised his foot to take another step and wobbled, his hands flailing, grasping at the air.

"Aba?" David grabbed his father by the shoulders, steadying him. "You okay?"

"I need to sit down," his dad said, his voice calm and measured.

David looked around. He felt a quiver in his father's body, under his hands. His own heartbeat quickened. There was a single tree a few steps away, its wild, dried branches brushed to one side by the winds, providing little shade. His father leaned forward, hands on his thighs. David's rubbed his back awkwardly. "Aba." His voice shook. "We just need to make it to that tree. You think you can do that?"

"Guess I better." His dad managed a strained chuckle.

"I'll help you," David said, first rolling the backpack off his father's sweaty back and tossing it over his, then wrapping his father's arm around his shoulder. Every muscle in David's body was tensed, engaged in the task of supporting his father's weight. The two of them were breathing heavily now, not talking. When they made it to the tree, David slid his hands under his father's armpits. "I got you," he said through clenched teeth, lowering him to the ground, leaning him against the trunk. His father sat with his knees bent, eyes closed, the tan gone from his face. David rummaged with numb fingers through his father's backpack. He found a water bottle, unscrewed the cap and handed it to his dad, who guzzled it in long sips.

David checked his cellphone. There was no reception. He stuffed it back in his pocket, placed his hands on his hips and scanned the area. He couldn't see the road from here, the hotels or the village. They were alone. What if his father passed out? What if their water ran out? What if he died? He felt a familiar heaviness, water pressing on his chest. Not now. David turned the volume down on the chatter in his brain. Not now.

"I'm okay," his father said.

"Are you sure? I could run and get help."

"I'll be fine, I just need a minute."

David squatted and rifled through the bag again, found a plump orange and started peeling it, digging his dirty fingernails into the skin. He handed his father one wedge at a time.

His father opened his eyes to a squint. "I had a heart attack a few months ago."

"A heart attack?" David repeated dumbly.

"At the swimming pool. Got out and collapsed. Hit myself here." He drew a line on his forehead, where David could now see a scar. "I was in the hospital for a couple of weeks. They opened me up." He lifted his shirt; a long worm sliced through the centre of his chest.

"Why didn't you tell me?"

His father shrugged feebly. "You were there. What could you have done?"

"You should have told me." His father looked old suddenly, his face wrinkled and worn out.

"This is why I moved here," his father said. "Things had to change. Life is too short."

David sat down next to his dad, leaned his head back on the tree trunk.

"That is why I invited you here," his father said.

The sun crawled up their legs. David pulled out another orange, peeled it and offered wedge after wedge to his dad, watching the colour slowly returning to his face, his breathing resuming a normal pace. They sat in silence for a while, the sea lapping at the shore beside them, the sharp smell of oranges permeating the dry air. David thought of Josie and felt a twinge of regret. He wished she were here.

"I'm okay," his father said. "I'm ready to go."

"We shouldn't rush," David said.

"I'm fine. I'll take it easy."

"You thought you were fine before."

His father chuckled. "Fair enough," he said. "We'll stay."

David shifted his bottom to find a comfortable nook in the dry earth. He inhaled deeply, then exhaled. For a few minutes, breathing felt like work, but then everything slowed down: the buzz in his body, the noise in his mind; his breath easing into a rhythm in sync with the desert. Steps away from them, the sea was still and glassy, offering near-perfect reflections: hazy, pinkish mountains and salt rocks, white clouds sailing in blue water.

He glanced at his father, who leaned forward now, looking more like himself as he searched through the pebbles by his feet. He ran his fingers along the edge of one stone and then tossed it over his shoulder, bounced another on his open palm to gauge its weight. Finally he found a flat, smooth stone he seemed pleased with, and he flicked it with a quick snap of his wrist. The pebble skipped twice across the sea, disturbing the silence. David watched the ripples spread and widen, overlap, smearing the reflections like a watercolour painting.

"The water is good." His father glanced at him while ransacking the earth for another stone. "Doesn't get too deep around here."

"Yeah?" David said.

His father brushed the sand off a large stone, blowing on it. "You can go in if you want," he said. "I'll wait right here."

The water appeared calm again, the reflections intact. "You sure?" His father nodded.

David glanced at the empty beach, up at the sky, and then he kicked his sandals off, removed his shirt and pants and flung them on the ground. He jogged to the water's edge, the stones hot on his feet. When he looked back, his father was watching him and smiling.

The water engulfed him, smooth and silky, like warm honey. He felt a sting where his sandals had cut him on the walk. He advanced deeper, until his feet were pushed up to the surface of the salty water, forcing him to lie horizontal. No matter how hard he tried, he couldn't put them down. It occurred to him that he couldn't drown in this water. He took a long inhalation of rich air, interlaced his hands behind his head and floated, weightless, buoyant.

A SIGN OF HARMONY

Maya sees Ian, pushed along by the crowd pouring out of Indira Gandhi Airport, and her heart starts beating faster. A good sign. In London, up until the day she left for India, they'd been together non-stop, hardly ever leaving the apartment, the bedroom growing stuffy, the windows steamed over, the bedside table stacked with empty plates, an overflowing ashtray, glasses with stale water. She'd missed him these past two weeks, though not as much as she thought she would. She'd enjoyed being back here, on her own.

Ian cranes his neck. A stream of people parts and flows around him. Maya doesn't raise her arm, just watches him scan the crowd with quick, nervous glances. He wipes his forehead, passes a hand through his hair. Despite his dark skin, long eyelashes and thick eyebrows, he stands out, overdressed in his stiff jeans, his gelled hair, his fluorescent green backpack. He spots her and his face lights up. He hurries toward her, drops his bags and hugs her. She pushes him away and whispers, "No, Ian. Not here."

"I don't care." He slaps a quick kiss on her lips. "I missed you."

She squirms, smiling and looking around. Two Indian porters stare at them, chewing, checkered lungis wrapped around their waists. One spits paan on the tattered asphalt, adding another stain, blood red, to the blemished pavement.

Ian looks her up and down. "You're wearing a shalwar kameez."

Her hand smooths the silky fabric on her thigh. "You don't like it?"

"No, no. It's just different."

"It helps sometimes." She blushes.

"And this." He laughs, pressing the tip of his index finger to the round red bindi on her forehead.

"Fuck off." She smiles, her matching bangles jingle as she waves his finger away. She doesn't tell him that she's wearing it for him, all of it: the bangles, the bindi, the V-necked top and flared pants, brilliant blue embroidered with green flowers, his two favourite colours. Wearing Indian clothing in public didn't always help, sometimes it was just the opposite, the locals stared, couldn't make sense of her: an Indian woman (or so they thought) in traditional clothing and a backpack, travelling alone. Once, while walking with a white guy, German, in a small southern town, she was called names by Indian men who spat at her feet, thinking she was a local woman who'd strayed. She has since learned to navigate between her personas, her borrowed and inherited identities; she only wears a shalwar kameez when she's alone in markets and cities, trying to blend in, and opts for a loose skirt and T-shirt whenever she travels or walks around with tourists.

By the curb, an army of taxi drivers surrounds them, calling Ian "sir," gesturing toward their Ambassador black and yellow cabs. They are closing in, touching Ian's forearms. "Bloody hell," he says, lifting his arms over his head, revealing circular sweat stains. One of them picks up Ian's backpack and marches toward his cab. "Hey," Ian yells.

Maya puts a firm hand on Ian's shoulder. She follows the driver and bargains with him, sneaks in a few words of Hindi. Ian gets into the cab and lets out a long sigh. "What a gong show."

She smiles. "Welcome to India."

He leans back and stares out the window, his hand clutching hers.

The New Delhi night is heavy with moisture, burnt-garbage smoke and car exhaust. Traffic is congested yet moving: rickshaws, bicycles and cars; brightly painted Tata trucks, adorned with shiny tassels like decorated temple elephants; entire families on the backs of motorbikes, the women sitting sideways, holding on to the free end of their saris. Passengers hop off buses while others hop on, the bus never quite reaching a full stop; some hang onto the bars from the outside as the bus drives off. Cows saunter in the middle of the roads. Ian watches the chaos with huge eyes, forgetting to blink. Then he leans his head against the headrest and closes his eyes, his eyelids fluttering. She understands how he feels. There was no reason to assume it would be different for Ian simply because he is Indian. He grew up in London, after all.

Maya had been fresh out of the army when she first arrived from Tel Aviv. She had started planning her trip in the last few months of her service. All her friends talked about going to India, it was the thing to do after the army, but she was the first one to make enough money to do it, working six days a week, twelve-hour shifts as a waitress on Mango Beach. She went about planning her itinerary as she had her army office work: circled places on the map, placed sticky notes in her travel guide.

Two weeks into her trip, her backpack was stolen on a train to Varanasi: her passport, her traveller's cheques, her address book, her clothes, her travel guide. Gone. She had nothing but the clothes on her back. It was as if someone had erased her. Not that anyone was looking for her. Her father had refused to talk to her since she had joined the army—no place for good Orthodox girls—and her mother had never been strong enough to fight him.

While she was stranded in New Delhi, sorting out the passport and traveller's cheques, sleeping in random travellers' rooms, she met Vijay, who ran a travel agency from a small glass cubicle in the Krishna Guest House. He and his wife, Amrita, took her in, letting her sleep in the back room, leaving homemade food in stacked tin containers by her mattress. Maya, in return, babysat their daughter, manned Vijay's office while he was out for lunch, arranged his files in a system she had learned in the army. Amrita gave her one of her shalwar kameez to wear, stamped a bindi to the middle of her forehead, and when Maya looked in her small hand mirror, moving it over her body to try and construct a full image, she was stunned by her reflection. Her small frame, her dark skin, her straight black hair. "Like Indian girl," Amrita gasped, wobbling her head from side to side, in that gesture Maya later adopted, somewhere between yes and no. Even her name was Hindi, Vijay said. In Hindu philosophy, Maya was the illusion we veiled our true selves with. Maya thought back to who she was before India, at the Orthodox girls-only high school her father transferred her to after he'd found God, then in the army, where she'd slept alone in an empty dorm room while the other girls went home for the weekends.

Now, when she walked the streets of New Delhi, the city made space for her, letting her in. She had never expected to experience a spiritual revelation in India, had thought it a cliché, yet here she felt she was unveiling her true self, stripping off the illusion. "Maybe you were Indian in past life," Vijay offered, and she smiled at that, pleased.

The Krishna Guest House attendant grins as she walks in. "Namaste, didi." He shakes his head, eyeing Ian.

"Namaste, bhai," she says, calling him brother in return. She passes Vijay's old office; he recently made enough money to move to Goa, where he opened an office in Panaji. She leads Ian up the dark staircase, stops at a wooden door, fumbles with a large key. The green tiled hallway is poorly lit, and she can hear the echo of conversations, Bollywood music playing from the reception area, the attendant singing along. Ian twists his nose at the smells she has become accustomed to: damp air sweetened with burning incense, Lysol, fried oil, urine.

It is bigger than the single room she usually rents, her home in New Delhi, and has a window facing the hallway. It even has hot water in the shower. Ian walks through it with a wary look, touches the sheets, squints at the ceiling fan, peeks into the washroom with its ceramic hole in the ground.

"It's clean," she says. "I've been staying in this guest house since my first trip."

"I think you've been spending too much time in India."

"You'll get used to it."

He kisses her, pushes her onto the bed. She squeals. The ceiling fan grunts above their heads.

They spend the next day walking up and down the main bazaar, a narrow street lined with shops and filled with backpackers, scooters, cows and emaciated dogs. The shopkeepers all know her; they invite them for chai, laugh when she speaks Hindi. Ian watches her inquisitively while the shopkeepers fling open embroidered bedspreads, urge her to feel wrap skirts and silk scarves, open boxes filled with jewellery, packages of incense and bindis. She smiles at their sales pitches. "Today, no business." It's too early to start shopping for the European festival season, during which she sells things from India every summer. This is her fourth time going through this cycle: she spends the fall and winter travelling through India, stocks up on merchandise during spring, and come summer—the unbearably hot monsoon season—leaves for Europe. She met Ian a few months ago while couch surfing in London. They were at a party in a huge artist loft in Soho, on the top floor of an old school. The place was bare: a record player on a desk, a stack of paintings in the corner, a double mattress and an L-shaped cream leather couch. She mistook him for an Israeli, maybe of Yemeni heritage, like her. Later he told her he'd thought she was Indian.

The real party was in the washroom, which was the size of an average bedroom, with brick walls and exposed pipes running along the high ceilings. She found herself standing beside him, crowded up against the raw concrete counter where people bent over, one at a time, to do lines of coke. He was small, compact, only a bit taller than her, his body defined and masculine. Later, when she touched his arm in conversation, she noticed his skin tone matched hers. He told her his father had left Rajasthan at sixteen with his parents and never returned. He'd met Ian's British mother at a house party in London—Ian smiled telling her this—

and married her against his parents' wishes. Ian had never met his grandparents, and now they were both dead.

She told him she hadn't been on speaking terms with her father either, found herself sharing details she usually was reluctant to expose, describing the double life she had led all through high school, how she carried a pair of jeans and an eyeliner in her bag and changed in the bushes before heading off to parties in Tel Aviv. She was high and a little bit drunk, just enough to feel daring and sexy. When the party died out, the house emptied, and the grey morning poured in through the large windows, she sat straight up on the couch and said, "Let's not go home yet." They went to a café and ordered espressos, and the young, perky barista smiled at them and said, "You look like brother and sister."

"Ew." Maya twisted her face.

"No, it's a good thing," the barista hastened to add. "It's a sign of harmony." Maya and Ian laughed, looking anywhere but at each other. Outside the café they kissed. They flagged a taxi to his apartment, and by the time they made it to his front door, her bra was unfastened, his zipper undone and their lips raw and swollen.

She had moved into his apartment within three weeks. He had three other roommates, so they rarely left his room, spending days in bed, making love, drinking coffee, watching TV, ordering in. In the evenings, when Ian went to work, she'd visit him, sit at the bar and drink fancy cocktails he'd make especially for her.

"So why India?" he asked one night while polishing wine glasses. She shrugged.

"But what do you do there? Apart from buying stuff to sell?"

"Nothing, everything. What do you do here? What do people do anywhere?"

"It's not the same, this is my home."

"People move. India feels like my home." She stirred her fruity martini with her finger. "You should come with me," she said, and he looked at her obliquely, smiling. "I'm serious. See for yourself what's so amazing about it. Imagine what an experience that would be, being in a place where everyone looks like you."

From the rooftop restaurant above the Krishna, New Delhi is bathed in amber smog. Square crowded roofs are punctuated by a few tall apartment buildings, and two round domes in the distance are a hazy mirage. On neighbouring roofs kids are flying kites. The sky is a thin golden sheet, the sun a cigarette-burn at its centre. Ian highlights the itinerary for the day in his guidebook, then puts down the pen. "It's so hot." He fans the menu in front of his face. "How do people live here?" He walks over and turns the standing fan toward them. "I can't wait to get to the beach," he says, lifting his shirt to balloon over the fan.

The rickshaw zips around Connaught Place, the driver's torso leaning toward the centre of the roundabout, the other vehicles swirling like debris around a drain. Maya lights a cigarette and inhales. She likes riding rickshaws; there are no doors, no glass to separate them from the street. The city is in their faces, like a gust of hot air. At the traffic light, beggars shove skinny arms into the rickshaw. Maya gives one man her half-smoked cigarette and lights another one for herself.

By the time they reach the Red Fort, the heat sits over the city like a fat, sweaty Buddha. They walk through the fort, its red walls faded to pink by the sun. The corridors are thronged with groups of middle-aged Europeans, their faces shiny and wide with awe, camera-toting Japanese in bucket hats, and young backpackers, their flip-flops smacking the marble floors.

"Let's eat. I'm starved," Maya says as they walk out of the fort, pointing at a makeshift restaurant across the street: a few plastic tables and long wooden benches, huge industrial pots steaming under a tent. A tourist bus is parked outside and its passengers, middle-class Indian families, all wearing baseball caps and sneakers, are lined up on the benches.

"Here?" Ian follows her, stands behind her in line. He peeks into the pot, waving away flies.

The waiter places two large trays in front of them: small tin bowls circle a mound of rice, each filled with a different type of vegetable. A piece of steaming roti is folded in the corner of the tray. Maya gathers rice with her fingers and shoves it into her mouth with her thumb. Ian rips a piece of roti and dips it in his saag as if it were a biscuit in a cup of tea.

The bus starts honking and the passengers board. A young Indian couple in jeans and T-shirts eyes them and smiles. Maya smiles back. They must think Ian and Maya are just like them.

They take a rickshaw to the Chandni Chowk bazaar: tangled wires, chains of coloured bulbs and large banners hanging between dilapidated buildings. The heat is at its peak and everything smells stronger, ripened. As soon as they step out of the rickshaw, people brush against them, push them, touch them. Porters carrying canvas sacks of fragrant spices shove their way through; their dark, bony legs poke out of their lungis. Ian and Maya turn into an arched alleyway and beggars latch on to them. Ian is hugging his camera like it might leap from his chest. A barefoot child wheels a man with no limbs on a plywood board past them. A blind woman, her eyes excavated, waves flies away from her listless baby. Another woman's nose seems to be eaten away by leprosy. A little girl with an amputated arm tugs on Ian's sleeve. Ian dispenses rupees at a panicky pace.

"Bas," Maya yells at a young woman who has been following her from the moment they turned down the alleyway. The woman twists her face in a pitiful expression, pointing at her mouth, at the toddler she's carrying, his hair matted, his eyes lined with kohl. Ian stuffs a rupee note into her hand.

By the time they make it to the Jama Masjid, Ian seems exhausted. They sit on the red sandstone stairs leading to the mosque, drinking chilled Fantas next to a group of young, fully veiled Muslim women. Ian massages the bridge of his nose.

"Headache?" she says.

"Just tired." He looks at her. "You've been there before. Couldn't you have warned me?"

She ignores the accusing tone. "It will get easier, you'll see." She thinks of her first time in this bazaar. She was mesmerized by it; she'd bought fabric and strappy sandals, sampled food from street vendors, walked until her feet blistered.

He takes a sip from his Fanta, wipes his mouth with the back of his hand and rolls his head from side to side until she hears a faint crack. "How about we stay somewhere nice in Jaipur?" He glances at her sideways, smiling. "I wouldn't mind having a real toilet."

The train to Jaipur is air conditioned and a lot fancier than the second-class sleeper she usually takes. As the train chugs through the slums on the outskirts of Delhi—decrepit structures made of corrugated iron and patched up with plastic and cloth—Ian snaps photos: a young woman shaking a yellow sari to dry; kids skipping over rocks, chasing the train; three men crouching to shit along the tracks, one of them waving.

The hotel Ian picked has rooms arranged around a stone-paved courtyard with wicker chairs and flowerpots. As they walk to their room, chatting about their plans for the day, they pass a group of backpackers, three boys and a girl, arguing loudly with one of the workers. "Babu," one of them says in a strong Israeli accent, towering over the much shorter Indian man. "You say two hundred rupee, no? Two people, four people, no difference." She walks straight ahead, pretending not to hear or see them, until they reach their door and she glances over her shoulder. One of them, a curly-haired boy with a tribal armband tattoo catches her gaze and smiles. Maya looks away.

They spend the afternoon sightseeing in Jaipur. It's a city Maya knows well, where she buys most of the silver jewellery she sells. In the evening, they walk into a restaurant Ian selects from the travel guide. It has dimmed lighting, an ancient air conditioning unit dripping into a plastic bowl at the entrance, a CD player playing old movie tunes. There is only one other couple in the restaurant, older and white, with sparse grey hair, wearing matching Bermuda shorts and pale buttoned-up shirts.

"Expensive," Maya whispers to Ian as the waiter leads them to a table covered with a maroon tablecloth and hands them laminated menus in padded folders.

He waves his hand. "I'm from London." He sits back in his chair, legs spread, flipping quickly through the menu. "I'm having tandoori chicken." He snaps the menu shut.

Maya raises her eyebrows. "I thought you didn't trust the meat in India."

"Fuck it." He grins. "You only live once."

He orders too much food: samosas, pakoras, a basket of naan, an assortment of chutneys. When the large Kingfisher beer arrives, he pours some into each of their glasses, sips from it, licks froth off his lip and sighs. "Starting to feel human again," he says, stretching his arm across the table and grabbing her hand. In this restaurant, at this moment, he looks like the man she remembers from London. After three beers he slips his foot out from his flip-flop, reaches under her skirt and strokes the side of her thigh with his toes. She stiffens. The older couple are busy eating. The waiter is nowhere to be seen. She swallows and moistens her lips. He hasn't been that bold since the first night. In fact, they haven't been having as much sex as she thought, or hoped, they would.

"You're bad." She lowers her chin, shuffles down in her seat so that his foot is resting on the crotch of her underwear.

He wiggles his toes.

"Screw dessert," she says. "Let's go back to the room."

"Holy shit." He straightens in his seat, his foot sliding down. "Did you see that? I just saw the hugest rat. Right there, across the beam."

She sighs and sips her beer.

"Did you see it?" His eyes are focused up, his jaw slightly dropped. "I swear it was the size of my forearm."

She shrugs. "They're everywhere. They're like cows."

"Let's get out of here," he says. When the bill comes he slips a credit card to the waiter, and Maya adds the bill up in her head and thinks of how many days she could have lived in India on that amount of money.

She flags a rickshaw outside the restaurant. "Raj Hotel."

"Forty rupees." The driver doesn't look at her. His oily hair is hennaed red and brushed over to one side. He sucks on his bidi.

She scoffs. "Fifteen."

The driver flicks his bidi onto the gravel and stares straight ahead.

"It's fine," Ian says. "Let's just get out of here."

"Twenty," she says.

"Forty."

"Pagal." She twirls her index finger at her temple and begins to walk away. Ian climbs in.

She stops and turns to him. "I can't bargain if you're already sitting there."

He sighs. "God, just let it go."

She puffs out her cheeks, letting out a deep breath. She climbs into the rickshaw and sits perched at the edge of her seat, looking out and smoking.

In the hotel room Ian lies on the bed and watches her as she undresses, his head propped against the headboard. "You realize you were bargaining for the equivalent of less than a pound."

"It's not about that." She takes off her shirt. "It's how it works here. They expect you to bargain. Didn't you read about it in your guidebook?"

"Well, you didn't have to talk to him like that."

"Like how? It's called negotiating."

"I don't know. You seemed a little harsh."

"I'm Israeli, this is how we talk." She takes off her small hoop earrings and places them on the shelf.

He shakes his head, picks up his guidebook from the bedside table.

"What?" she says. "You guys are just as patronizing as Israelis. We're just more direct about it."

"I'm Indian," Ian says.

"I'm more Indian than you are," she says and immediately regrets it.

"Wow." He raises his hands.

"I'm sorry," she says. "I didn't mean that."

He puts on his headphones and turns his back to her. She watches him shutting down, pulling the blinds over.

The courtyard is lit with lanterns, swarming with dark clouds of bugs. She crosses the street to pick up another pack of Gold Flakes and, as she pays the clerk, hears laughter and talking from the back of the store. Without thinking, she follows the sounds to a small garden restaurant with backpackers sitting around candlelit tables. She orders a Kingfisher, unwraps the plastic off her package of Gold Flakes and glances at the table next to her. The Israeli group from this afternoon.

"Achi," the guy with the short army cut tells the curly-haired man. Achi. *Brother.* "If you're in Manali, you should go to Kullu and Parvati Valley. The best charas you'll ever taste."

"It's true. I was there in the spring," she offers in Hebrew. The language feels new and clunky in her mouth. When was the last time she used it?

"You were?" Curly hair eyes her; he's wearing faded Thai pants and a sleeveless shirt, a large woven necklace with a turquoise stone around his neck. "Second time in India?" he says, passing her a joint.

She sucks in the sweet, smooth smoke. "Fourth actually."

He whistles, slides into the chair opposite hers. "Omer," he says.

"Maya."

A waiter carrying a tray with four lassis stops by their table. The three guys each take one. The girl says, "No fucking way. After last time?" She blows a large bubble with her gum and sucks it back in.

The waiter hovers.

"Maybe Maya wants it?" Omer says. "Bhang lassi?"

She looks at the tray. She's already stoned, still holding the joint Omer passed her. "Why not." She takes a long sip. Banana, yogurt and hash. Omer watches her. She'd forgotten how intense Israeli men can be. "You stay at our hotel," he says. "That guy, he's your boyfriend?" Or how direct.

"Yes," she says.

"Oh, you're one of those."

"One of what?"

"What is he, British?"

"He's half Indian."

"British guys, they're like refrigerators," the girl volunteers and the guys howl with laughter. "I dated one in Israel. No passion. They're not like our boys. Now I could never date a guy who isn't Israeli."

"You mean, not arrogant and obnoxious?" Maya says.

The girl stares at her, her mouth slightly open. Omer laughs. "Well, maybe Maya loves him. Right?"

"Right," she says.

"That's what's important. Love."

The courtyard is covered in soft Cellophane. The lights turn dimmer, but the sounds crystallize, spoons hitting glass, a man's laughter, cars honking from the main road. She sinks into her chair, comfortable, content, resigned to staying awhile. Maybe she should bring Ian here tomorrow evening for a bhang lassi. It would loosen him up a bit. The guys and the girl get into a heated argument. Something about Palestinians. Or Lebanon. Or maybe some Israeli reality show Maya doesn't know. The girl keeps yelling, "No, no, no," half-rising from her chair and leaning over the table. They are the loudest table in the restaurant. People at other tables keep glancing at them. Omer lights a Winston and holds the package open in front of Maya. She takes one and he strikes a match. She leans over. Too close. Her cigarette hits his hand. His face is long and oval, his features sharp, like a fox.

"So how long have you been travelling?"

"About three years." She leans back and inhales deeply. She's missed American cigarettes. She's missed cigarettes that don't taste like sand.

"Ahhh, that explains it." Omer blows out smoke.

"Explains what?"

"It fucks you up, not having a home for that long."

Maya smiles with her mouth closed.

"You travelled all this time with your boyfriend?"

"No, he just got here." She peels the label off her beer bottle and eyes him, considering how much to share. "He hates it."

"I thought you said he was Indian."

For some reason this makes her laugh, and then she can't stop. Omer joins in. They laugh for a long time, and her eyes are tearing up.

"Well, guess he doesn't belong here any more than we do," Omer finally says. "It's like you going back to . . . what are you, Yemeni?"

She nods and shuffles in her chair, annoyed that he places her in the same category as him, with all of them, as if she's just another one of those backpackers who come here for a few months after army service and then return to their real homes, start university, rent an apartment in Tel Aviv, hang a series of stylized photographs of barefoot Indian children on their living room walls, cover their mattresses with Rajasthani mirror-studded bedspreads.

When the waiter walks by, Maya waves at him and orders another Kingfisher in Hindi.

Omer takes a swig from his beer and stares at her in a new way. "You speak Hindi."

"A little bit."

"Do people think you're Indian?"

"Sometimes."

"Bet you love it."

She shrugs, takes a long sip from her beer.

"So what's your story? What are you running away from?"

She frowns. "Isn't it what we're all doing? Running away from everything back home?"

"Yeah, but that's a long time to be running away," he says. "I'm going back next month."

She looks around and realizes the restaurant is almost empty. The lights are off. The candle on their table is flickering, dying out. When did everyone else leave? She feels a pang of fear and exhilaration, a thrilling sense of dread, like her first day in the army, her first day in New Delhi. She swallows. "I'm really stoned," she says. She realizes she's been staring at his lips; they're full and dark purple, as if bruised.

"You okay?" Omer leans over the table and gives her a warm, caring look. She thinks of her mother, of the last time she saw her, the day before she flew to India. It was Saturday morning, her father was at the synagogue, they ate kubaneh her mother had baked overnight with spicy, lemony hilbe; dipped a brown, hard-boiled egg in grated tomatoes mixed with green schug, speckled with red chilies. The sweet smell of kubaneh stayed in Maya's hair, the oil in her fingers, the tang of fenugreek oozing from her sweat throughout the next day, on her flight here.

"Hello. Earth to Maya," Omer says. "You okay? Do you want me to get you coffee? Water? Anything?"

"I'm fine." She looks at her hand and sees that she's holding a filter with perfectly formed cigarette-shaped ash. She jerks and the ash crumbles and falls off.

Omer leans forward, offers her his hand, palm up, across the table. He examines her, eyes narrowed.

"No, really," she says, and she places her hand on his. "I'm okay."

He looks down at their hands; they lay on top of each other cupped, as though holding something fragile. He swallows, his Adam's apple retreating and bulging.

"So . . ." he says. "I bought an Enfield in New Delhi and rode it here."

"Oh yeah?"

"You should come with me. To the Himalayas."

She laughs.

"I'm leaving tomorrow morning."

"Very funny."

"You know you want to."

A sudden alarm goes off inside her head. She glances at the clock. It's past 2:00 a.m. "I have to go." She pulls her hand away, palm moist, stands up too quickly, dropping her smokes. She tries putting money on the table, but Omer puts his hand on hers and says, "It's on me." She doesn't argue. She crosses the street, half running, slows down as she reaches the gate. The hotel is dark, the courtyard empty. She hears steps behind her and her heart begins to pound. Omer catches up to her in the corridor. He pushes her gently against a wall. His breath is hot, sweet from charas, banana, Kingfisher beer. "Hey," he says.

"This is a bad idea." She puts her hand on his shoulder as if she's about to push him away but then kisses him instead. His tongue tastes good swirling in her mouth. He grabs her hand, leads it down to the bulge in his pants. He lifts her skirt with his other hand, moves her underwear aside with quick fingers.

She hears shuffling footsteps, lets out a gasp and pushes Omer away. A flashlight turns on, its beam skittering across the court-yard. Maya arranges her skirt and, when the light finds them, puts her hands together in Namaste and greets it in Hindi. The night guard lowers the flashlight to his feet and squints at Maya and Omer as if trying to read the situation he's walked into. Omer nods at him. "Everything okay, Miss?" the guard asks Maya in Hindi.

"Everything's fine." She wobbles her head. He lingers, studying Omer, then says, "Good night," and walks away. They're silent until he disappears behind a corner.

"Aren't you handy to have around." Omer grabs her by the waist, pulls her to him. "You're really good at this whole Indian thing."

She removes his hands. "Indian thing?"

"You know, your whole . . . act. Must be good for bargaining."

"Look, Omer . . ." She crosses her arms on her chest. "I can't do this. I have a boyfriend."

He nods with a thin smile. "Right."

"I should really go."

She rounds a corner and leans against the brick, catching her breath. Through the window of their room she sees Ian sleeping. He's stretched out on his back, his face turned to the window, the sheet pulled down to reveal his chest, a few curly hairs sprouting in a clump like a wilted flower. She's taken by how handsome he is, like a Bollywood actor. He could be a local, especially now, undressed, stripped of his accent, his guidebook, his backpack. He looks the part, just like she does; both wear the right skin colour, the right features, yet neither of them belongs here, not really. She wonders if this is all they ever had in common. Ian shifts in his sleep; in this light the harsh lines of his features are softened, boyish, like the child he must have been. She's filled with sadness. She lowers herself to the floor, pulls a pack of cigarettes from her pocket and realizes she took Omer's Winstons by mistake. She smokes one, two, three cigarettes before she goes in.

BORDERS

It was Karin's idea, hitchhiking to Eilat for the last summer before army service. The last summer. It sounded romantic to Na'ama, like one of those old Israeli movies they played on cable Friday nights. A summer of firsts and lasts, of falling in love and saying goodbye, skinny-dipping in the sea and staying up until sunrise. In the movies, one of the characters was bound to die in the army, always the sweet, gentle one no one had imagined as a hero.

But there was nothing so dramatic in Na'ama's and Karin's future. The Gulf War had ended a few months ago, and for a brief, hopeful moment it seemed like there would never be another war. Karin was enlisting in September, predestined for the infantry corps, which was exactly what she wanted, to be surrounded by cute boys in uniform. Na'ama was due to report in November; she was assigned to general basic training, which suited her fine since she wasn't sure what she wanted to do anyway.

Eilat was the farthest they could go in the country, the farthest from their families and the memory of high school, of stuffy classrooms and textbooks and final exams. Neither of them could afford to travel to Greece, like some of the girls in their grade. They had been to Eilat several times that year. The summer before, Karin had filled in a ballot at the mall and won a basic scuba diving course for two at The Deep. Na'ama was reluctant at first. She remembered Eilat from childhood visits: the noise, the dirt, the crowds, the throngs of high school students and soldiers on leave who slept in packs under gazebos, drank beer and shandy at seawall cafés and picked up topless European tourists at the beach. But Karin said the diving club was outside the city, on Coral Beach, minutes from the border with Egypt, and that it was serene, beautiful. "More like Sinai." And after two days at The Deep Na'ama was hooked. Coral Beach wasn't Sinai, but it was close enough to trigger her body's memory: the same red, jagged mountains towering quiet and majestic behind her, the same warm sea licking her feet. They had come back for Sukkot, Hanukkah and Passover, but always for just a few days, never for an entire month.

It was their first time hitchhiking. Karin said it would be cheaper and faster "and more fun" than taking the bus—a five-hour night ride from Tel Aviv, which dropped them in the southern city well before sunrise and left them wandering the darkened streets as they waited for the first bus to Coral Beach. In the end it took longer; they hadn't accounted for the waits at the sides of dusty roads, and for losing rides to soldiers in uniform. Finally, they were picked up by a gold-toothed truck driver who chain-smoked Time cigarettes—the smoke swirling inside the cabin, clinging to their hair—and who never stopped ogling Karin's brown legs.

By late afternoon the Gulf of Eilat emerged in the distance, a surprising blue amidst the browns and yellows, like a fallen piece of sky wedged between the mountains and the city. Na'ama rolled down the window and inhaled the hot, dry desert air. She could feel her heart expanding, her breath softening, her muscles winding down. It was as though her body had retuned itself, resonating with an old melody.

Na'ama was born and raised an hour south of Eilat, in the Sinai Peninsula, in what was now Egypt. She was a child of the desert, her feet callused by hot, white sand, her eyes used to squinting through the fog of sandstorms, her body accustomed to moving slowly, preserving its energy on hot summer days. The small Israeli moshav she had called home was nothing more than a cluster of plain houses, a modest guest house, a dive shop and a grocery store, built on the Red Sea shore by a few dozen families and some young hippie drifters. Mira, Na'ama's young, Tel Avivian mother, had been posted to Sinai during her army service, a couple of years after the peninsula was seized in the Six Day War. She had fallen in love with it—the remoteness, the simplicity, the unbearable beauty—and decided to stay, undisturbed by the fact that it was Egyptian land, taken over in an act of war. There weren't many Egyptians living in the peninsula, just Bedouins, who lived in tents, adhered to tribal laws and didn't care which government ruled them. The land itself didn't change, they said. Egyptian, Israeli, it was all the same.

Her mother had named her after Na'ama Bay in Sharm el-Sheikh, at the southern tip of Sinai, where the Gulf of Aqaba and the Gulf of Suez—flanking the triangular peninsula like two fingers held up in a peace sign—both spilled into the Red Sea. Na'ama had visited

Sharm once with her mother; their friend Tariq had given them a
ride in his pickup truck. On the way there, Na'ama sat crammed
between Mira and Tariq in the front seat, the road, paved by the
Israelis, glistening along the shore, her mom's long hair flapping
around like octopus arms. In comparison to their moshav, the
small town of Sharm seemed a dazzling metropolis, with a prom-
enade, restaurants, even an airport.

It was Na'ama and Mira's last journey in Sinai, a goodbye trip
before they had to pack up and leave. Israel's final withdrawal
from Sinai was weeks away, following the peace agreement with
Egypt: Begin and Sadat shaking hands in pictures that made history, raising hope for a new Middle East. On their way back from
Sharm, nobody spoke. The sun sank behind the mountains, the
world a muted pink. Tariq drove too fast, his kaffiyeh stiffly fluttering, while Mira leaned her head out the open window—wet
trails on dusty cheeks—and took in every curve in the road, every
rock and mountain and lagoon, as though creating a mental inventory, a catalogue of home.

It had been nine years since they'd left Sinai. Some moshav
members went back to visit regularly, but Mira never had. Na'ama
understood. She too was afraid of disappointment, scared to find
the place a faded version of her childhood home.

The plan was to get a job behind the counter at The Deep, filling air
tanks, signing out diving equipment. They also had some money
saved from working at a movie theatre over the past few months,
and the hostel—a damp, dark one-storey with a row of dorm
rooms and two mouldy communal showers—was dirt cheap. But
when they got there, there were no jobs: a leggy blonde was work-

ing the counter alongside a guy with dark curls and intense green eyes. Everyone called him Samir, even though Na'ama was pretty sure he wasn't an Arab. He looked up when they came in, followed them with his gaze.

"Plan B," Karin whispered and waved at Ari, the owner, with whom she'd been having an ongoing affair since last summer. He had let them use the equipment for cheap before, join some dives he led, and had even given them a special deal for their certification dives during Passover. Ari's face broke into a smile when he saw Karin; he strode over and picked her up by the waist, spinning her around. Karin squealed. Ari was twenty-seven: a real man, with big, tattooed arms, a shaved head perpetually shadowed with new growth, and a patch of curly chest hair. Na'ama was intimidated by him, envied Karin for being so comfortable around him, around men in general. She often felt as if she was Karin's plus-one at The Deep, the same way she felt when they waited in club lineups in Tel Aviv. Now Karin threw her head back laughing, her black curls bouncing like a shampoo commercial. She punched Ari in the arm, and he rubbed it as if it hurt. She gave him a peck on the cheek, turned to face Na'ama and grinned. Ari slapped her butt and she lurched forward, then flipped her hair back and sauntered away. He stared at her hips.

Their room smelled of salt and wet bathing suits and coconut sunscreen. A little window framed two shades of blue. Karin claimed the top bunk, flinging her sunglasses and purse onto the mattress. Two other beds were already occupied, backpacks stuffed under the frames and toiletries lined up on the bedside tables.

"What do you think of the guy behind the counter?" Karin asked as they zipped open their backpacks.

Na'ama shrugged.

"He's cute. You should do it with him."

"I haven't even spoken to him!"

Karin laughed. "Then go talk to him."

Na'ama shook her head.

"What?" Karin gave her a little nudge with her hip. "You should be thanking me. You'd never do it if I didn't harass you. You need to take the initiative."

For weeks Karin had been telling Na'ama that she had to lose her virginity before the army. And this was the place for it: Na'ama's first kiss had been in Eilat, her first make-out session. She could trace her sexual history along this shore.

Na'ama pulled out her toiletry bag and her diary, a leather-bound notebook with a floral design she'd bought last summer. Some photos tumbled out of it onto the floor, and she bent down to retrieve them. They were all a variation of the same image: her mother's girlfriends from the moshav holding Na'ama as a newborn baby, displaying her to the camera in awe and delight. She blew the dust off the last photograph as she picked it up: Tariq was sitting in his galabeya on a frayed rug with Na'ama in his arms, his shoulders hunched as if to protect her. The photos were grainy, yellowed and faded, as though desert sand had coated the lens. She had found the stack a few days ago while rummaging through her mom's closet for a backpack. She'd never seen them before; her mother hadn't kept photo albums for the same reason she owned little furniture: such things made picking up and moving at a moment's notice more difficult. The only picture Na'ama had had of Tariq was taken when she was five or six, the two of them sitting on the beach, backs to the photographer, both looking over their shoulders.

She felt the familiar tug of memories threatening to pull her in like an undertow. It wasn't just the photos—this happened every time she visited Eilat. She missed Sinai, now more than ever, and she missed Tariq, who had been a big part of her life growing up. Na'ama used to perk up at the sight of him: his tall, narrow frame, the loose galabeya hanging like a tent from his broad shoulders. Everyone at the moshav was fond of Tariq, and not just because he supplied them with smuggled hash, the smell of which frequently wafted across the beach, as much a part of the place's aroma as sea salt and desert dust. He knew everyone by name, stopping to ask about their day, share a cigarette or a coffee. On cold nights he told stories around the fire with a dramatic tenor and expressive gestures, and when he burst into his belly-deep laughter, everyone wanted to join him. The men chatted and played backgammon with him, the kids chased him around, begging him to let them ride his camel, and the tourists, whom he guided to the Santa Katarina Monastery in his pickup truck, took pictures of him, regal in his galabeya.

"Who's this?" Karin snatched the photos from her hands.

"Tariq." Na'ama watched her careless fingertips on the print. "From Sinai. He used to babysit me sometimes."

"Seriously?" Karin raised her eyebrows. "Your mom let a Bedouin babysit you?"

"He was our friend," Na'ama said. "It was different over there."

Karin browsed through the photos quickly and stopped at one of Mira, sitting cross-legged on a bed, wrapped in a tie-dyed sarong, her long, straight hair parted in the middle, her eyelids heavy, smoke curling from the cigarette she was holding up to her lips. She looked like a seventies movie star, an olive-skinned, voluptuous beauty, with long, thick eyelashes, defined cheekbones and a dimpled smile. It was a cruel genetic injustice, Na'ama had always thought, that she looked nothing like her mother. Her own features were too large for her narrow face; her skin was the colour of sand, and her body angular, boyish, with jutting hip bones, a flat chest, and sharp, triangular shoulder blades that didn't make for good cuddling.

Karin handed the photos back to Na'ama. "Your mom is so awesome," she sighed.

Na'ama squared the stack of photos and put them away, saying nothing. From the very first time she had brought Karin home, Karin had been enthralled by Mira, mesmerized by their home: the emptiness, the quietness, the femininity of the decor. The three-bedroom apartment in Shikun Lamed in Tel Aviv was their fifth try at a home since leaving Sinai. Before that, with the compensation money the Israeli government had paid them for evacuating, Mira had bought and sold apartment after apartment the way some mothers discard old clothes. With every move, Na'ama grew more restless, more resentful of her mother, envious of her classmates who lived in apartments filled with photos and memories, packed with old, heavy furniture, door frames etched with proof of their growth. Na'ama became adept at moving, until the act of packing and unpacking, claiming space by arranging books on shelves, laying down frayed rugs on tile floors, became her idea of home.

"So what's the story with your dad?" Karin had asked the first day she visited Na'ama's home. They were swinging on two straw hammocks Mira had hung on their fourth-floor balcony, out of place in the urban setting, facing a smoky city view.

Na'ama had kicked the wall with her foot, rocking her hammock. "He was a Spanish tourist my mom met in Sinai," she said. Mira had no photo, no address, just a name: José Luis, one of many tourists, eccentrics and nudists who had flocked to their moshav, staying for weeks or months or years, working with her mother in the guest house the moshav residents called the Holiday Village.

"Wow." Karin leaned her head back, her eyes glazed. "Your mom is so cool."

"How is that cool?"

"I don't know, moving to Sinai on her own, having random sex with hot Latin lovers. My mom is like the opposite of cool. Must be nice to have a mom you can actually talk to about boys."

Na'ama fingered the rope over her head and watched the city roofs sway back and forth. She didn't tell Karin that her mother was the last person she would ever seek relationship advice from, because Mira hadn't been able to hold on to a man for longer than a year, a track record that mirrored her meandering career path and frequent moves. She didn't tell her about the dreams she used to have as a child, where her father came back from Spain to find her and take her back to live with him. Or about the nights Mira had spent crying behind her bedroom door after Na'ama had tried to probe her for information about her father. Na'ama had stopped asking, eventually. Her father became an empty pit she learned to walk around.

Still, she said nothing about this to Karin. She enjoyed having Karin envy her; so often with friends it had been the other way around.

On their second day in Eilat, they went for a shallow dive, just the two of them, close to the shore. Na'ama had been itching to get in the water. Diving, to her, was a kind of miracle, the way the surface of the water rippled above them, instead of below, the sky liquid blue, like a reflection of itself. She found comfort in knowing that underwater everybody was a guest, an alien, everyone there on borrowed time. If anything, she belonged there more than most: she had learned to swim in these waters after all, amongst these corals and fish. And she was a good diver, a natural, Ari had once told her. Her body knew how to control its buoyancy, how to breathe slowly and steadily, how to move through water with the gliding, elegant grace she sensed she lacked on land. Some days she felt more at home underwater, where verbal communication and social skills were of no use, where more value was placed on being inconspicuous, on leaving no impression.

After the dive they sat at a shaded picnic table and sipped Cokes, quenching the intense thirst that being immersed in salt water induced. In the brightness of the afternoon, the beach appeared blanched, the sounds muffled by the wavering heat. Na'ama was straddling the wooden bench, her diving suit folded down to her hips, when someone sat down behind her and said, "You have a beautiful back."

She turned around and saw Samir. "Sorry," she said, blushing, thinking he was being sarcastic, that he thought her rude for sitting with her back to him.

"Why are you sorry? It's a compliment." He smiled, exposing a gap between his front teeth the width of a wooden match.

Karin got up. "I'm going to get smokes."

Na'ama half-smiled in Samir's direction. She noticed a sandal-wood necklace resting on his collarbones, a coppery tint in his green eyes. "So why do they call you Samir?" she asked.

"It was my Arabic name in the army," he said, squinting at the sea. "I was a mistarev, you know, undercover."

She picked at the wooden table and watched Karin at the counter, unwrapping her pack of smokes, laughing with one of the instructors, who quickly produced a lighter for her cigarette.

Ari joined them, handing Samir a chilled Goldstar. He offered her one too, which she declined. Karin landed in Ari's lap, hooking her arm around his neck.

"There's a group heading to Sinai to dive this weekend," Ari said to Samir, his hand on Karin's ribs. "You coming?"

"Na'ama grew up in Sinai," Karin said, poking her with a foot under the table.

"Did you really?" Samir said.

"In Nuweiba," Karin said.

"No shit," Ari said. "My uncle was at that rock festival they had there in . . . what was it, '78?"

Na'ama nodded.

"He said it was wild. He still talks about it. Israel's Woodstock. Everyone sleeping with everyone, sex, drugs and rock 'n' roll. Man, I wish I could have been there."

Na'ama pushed her nail into a groove in the wood. She remembered that festival. Her mom had left her with Tariq for the evening, and Na'ama had asked him why he didn't go, but he just laughed. For dinner they drove to his family's tent, where Na'ama watched the veiled women squatting in their long dresses, slapping dough between their palms and burying it under the embers. One of them, a young woman with too much kohl around her eyes kept glancing at them, smiling and lowering her gaze—his fiancée, Tariq told Na'ama when she asked. Later, Na'ama could hear Tariq's mother reprimanding him in quiet, stern Arabic while eyeing her. Tariq ended up sleeping on the couch in their living room that night; Mira hadn't come home as promised. All night long the bass boomed through the desert, reverberating against the mountains. Outside her window, the night sky was steely and brimming with lights, the air thick with bonfire smoke and the smell of something electric.

"How old were you when you had to leave?" Ari propped his sunglasses on his head.

"Eight," she said.

"That must have been hard."

"They were settlers," Samir said. "They must have known that it was temporary."

"I wouldn't call them settlers." Na'ama shifted in her seat. Settlers made her think of gun-toting fundamentalist Jews living in the West Bank. "It was different then. They didn't go there for ideological reasons."

"Still, they settled on occupied land," Samir said. "Everyone makes it sound all romantic, but facts are facts. That famous guest house in Nuweiba that everybody talks about? That was built on Bedouin land."

"It wasn't like that." She sat on her hands, annoyed. "They were just a bunch of hippies looking for a place off the grid."

"Hippie settlers." He grinned.

"Don't be an asshole." Ari smacked Samir on the back of the head. "Forgive my leftist buddy here," he said to Na'ama. "He spent too much time pretending to be an Arab in the army. It made him all fucked in the head."

"Samir," the blonde from the counter yelled, waving a telephone, and he hopped off the bench and left. Karin leaned over and whispered, "He's better looking when he isn't talking," and Na'ama forced a smile.

The next morning they joined a group on their certification dives. Karin was Ari's partner, so Na'ama teamed up with Samir. She avoided his eyes as they performed the buddy check, conscious of the intimacy in these routine tasks: inflating and deflating each other's buoyancy compensator vests, pulling on straps to ensure they were secure, breathing through each other's regulators.

It was a deep, short dive down to thirty metres, where the reds, yellows and oranges faded, blended into a murky purple. On their way up, they hovered for a three-minute safety stop, allowing their bodies to decompress. Na'ama watched the blue deepening in the distance, the water above shimmering like Cellophane. With the sea floor so far below her, she was flying, weightless, suspended in mid-air. She stretched out her arms and closed her eyes, listening to the rhythmic gurgle of bubbles releasing from her regulator. She didn't notice she was sinking until something tugged at the strap of her buoyancy compensator. She looked up and saw everyone's feet float-ing above her. Samir swooped down and grabbed her by the hand. With a quick press on her inflation valve, she filled her vest with air, glad that no one could see her face turning red. Samir's eyes smiled at her through his mask, and she was aware of his hand still holding hers. When he let it go he slowly ran his finger across her palm.

Later, at lunch, he slid into the seat next to her. "Good dive," he said, chewing on a toothpick.

"That was kind of embarrassing," she said, briefly glancing at him.

"What, that? Don't worry about it."

She crossed her legs and stared at the boats, the windsurfers' bright-coloured sails bobbing in the distance.

"A few people saw King Hussein's boat this month," he said, cupping his eyes with his palm. "Sometimes he sails from Aqaba toward the sea border between Jordan and Israel and waves."

"Really?"

Samir nodded. "Wouldn't it be cool if he could just keep sailing and dock right here? Sit and have a beer? It seems so strange that there's this invisible border you can't cross."

She studied him, following the blue veins that sliced through his forearms. His skin was smooth and hairless. He smelled good too, clean and salty, like he was carrying wet seashells in his pockets.

He drew the toothpick out and nodded at her plate of french fries. "You shouldn't be eating this shit every day."

She blushed.

"How about dinner later? Tonight?"

"Um . . ." She swallowed, looking over at Karin, who was sitting at the other end of the table with Ari. Karin glanced back.

He stood up, plucked a couple fries off her plate and ate them in one bite. "I'll pick you up at eight."

By the time she thought to say something in response he was already gone. She watched him walk back to the counter, chin up, arms slightly bent away from his body. Karin examined her from across the table, eyebrows raised. Na'ama nodded and Karin gave her an exaggerated, excited smile.

Over dinner at a fish restaurant across the road, Na'ama started to wonder if Karin was right. It was embarrassing, being a seventeen-year-old virgin. And Samir was twenty-five and obviously knew what he was doing. She enjoyed sitting at a candlelit table across from him, sipping red wine, her cheeks flushed, her skin tanned against Karin's white summer dress, her hair wavy and soft on her shoulders. She felt almost beautiful, a woman.

"Have you ever been back to Sinai?" he asked.

She shook her head. "My mother never wanted to. Too hard."

"Was it a difficult adjustment for you? When you left?"

She swirled the wine in her glass. "My grandma used to say that when I came back from Sinai I was like a little Bedouin, walking everywhere barefoot, playing in the sand. We had no TV or phone or anything like that in Sinai, so I just wanted to be outside all the time. She said: 'We left Egypt to come to Israel, but somehow we ended up with a Bedouin granddaughter.'" Na'ama smiled, trying to lend the story a light-hearted tone, when in fact her grandmother often sighed when she said it, shaking her head. Mira's lifestyle had been a source of great sorrow to her devout, traditional parents. They disapproved of the way she raised Na'ama, were heartbroken that their daughter had never married, devastated that their only granddaughter had been fathered by a goy.

"So wait a second," Samir said. "Your family is from Egypt?"

She sipped wine. "My mom was born in Israel, but my grandparents came to Israel from Alexandria. Totally different from Sinai, though. Two different continents." The wine was loosening her tongue; she was talking too much, tangling one story with another. By dessert, she had counted on her fingers the many places she had lived after they left Sinai, coastal towns of various sizes clumped against the Mediterranean shore. But not Eilat, never Eilat. Mira hated the tourist town, the monstrous hotels that claimed the waterline, bullied the desert, destroyed the view; so close to Sinai, yet miles away. Samir listened to her, nodded and smiled in the appropriate places.

They continued talking as they left the restaurant. The night was warm, but brief gusts of wind cooled it, carrying the smell of sea salt and fresh fish and downtown dinners. The sky was shot with stars, and across the gulf the lights of Aqaba flickered, festive. Her body, warmed by the wine, felt at ease; she hadn't once worried about what to do with her hands. So when they made it back to the hostel, she asked if he wanted to come in.

The air inside her room was stale and hot. Karin was spending the night at Ari's, and both their roommates had checked out earlier that day. Na'ama unlatched the window, placed an incense stick in a wooden holder and lit a match. When she turned to look at Samir, he was on the bed, leaning against the wall, browsing through the stack of photos she had left on her nightstand.

"Is this you?" He turned one of the baby photos to her.

She nodded and sat next to him.

He flipped through the photos. "Who's that holding you?" he asked. "Your dad?"

"What?" She snorted. "Of course not." She paused. "Why would you say that?"

He squinted. "I don't know. The way he's holding you, I guess. And you said before you were like a little Bedouin when you came back."

"That's not what I meant—"

"The nose, the eyes." He cocked his head. "The long face. You look like you could be related."

Na'ama leaned in to look at the photo, zeroed in on Tariq's face. Tariq's black eyes stared back at her—at her mother behind the camera—his gaze soft and knowing. Na'ama felt as though she was barging in on an intimate moment she was not meant to witness. Her stomach caved in as from a direct blow, leaving her breathless. Her body went numb.

"So who is he anyway?" Samir asked.

She turned sharply toward him and slapped a hard kiss on his lips.

"Whoa." He recoiled and laughed, rubbing his lips. "Easy."

She stared down, cheeks tingling. Then he leaned in and kissed her, and she parted her lips and closed her eyes and tried not to think about Tariq or her mom or the hole in her gut. Samir laid her on the bed and hovered over her body, close enough that she could feel the heat radiating from him as he kissed down her neck, his lips sinking into the nooks over her collarbones. He took off his shirt, and she reached out and touched his chest, tracing the line down the middle with one finger, stalling when she reached his belly, unsure of how to proceed, and finally pulling away. Stop thinking. She took a long breath in. Stop thinking. She watched with silent fascination as he lifted her dress and rolled down her underwear; then he grabbed her protruding hip bones as though they were handles and lowered his head between her legs. She gasped, surprised, rising on her elbows to look at him, feeling something wet and tickling, a flutter, hot and cold all at once, pulsating and swelling, like something in her was about to break open, spill out. Stop thinking. She leaned back and stared at the metal bars overhead. Stop thinking. Goosebumps spread over her belly, her nipples, down to her toes. She wiggled her pelvis one way, then another, knees closing, muscles contracting, fingernails digging into the mattress, crumpling the sheets. "Relax," he whispered, looking up at her. Stop thinking. She closed her eyes. Stop thinking. But her mind kept looping back to the same place. Was there ever a José Luis? Had her mother lied to her all these years? How could she? Her body stiffened, her anger defusing the pleasant sensation, turning it off like a dimmer switch, until she felt nothing but mild irritation, his tongue rough and gritty on her skin. She closed her eyes and shook her head. Stop. Thinking. But then she worried that Samir would want her to reciprocate, because she wouldn't know what to do. The farthest she'd ever gone was to give a kibbutznik a hand job on the beach last year, and she hadn't been very good at it; the guy had had to finish himself off. And how well did she know Samir, anyway? She had talked so much over dinner that she hadn't even asked where he was from. She knew nothing about him. Nothing. She didn't even know his real name.

"Stop," she gasped.

He looked up at her, his chin shiny. "You want me to stop doing this or stop altogether?"

She stared at the bars, breathing. "Just . . . stop."

He stood up, wiped his mouth with the back of his hand. "Okay," he said. She could see the outline of his erection under the fabric of his jeans. He went to the washroom, and she stepped into her underwear, sat on the bed with her ankles crossed. When he came back his shirt was on.

"I'm sorry," she said.

"Whatever," he said. "It's my fault. I should have known. You're just a kid."

She looked at her feet, stung.

Once Samir's footsteps faded in the hallway, Na'ama grabbed the photos and fanned them out on the bed. She fished out the one of Tariq and her and studied it, scrutinizing his face, trying to see what Samir had seen. But the picture was grainy and the light in the room dim and her eyes started to ache. Still, she thought she recognized some of the features that made Tariq handsome—the long nose, the squared jaw, the natural curve of the lips suggesting a smile—clumsily rearranged in her own face. She looked at the photo of her mother: Mira was in her bedroom, the room sparse and washed in a golden, soft light, the bed behind her unmade. Her hand was stretched out toward the lens, large and blurry, as though trying to take hold of the camera, or maybe draw whoever had taken the photo back to bed. Tariq. Of course. It had to have been Tariq all along. Na'ama overlapped the two photos, holding them under one thumb. The proximity of the two photos, in the same strip of film, in the same envelope hidden in her mother's closet, told a story, a story she realized then made so much sense she couldn't believe it had taken her so long to figure out.

She leaned against the wall and her heart unclenched, like an unfurling fist. She rifled through her memory, searching for moments she knew were there all along, dusty, unexplained snapshots she had almost forgotten: furtive smiles and glances, late-night knocks and hushed conversations she couldn't make out from her bedroom. For a moment, in that dim, bluish moonlight, she could see her mother in the photo as though she was someone new, unrelated to her, a young woman posing in front of her lover in a sun-soaked room, and Na'ama's heart ached for her. All those years, Mira had been searching for somewhere she'd be as happy as she was in Sinai, longing for the one man she must have really loved.

Na'ama stared at the piece of starry night sky that hung by the door. The noise from the outside dwindled as the night deepened, until it was quiet enough to hear the sighing of the sea. She couldn't sleep. She lay awake considering every quirk of her character that she couldn't trace back to her mother, revisiting every memory she had of Tariq. Tariq, who had taken her walking through the desert, teaching her Arabic as he pointed out rocks, lizards, shrubs, trees; Tariq, who had shown her how to play backgammon and let her win every time, always making a scene of losing, throwing his hands up in the air in mock frustration. It was Tariq, not her mother, to whom she confessed her secret crush on Gil Yanay, Tariq who consoled her when Gil asked Dorit Cohen to be his girlfriend instead.

She stayed up until dawn sneaked in through the window, a cool, light, silky sheet, and then she got up and stuffed the rest of her belongings into her backpack. Outside, the metal shutters of the rental counter and snack bar were pulled down; the fresh water pool was freckled with stars, a sliver of moon askew on its surface. She walked out of the club, heading south along the highway. The sun was just peeking above the Jordanian hills, its rays skittering over the mountaintops, colouring the tips a fiery red. A couple of taxis zoomed by toward the Taba border crossing in the distance. She clutched her passport, grateful she had brought it; it was a habit she had picked up from her mom, the eternal nomad. Now she wondered why she had packed not only her passport, but the photos and the one thing she had from Tariq: a cone shell necklace he had given her the day she and her mother left.

Na'ama remembered burying her face in Tariq's white galabeya, inhaling its smell—coffee and sweat and smoke. Tariq had put his forehead to hers and then, when he let her hand go, touched his heart. As they drove away, the moshav looked desolate: the plastic sheets that covered the hothouses had flown off across the desert plains, caught on bushes and fences; the Holiday Village was abandoned, ghostly curtains billowing from gaping windows. Her mother cried as Na'ama watched the road disappearing into the mountains from the back window, cried as they crossed into Eilat, and continued to cry halfway through the Negev desert,

Sinai's less dramatic sibling, plains of brown and yellow strewn with shrubs.

The fluorescent-lit Taba crossing was steps away, a narrow pathway jammed between the sea and the mountains, interrupted by cordons and customs, a couple of idling cars waiting in line. Things were different now, she knew. She heard from people who'd gone back that the houses they had left behind—her house too—were inhabited by Egyptians. A town had been built around the skeleton of the moshav, and rows of straw huts were erected on the dunes, where young Israelis and Europeans vacationed, and a restaurant playing Bob Marley tunes served freshly caught fish. They said the guest house her mother had worked in was still standing, renovated and revamped, and that the fields the Israelis had cultivated—growing melons and flowers—had dried out and turned to thorns.

She changed her Israeli shekels into Egyptian pounds, then walked the few dozen metres from the Israeli side to the Egyptian terminal. To her left, a chain-link fence descended into the water, as though the sea could be divided, as though water didn't flow between the two countries. An invisible border. It seemed like such an arbitrary place to stop, to separate the land and the sea and the mountains, when it was clearly the same landscape, the same sea.

The Egyptian clerk eyed her as he stamped her passport with a two-week visa, and she smiled and thanked him in Arabic. She gazed over her shoulder at the familiar skyline of Eilat, the hotels ablaze in the morning sun, an orange flame caught in each window. She looked past the Egyptian terminal, to where Bedouin taxi drivers leaned against their dusty station wagons, waiting to take her where she wanted to go.

WARPLANES

On the way home from school, three warplanes slice the sky, leaving a trail of chalk across the blue as they head north. Orli squints and cups her hand over her eyes. "F-15s again," she says, disappointed. Her dad flies F-16s.

I glance up, say nothing. We've been watching warplanes all summer long.

When we get to my building, we throw our school bags on the lawn outside. It's September and everything seems tired and dull, sucked dry by summer. The grass is yellow and sparse, speckled with patches of cracked earth. Orli ties her hair into a bun, pulls a deck of cards from her bag and shows off her shuffling skills.

"I think it's going to rain," she says.

"But it never rains before Rosh Hashanah," I say. The air does feel heavy with moisture; it's like being draped in a sheet just out of a washing machine. I pull a card from the pile and discard it, then change my mind and take it back.

"You can't do that," Orli says. "Once the card is down, it's down."

"You don't get to make the rules," I say.

"They're not my rules."

I put my cards down and get up, brush the grass off my jeans. "I changed my mind," I say. "I have to go in."

I skip up the stairs two at a time to the second floor, open the door and yell, "I'm home."

Mom says, "Don't leave your bag by the door. Every day I have to pick up after you."

I drop my bag in my room and go into the living room. I turn on the TV. News. Since the war started they break for news all the time, interrupting shows I love, like *Little House on the Prairie*. On the screen a guy from parliament is saying, "This war is leading Israel into an abyss!" and other members of parliament start yelling at him and waving their hands. I turn off the TV and head to the kitchen. Mom stands by the stove, staring into a pot. She wipes her hands on a towel and sits down at the Formica table to read the paper. I read over her shoulder. The front page headline is a big black box with white letters. Black on the front page means many soldiers died in Lebanon. Red is usually some sort of murder. A bad car accident can go either way. If someone dies from a heart attack or a disease, they put it in the obituaries in the back, in little squares with black frames. That's where they had my dad's obituary last spring, next to one sponsored by the factory where he worked that said, "To Sara and family, with you in your grief over the loss of your husband and father." The front of the paper that day had a big black headline with a picture of an artillery officer who was blown up by a land mine in Lebanon.

The day my father died I called Orli. I was crying really hard, so at first she couldn't understand me. She came over and took me outside because our apartment was full of people talking and praying, and women carrying steaming Pyrex dishes. We walked on the neighbours' fence, and I laughed when I lost my balance and almost fell down. Later, I overheard my aunt telling my mom that she had seen me laughing, and that it was inappropriate.

Other things that are inappropriate when your father dies: going to weddings or bar mitzvahs, dressing up all fancy, listening to music really loud, thinking about boys, having fun of any kind.

I get bored with the paper, so I walk over to the counter. There's a plate of schnitzels by the stove, layered on top of a paper towel. I touch one, and Mom says, without turning her head, "Don't."

"I'm hungry," I say.

"It's not ready yet."

"It looks ready."

Mom doesn't answer, just flips a page in her newspaper.

She wasn't always like this. Before Dad got sick we talked about things. Sometimes after ballet class she took me for ice cream, and once we drove all the way to Tel Aviv for no reason and had milkshakes on a terrace overlooking the sea. On the way back the roads were empty and we hit a green wave on Jabutinsky, the traffic lights turning in our favour one after the other. Mom rolled down the windows and cranked the radio way up, and we sang at the top of our lungs until my throat got scratchy.

Now, days can pass and the only things she'll say to me are, "Don't touch that," "Dinner is ready," "I need you to get milk from the store." And it's not like I don't try to get her attention. I sit in the kitchen while she cooks, follow her around while she does laundry or cleans. Once, I told her I thought I was in love with Amir from my class. I thought it was pretty big news. Silence. Another time I asked, "Ima, do you believe in God?" because I had started to have my doubts. Nothing.

Instead, she makes other kinds of noise. She digs in the pots and pans drawer really loudly, for a long time, like she just can't find the right pan, or bumps the broom into the walls when she sweeps, or drags chairs on the floor instead of lifting them. When I still believed in God, I used to make deals with him to bring Dad back. I promised I wouldn't watch TV on Shabbat, mix dairy and meat behind Mom's back, or steal money from her purse. When that didn't work, I offered up Mom. If I had to have one parent, I wanted one who saw me.

Now I don't bother talking to God. I was hanging out in the empty lot behind our house one day soon after Dad died. The shiva was over. People stopped coming, life went on. I was angry at everyone. Especially God. I threw cans into the abandoned house at the edge of the lot, ripped weeds from the ground and kicked stones. Then I said aloud, "God is an asshole." I looked up but nothing happened, and I saw that the sky was just a sky, and there was nothing there, just clouds and planes.

I walk to my room, slam the door and turn the radio on loud to listen to the top ten chart on Reshet Gimel, but it's the news again. The anchor is reading in a very serious voice, "Captain David Yehu, Sergeant Gal Bergman, Lieutenant David Abutbul." One time last year I actually heard Meirav's dad's name on the list. The next day at school, the teacher told us what happened. It was a big deal when he died, because he was a war hero, so they wrote about him in the paper and had a special ceremony in the community centre with a big picture of him, like a fold-out poster from a teen magazine. Unlike regular people, who get buried covered in a white sheet, Meirav's dad got buried in a coffin, in the cemetery's army lot, which looks like a garden, with flowers and trees. My father's lot is all stone. Meirav's family got lots of money because they were now a bereaved Israeli Defense Forces family, and the kids were IDF orphans. IDF orphans get to go to a special camp every summer in a nice kibbutz by the beach, with lawns, a pool and a water park, and cool activities like a makeup-for-film workshop and flamenco dancing, all paid for by the army. I wish my father had died in the army instead of in a hospital. There is no Remembrance Day for people who died of a weak heart.

The teacher made us go to the shiva at Meirav's house, and afterwards Orli and I walked home and Orli was quiet the whole way. It was already dark. You could hear people's TVs playing the opening jingle for the evening news. We sat on the fence by her house and she said, "You know, I'm scared about my dad, too." Her eyes were pink and wet. I just sat there and stared at my sneakers, and I thought I should hug her but I couldn't. I was frozen.

In the afternoon, Orli comes knocking on my door and suggests we go for a walk to Fege, a neighbourhood pretty far from where we live. She threads a token for the pay phone on my shoelace in case of an emergency. Orli always has one because her mother doesn't come home from work until four.

I grab my hoodie and tie it around my waist, and meet Orli in the parking lot.

"You told your mom?" Orli asks.

"She's napping," I say. "Besides, she won't mind." My mom likes Orli. She thinks she's a good influence.

We walk for a long time. Orli has some money, so she buys us chocolate milk in plastic bags and we puncture holes in them with our teeth and suck on the plastic, letting the bags hang between our lips. We talk about school and gossip about our teachers and classmates. Halfway to Fege, it starts smelling like the bomb shelter in our building, which is always damp and dusty. We look up and it starts to rain, a cloud bursting over our heads. Everything turns dark, as if someone flicked off the light switch. The asphalt is shiny and wet like a giant dead fish, and we have to hop over puddles on the sidewalks. On the sides of the road, rivers flow, full of leaves and plastic bags and candy wrappers. We start laughing, running until we make it to the nearest apartment building and take shelter in the lobby. We sit on the marble floor next to a row of metal mailboxes and a big fake palm tree and wait for the rain to stop. Inside the lobby it's quiet and cool, and even the smallest sound has an echo. Every now and then people come in, shake their umbrellas and let them drip on the floor while they check their mail. They glance at us and then go upstairs to their apartments, the echo of their footsteps fading away. Nobody asks us anything. Only one older lady smiles and says in a thick Russian accent, "Guess summer is over, eh?" and Orli says, "Guess so."

A young soldier walks by us without checking the mail. He's wearing a khaki uniform and his gun dangles behind him. There are two lines sewn on his sleeves. Orli follows him with her gaze, and once he's gone she says, "Corporal, engineering corps."

Orli knows all the different ranks and units in the army. She says the air force is the best, then the navy and the ones with coloured caps, like paratroopers, who also have red boots to match their caps, and then the artillery corps and armoured corps. Orli's entire family is in the air force, even her mother was a secretary in the air force during her army service, which is where her parents met. Orli's father is a major and has a profile of ninety-seven, which is the highest medical rating and determines your suitability for fighting. My dad only scored sixty-four. He had a weak heart and thick eyeglasses. He served in the signal corps.

My dad once took Orli and me to the movies at Shalom Cinema and later to a café on Hertzel Street, where we sat at a table on the sidewalk and shared hummus and fries and falafel. When he ordered for us he said, "The lovely young ladies would like some Coke, please." He asked our opinions of the movie and talked to us like we were grown-ups, and he was really interested in what we had to say. Afterwards Orli said I was lucky that my dad was around. I only met Orli's dad once. He was wearing a grey uniform, all decorated with glinting pins on his chest and some round buttons on his shoulders. He picked Orli up and spun her around and didn't even say hello to me.

Orli is braiding her hair in neat little braids. I find a pen in my pocket and start drawing hearts on my jeans. The marble starts to feel cold on my bum.

"Aren't you cold?" I ask.

"No."

"How come you didn't bring a hoodie?"

"I'm not cold."

"I don't believe you," I say.

"You think I want to suffer?"

"I think you like to show off, like you're tough or something."

Orli rolls her eyes at me but says nothing, just keeps braiding her hair.

A teenage boy with acne on his forehead and a skateboard walks by and looks at us. He lingers by the mailboxes and keeps glancing at us. Orli and I smile at each other. I think he's going to talk to us, but then he just skips up the stairs to his apartment.

"You want to know a secret?" Orli says.

I nod.

"Amir asked Dalit to be his girlfriend."

I press the pen into my jeans until the tip pokes through the fabric. "When?"

"Friday at the party."

I press harder. I can feel the pen jabbing my skin.

"When are you going to come to parties again?" Orli says.

I shrug.

"You should come next week. Danny is having one at his house. There's going to be a DJ."

"I'm not allowed to go to parties," I say. "You're supposed to wait a year according to the Torah."

"A whole year?"

I shrug.

"We miss you," Orli says. "I miss you."

I stare at the floor between my legs. Suddenly I have tears in my eyes. They burst out all at once. I pull the hood over my head so Orli won't see them.

"Are you upset?" she says.

"No."

"You can tell me if you're upset."

"I'm not upset!" I yell.

"Why are you yelling at me?"

"Why don't you just shut up and leave me alone?"

Orli stands up. "Fine. I'm tired of defending you anyway."

"Defending me?" I snort.

"Yeah, everyone says you've been weird since your father died. Even Meirav is not acting like this and her father was a hero."

"That's the stupidest thing I've ever heard." I stand up and push Orli out of the way and run outside. By the time I get to the pay phone I am soaked again, my face wet. I take the token off my shoelace and call my mother to ask her to come get me, but the phone rings and rings. I sit on the dirty floor of the phone booth. I can't see through the condensation on the glass or hear anything through the rain pounding on the booth. I feel like I'm in an aquarium. I wonder if this is what it feels like to be dead. Shut in and all alone. At first my heart beats fast, but then I lean my head against the cool wall and watch the glare of the traffic lights through the steamed-up glass; it's beautiful, how it paints everything green, then orange, then red, then green again. I start to feel quiet and a little sleepy. I almost don't want the rain to end. I stay in the booth even after the rain slows down to a drizzle and finally stops. I wipe a window with my sleeve and look out. The street looks different now—new, as if the rain injected fluid into its veins. The sky is the colour of peaches and blood oranges.

Up high, two warplanes fly north and disappear behind trees.

THE BEST PLACE
ON EARTH

The plane started its descent, and Naomi looked out the window at the dramatic patchwork of land and water. Vancouver was as blue as Jerusalem was golden. The only other time she'd visited her younger sister, ten years ago with Ami, she had been stunned by that view. They had been happy then, married for five years, their first time away from three-year-old Ben, whom they had left with Ami's brother and family. Ami had given her the window seat, and as he had leaned over her to look out, Naomi had squeezed his hand on her thigh. Now, as she watched the neat rows of boxes on the ground, the toy cars zipping on the highways, the buildings like Monopoly pieces she could crush with gigantic feet, the beauty of the city—like a mass-produced postcard—was lost on her. She pressed her forehead against the cool window, feeling alone, missing him.

Only four weeks ago, they had been sitting in their living room, as they did every evening, watching a romantic comedy she had picked up on the way home from work. Street lights filtered through the arched living room windows, and the evening fell over Jerusalem like warm syrup drizzled over baklava. Naomi had made tea, brought out a plate of cookies. She lay across the couch, rubbing her feet together while Ami sat in the reclining chair, his legs in a diamond shape.

Not long into the movie, the character of the husband came back from a business trip and said to his wife, "I'm afraid you're going to leave me. I slept with someone else." Naomi peeked over at Ami like she did sometimes when they watched movies together, searching for the comfort in his shared reaction, and saw that her husband was wearing the wrong expression, one suitable for a horror film, perhaps. Her heart plunged into her stomach like a dead bird.

"Babe?" Her voice gave, got tangled with her breath.

When he finally turned to look at her, his eyes gleamed like two murky puddles.

"Oh dear," he said, and started crying.

Her sister sounded surprised when Naomi called to say she was thinking of visiting her on Hornby Island. Without Ami. Without the kids. "Is everything okay?" Tamar said.

"Yes," Naomi said, putting on a cheerful voice. "I just need a vacation. I miss you."

She didn't want to tell Tamar over the phone. She could hardly bring herself to tell her friends. She had lied to the kids too, telling them their father was on a business trip, when in fact he was sleeping on the rickety futon in his brother's living room, a few blocks away.

They hadn't spoken since she kicked him out; Naomi refused his calls, ignored his emails. Every day, as she drove by his brother's house on her way to work, she found herself—against her better judgment—searching for his lean frame, his confident stride, his short curls. At the same time she dreaded seeing him, afraid to awaken the part of her that wanted to stop the car and run to him sobbing, seeking comfort from her best friend.

In the evenings, as she came home from work—the jiggle of her keys in the lock echoing in the empty house—she was greeted by musty, stagnant air. The boys were out for hours at a time, busy with their soccer games, boy scouts, summer camp. She found herself saving her daily anecdotes and observations for Ami, and then watching them go stale like leftover food in the fridge.

One evening the toilet wouldn't stop flushing, and Naomi stood over it, staring at the innards of the tank, perplexed. She grabbed the phone and held it for a while before putting it down. In the car, she didn't know how to check the oil or water. She had always thought of herself as a modern woman. She worked *and* kept house; she was the one in charge of the finances. Her mother hadn't even had her own bank account.

As a teenager, Naomi had been angry at her mother for turning a blind eye to her father's affairs. But perhaps her mother's quiet resignation was better than the fights Naomi and Tamar had witnessed as children. Back then, there had been tears and yelling, slammed doors, and once a cloud of smoke Naomi had seen from afar, as she walked home from school. "Someone's house is on fire," her friends had yelled, and they all ran, until they were close enough and Naomi realized it was coming from her own house.

Her friends stood in a row, giggling and shoving each other as they watched her mother throwing her dad's clothes into the firepit in their front yard.

Some days, burning Ami's clothes didn't seem like such a bad idea. She was a nobody, Ami had sworn over and over again. It was so long ago. He hardly remembered her face. "What, you want a name?" He flapped his arms. "Rona, I think."

"You think?" she screamed. "*You think?*"

Naomi pushed her cart out through the automatic glass doors to the pristine arrivals area, searching for her sister's full head of blonde curls. It had been a while since she last saw Tamar. Her sister didn't visit often. "This country drives me nuts," she had said the last time she came to Jerusalem, over three years ago. "No, let me rephrase." Tamar had cleared her throat. "I love the country, I hate the people." Naomi wanted to tell Tamar that she was, and always would be, an Israeli. They had grown up running in the narrow streets of Sha'arei Tsedek, spent afternoons riding their bikes in the Mahane Yehuda Market, pinching cashews and peanuts from the Armenian vendor on the corner of Yafo Street.

Tamar waited at the end of the corridor, her long arm waving like a flag. Naomi quickened her pace when she noticed a slender, bearded man standing next to her sister. His long hair was thinning on top and tied in a ponytail. He wore a sleeveless shirt with a faded print and loose Thai pants.

They hugged, and Naomi held Tamar out at arm's length. "Look at you. How come I grow old but you never age?"

Tamar laughed, pushing Naomi's arm off her. "Shut up. You look great."

"I'm Carlos." The man shook Naomi's hand firmly, his black, small eyes penetrating hers. He was older than his attire suggested, fine lines etched into his tanned skin. Tamar cuddled up to him. Naomi busied herself with her luggage, rearranging her suitcases on the cart.

Outside, summer was at its best, the sky a flawless blue, the dry air smelling of mowed lawn. The three of them sat together in the front seat of a pickup truck, Tamar's long legs straddling the gear stick. Naomi rested her head against the truck's window, giving in to the fogginess of jet lag. She squinted to read the slogan on a passing car's licence plate. "Beautiful British Columbia. The Best Place on Earth." She scoffed quietly. According to whom? She was from Jerusalem, after all, the holiest place on earth, a place so laden with history it made tourists crazy. She grew up seeing delusional tourists loitering by the Old City's gates, touching the ancient bricks, delivering mumbled sermons in foreign languages about Jesus and redemption. Once, she wrote a psychology paper about the Jerusalem syndrome, suggesting it was often resolved by simply removing the patient from the city. "If leaving Jerusalem is all it takes to cure a psychosis," her professor had scribbled next to it, "then we should all leave."

She had hardly ever left Jerusalem herself. She didn't even like going to Tel Aviv. Maybe this was exactly what she needed to cure herself of her delusions, or at least get some perspective. She watched the mountains in the distance shimmering in the hot afternoon. She rolled her window down and inhaled; the air tasted green, fresh.

Naomi slept for much of the ferry ride, and Tamar was grateful for the opportunity to study her sister's face, inventory the changes. Naomi frowned in her sleep. Tamar wondered again what had brought on this visit. When she had pressed over the phone, Naomi had said dryly, "I'm not dying. I'm just coming for a visit."

Naomi's hair had new white strands threaded through it, and the laugh lines that fanned from the corner of her eyes had deepened since Tamar had last seen her. It always surprised Tamar to see that her sister had aged. Whenever she thought of Naomi, she pictured her at twenty-five, even though she was three years older than Tamar. Tamar had called to wish her a happy fortieth birthday a couple of months ago.

"I can see the resemblance." Carlos, back from the ferry café with two chai lattes, sat beside her and cocked his head as if to mimic Naomi's.

"Really?" Tamar said. "I look like my dad. Naomi looks like my mom."

"Still," he insisted. "You have the same cheekbones. Something about your facial structure."

Back in Jerusalem, a stranger would occasionally recognize Tamar by her resemblance to her father. Everybody knew her father. His family was one of the oldest Jewish families in the city, having arrived in the sixteenth century, after the expulsion of Jews from Spain. Once, a woman on the number 18 bus had stared at Tamar for five stops before saying with curled lips and narrowed eyes, "You must be Shlomo Delarosa's daughter." The woman's hair was bleached and her nails long and golden; she wore tacky high-heeled boots. Tamar didn't ask her how she knew her dad, didn't want to know. She hated that she looked like him, that their relationship was evident in her face, that sometimes she caught her mother looking at her with a mixture of affection and derision.

"You two are so much alike," her mother had said after she

witnessed one of Tamar's many fights with her father. Although Tamar protested, she knew her mother was right. She had inherited her father's temper, his intensity and his charm. This temper, her contempt for authority, had made her army service insufferable: a series of trials, detentions and reassignments. Her father, who had been an officer in the army—had fought in three wars— was appalled by her behaviour. A temper wasn't the only thing they'd had in common. She had never thought herself very good at relationships. Not until Carlos.

Outside the ferry window, Galiano Island was dark blue against the lighter sky. Small houses clung to the shore and a row of boats was moored at the marina. She rested her head on Carlos's shoulder. She didn't like remembering how angry she'd been back then, before coming to BC. When she first arrived in Vancouver, she hadn't planned on staying long; it was just another stop, like the year spent selling sandwiches for office buildings in New York City, the months spent driving an ice cream truck in California. But in BC she noticed herself slowing down, unwinding, as if she'd been holding her breath for twenty-four years and could finally let it out. It was in BC that she learned to forgive her father, though he never forgave her for leaving; when she called home he often didn't want to speak to her, and when he did, he was short, demanding to know when she was coming back. The day Naomi phoned to tell her about her father's stroke, Tamar had just moved into a new apartment in East Vancouver, her few boxes piled unopened in her new living room. Tamar boarded a plane to Tel Aviv the next morning. By the time she landed in Israel, eighteen hours later, he was gone.

Tamar's house, wooden and painted red, was on the other side of the
island, a twenty-minute ride from the ferry terminal on skinny
roads that curved around bays and hills. Inside, it smelled like
fresh herbs, garlic and essential oils. Naomi noticed that there
was nothing Israeli or Jewish about it, no mezuzahs on the door
frames, no hamsas like the ones their mother had hung all over
their home for good luck, no dangling strings with blue beads to
repel the evil eye, no calendar with Jewish holidays marked upon
it. Tamar proudly showed her the patio, which was framed by
luscious forest. Even though it was past nine, the sky was a quiet,
steady pink. The lingering daylight made Naomi uneasy. In Israel
the sun had never set later than 8:00 p.m.

Tamar asked about Yoav and Ben, and Naomi was relieved
to talk about her children. She told Tamar about Ben's new girlfriend, Yoav's new interest in cooking. She felt a stab of guilt; she
couldn't remember the last time she had left the kids alone with
Ami for more than a day. She calculated the time difference; the
kids would just be waking up now. She hoped Ami had made them
sandwiches, wasn't just giving them money. She pictured her boys
scampering around the house, Yoav pounding on the bathroom
door, the two of them downing their juice standing up, bickering
and pushing each other on their way out the door.

They sipped their tea in silence. Naomi looked into the living
room. Through the glass it looked staged, like a display in a
department store: the earthy toned walls, the row of black-and-
white travel photographs in silver frames, the wooden Buddha
head above the mantle.

"You never told me you had a new boyfriend," Naomi said.

Tamar smiled. "I wanted to tell you in person."

Naomi took a sip, looking at Tamar sideways. "Is he Jewish?"

Tamar laughed in a short burst and shook her head. "I forgot Israelis always ask that. You know, people actually consider that rude in other parts of the world. It's like asking people what their sexual orientation is."

Naomi turned to face the forest and bowed toward her mug. The treetops swayed like a coordinated dance troupe, their rustling leaves a thousand tiny jazz-hands. "It's so quiet here," she said with a nervous laugh. She fought a yawn, wishing for darkness to come.

"When I first moved here the quiet used to freak me out," Carlos said. He had snuck up on them, creeping barefoot like a thief. He grinned at Naomi, his teeth large and perfectly white. "Hopefully one day we'll be able to live here full time. Right now, we have to keep going back to the city for work."

"Carlos joined my business," Tamar said, leaning toward him. "I do video and he does stills. We offer package deals."

"That's great," Naomi said, running her finger along the wooden railing.

"Especially for weddings. People like to hire a husband and wife team."

"But . . . you're not married, are you?" Naomi stared, confused.

"Well, not *officially*," Carlos said. Tamar tilted her head and smiled at her. Naomi felt ancient, backward. She looked up, relieved to see stars starting to appear, filling up the sky. A distant choir of crickets and frogs followed, breaking the silence.

Tamar and Carlos tiptoed around their bedroom, speaking in whispers, not used to having another person in the house. It occurred to Tamar that this is how it would be if they ever had children, the house no longer theirs alone. She squeezed toothpaste onto her brush and caught a glance of her face in the mirror, brow furrowed. The visit had just begun and already it wasn't going as well as she'd hoped. She wasn't sure that Naomi liked Carlos, and for the first time, she really wanted her to approve of a man.

When she first met Carlos, on a shoot at a wedding in West Vancouver, Tamar wasn't thinking romance. She had enjoyed working with him, impressed by how thoughtful he was in his movements, possessing an awareness of space that she had rarely witnessed in men. Over lunch, as they sat together at a table, he pulled out a card and handed it to her, suggesting they keep in touch, maybe recommend the other to prospective clients. When he called the following week to ask her out, she thought it was business related, but over a vegetarian Indian dinner at a Commercial Drive restaurant, she reconsidered. He may have been twelve years older, but she found herself envying his youthfulness, his enthusiasm, his energy. But it was his goodness that got her in the end, the kind of sincere kindness she had always admired in others and was afraid she didn't possess.

Carlos walked into the bathroom and reached around her to grab the floss from the medicine cabinet. "I changed my mind," he said as Tamar spat toothpaste into the sink. "I can't even see the resemblance anymore."

"I know," she said, looking at him through the mirror. "We were really close once."

"Really?"

"Inseparable." She nodded. "We got into so much trouble together."

"You? Trouble?" He glanced at her with a lopsided smile. "Impossible." He threaded the floss between his teeth. "I would expect Naomi to keep you in check, being the eldest and all."

"She did," Tamar said. "Especially when we were kids." She dried her face. "Okay, maybe *I* got us into trouble." Carlos laughed. Some of Tamar's best memories were with Naomi, or if not the best, then at least the most intense. Tamar, at sixteen, convincing Naomi to take her to a bar at the Russian compound, and then getting so drunk that Naomi had to hold her hair while she puked in an alley. Tamar (seventeen? eighteen?) dragging Naomi, recently dumped and heartbroken, out of her room late at night to the Mahane Yehuda Market, handing her cracked dishes she had stolen from their mother's kitchen, and urging her to smash them against a wall to vent her anger. When windows in the nearby buildings turned yellow and a woman screamed, "We're calling the police!" the two of them ran back home, laughing so hard they couldn't breathe. Hitchhiking together to Eilat on a whim the summer before Naomi enlisted in the army, sleeping on the beach with a bunch of stoned hippies they had met along the way; and then later, in their early twenties, driving to Sinai in a beaten Fiat their father had advised Tamar against buying, and picking up cute hitchhikers: uniformed soldiers and European backpackers Tamar flirted with. The car died on the way back, outside Dimona, and the two of them stood and watched a finger of smoke rising from the engine up to the desert sky.

And then, an older memory flickered, out of place: eight-year-old Naomi sneaking Tamar outside through the kitchen door to play in the street, two girls in nightgowns under a lone street light, the sounds of fighting and crying from their home faint, blending with the buzz of traffic and mosquitoes and television sets from other homes.

After Tamar moved to BC, she had called her sister almost every

week, but eventually life took over. Every now and then they'd
make vows that they'd call every Tuesday, email every Friday, but
nothing stuck.

Then, on Tamar's last visit to Israel, something had shifted
between them. She had missed Jerusalem so much when she was
in Canada, but having finally made it there, she couldn't wait to
go back to BC. For the first time, she saw the city through a for-
eigner's eyes: the chaos, the traffic, the aggression, what Israelis
loved calling "passion." It was as if the city was stuffing itself into
your throat. She no longer belonged.

"You have an accent," Naomi had said one evening over dinner.

"What?" Tamar laughed. "That's crazy."

"You do. Your *l* is too soft, your *t* is too sharp. You speak funny."

Tamar had tried talking to Naomi about the distance between
them, bringing it up in a polite, Canadian way, but somehow
Naomi got annoyed, accusing her of being passive-aggressive.
Tamar wondered whether Naomi resented her for not having children or a husband, for never having wanted a family, for being
carefree and travelling the world while she was stuck in a life that
so much resembled their mother's.

After that visit, it was hard to just call. Or rather, it was easy
not to, to let months pass by. Tamar felt guilty about it, aware of
the passing time, dreading the day something happened, because
things happened, especially in Jerusalem, and then she'd realize
how much she was missing out on, the way she had felt when her
mother died of a heart attack—two years after their father—leaving no time for goodbyes. Naomi was the only family she had left.

Sometimes Tamar tried to imagine what life would have been
like if she and her sister lived in the same city, like their mother
and her sister, who had visited each other almost daily, had taken

care of each other's children. Tamar hardly knew her nephews. She hadn't been there to help raise them. She never sent them birthday gifts. And they grew so fast, in three-, four-year increments. Carlos spoke to his niece and nephew in Toronto often, calling his mother and sister at least once a week. A few months ago, the entire family had visited their apartment in Vancouver, hijacking their home for a few days, filling it with lively chatter and loose laughter, drinking wine in the afternoons and talking late into the night. They had such an easy way of communicating, such intimacy and comfort, that it made Tamar feel lonely, then guilty.

She watched Carlos now as he turned on his reading lamp, stripping off his clothes and hanging them over the chair. She hadn't shared these thoughts with him, harbouring an irrational fear that he'd leave her if he knew how strained her own family relations were. He desperately wanted a family, had told her so early on. And although a part of her—for the first time in her life—yearned to share the experience with him, she was terrified that she was not right for the task, that like her father, she was bound to fuck it up. Things with Carlos were so good. She didn't want anything to change.

Naomi woke up at dawn. At first, she thought she was in her own bed, Ami by her side. She rolled onto her back, startled by his absence. It reminded her of the bus rides she used to take through the desert to see Ami in Be'er Sheva, where he'd been at university. She often fell asleep in her seat, letting her head drop on a stranger's shoulder, mistaking him for Ami.

She got up and tiptoed into the kitchen, made tea and stepped outside with her mug. The sky was pastel, a watered-down version of its daytime self. A couple of faded stars flickered weakly and a brilliant orange belt embraced the horizon. She warmed her hands around the cup and breathed in the cold, foreign morning air. It was peaceful, serene. The best place on earth. Yet, somehow, it made her feel anxious and lonely. What was she doing here? What was she thinking? She sat on the deck and cried.

She felt the warmth of the sun tickling her skin and looked up. On a patch of grass she saw Tamar and Carlos frozen, each with their legs spread in a wide stance, one arm extended up to the sky and the other touching the earth, their faces golden with sunlight. They looked like twins in their matching yoga outfits, their long ponytails. Naomi ducked. They hadn't seen her.

After breakfast she asked to use the computer to check the news. "Please don't," Tamar said. "You're on vacation." She had stopped reading news from Israel years ago, she said. "It's all bad anyway." Naomi turned on the computer, typing in Ynet's URL. A pigua in Jerusalem. Her heart stopped. She scrolled down with shaky hands, skimming over the first few lines. She had to call home. Make sure the kids were okay. Then she noticed the date. The attack had taken place yesterday.

Ben answered in monosyllables, on his way out to see his girl-friend. Yoav told her Ami had taken them to a restaurant last night; they'd had steaks. "We're having fun," he said and she couldn't help but feel jealous. Neither of them mentioned the attack.

After she hung up she turned back to the news online. Ten injured, nobody dead. For a moment, she could see how her country might look to a Canadian. How Jerusalem could be perceived as the worst place to live, raise a family, a dangerous, troubled city, torn between faiths, a hotbed for fanatics and fundamentalists.

Ten years ago, on their visit to Vancouver, Naomi and Ami had asked Tamar to take them out. They had been younger then, intoxicated by the sense of freedom new parents experience on their first vacation away from their child.

"Let's party all night!" Ami said.

"This isn't Jerusalem. There's no all night here," Tamar said.

"Well, that sucks."

"Maybe. But it's also safe. And civilized."

"Safe," Ami scoffed. "Overrated." They all laughed.

Later, he said to Naomi, "Maybe people in Vancouver don't party as much because their lives are too comfortable. You know, the whole 'drink, dance and be merry because tomorrow you might die' kind of thing. Maybe there's something good about knowing it could all end at any minute."

She had thought he was being morbid, but now it made sense. She was so used to living in a constant state of urgency, verging on emergency. No wonder the quiet made her uneasy. She looked at the screen: Israeli soldiers and paramedics frozen in mid-action, their faces grim and alert, a carcass of a car, broken pieces of twisted metal, a dark stain on asphalt. How could this be a good thing? She didn't miss *this*. Yet she couldn't even fathom living anywhere else.

"It's too much," Tamar had said to her on her last visit. "It's just too intense for me." She was right, Naomi had thought, sometimes it was too much. She loved and hated Jerusalem: a city that would forever be contested, forever divided, never at peace. But there was more to Jerusalem than what one saw in the news, like how beautiful it was, not in the way BC was, but in a hard, raw and broken way. How it felt alive, a kind of beast, pulsating, breathing, vibrating under her feet. How sometimes, when she walked through the old city and saw tourists snapping photos and looking at everything with awe, she would see Jerusalem through their eyes and be reminded that people used to walk there two thousand years ago in togas, and it would make her feel small and insignificant, but in a good way. How at times, the city truly felt sacred, magical, the centre of everything, like at sunset, when the sun reflected crimson and gold on the limestone, and the Dome of the Rock shone like a rare amber in the middle of the city. Or on a winter night, when it snowed and everything was briefly muted and still, the sharp edges softened. Or how on Friday evenings, when the buses disappeared into the jaws of Central Station to park for Shabbat and the Hasidic neighbourhoods blocked their roads from traffic, and everywhere smelled of home-cooked dinners, it felt like the most peaceful city in the world. The best place on earth.

Her sister had a full day planned. They walked around Helliwell Park, where Carlos stopped to take pictures at every turn; had lunch at a little café at the island's centre; drove to the marina to look at the boats; shopped at the Co-op, the island's only grocery store. Naomi watched Carlos and Tamar's ritual as they circled the vegetable aisle, calling to each other: Avocados? Tomatoes? By the greens, their hands touched as they picked through the spinach.

"Oh no," Naomi said in Hebrew when they arrived at home that evening. Carlos and Tamar were unpacking the groceries. "I forgot to get ground beef."

"Beef?"

"I was going to make mafrum, like Mom's."

Carlos followed their conversation with the blank open face of someone who didn't understand the language but was fascinated by the sound.

"It's too late, anyway," Naomi said. "I'll just go tomorrow. It takes three hours to make."

"Actually," Tamar switched to English, glancing at Carlos. "We don't eat meat."

Naomi stared at her.

"I'm a vegetarian."

"Since when?"

"Since about a year ago."

"Oh," Naomi said. But mafrum, a Tunisian dish they had grown up eating—potatoes filled with ground beef, dipped in egg and topped with tomato sauce—had been Tamar's favourite comfort food. Whenever Tamar visited, it was the first dish she requested. Naomi had been looking forward to making it for her.

"Why don't you let us cook for you? Carlos is a fantastic cook." Tamar passed by him on her way to a cupboard and ran the tips of her fingers across his back.

"You're our guest," Carlos said.

Guest. She shouldn't be a guest at her sister's house. That's not how they were raised. Naomi fingered a loose thread from her cardigan. She watched Tamar and Carlos by the counter, their backs facing her, four poking shoulder blades. "Fine," she said. "But I'm definitely cooking tomorrow. It's Shabbat dinner. We can pretend we're having a kiddush, minus the prayers."

"Kiddush?" Carlos asked.

Naomi waved her hand. "It's a Jewish thing."

Carlos looked at her and then at Tamar. Tamar brushed hair off her forehead. "It's a ritual to welcome the Shabbat. You sip some wine, say some prayers, eat some bread."

"I'm sorry," Naomi said in Hebrew. "Did I hurt his feelings? I was just . . ."

"Don't do that." Tamar put the knife down and turned to her.

"What?"

"Speak about him in Hebrew while he's in the room."

"I didn't mean to . . . I was just . . ."

"It's fine," Tamar said. "Just speak English."

Naomi sat down, feeling like a scolded child.

Dinner was a bowl of chewy brown rice sprinkled with cumin seeds, with a heap of vegetables and tofu on top. Naomi complimented Carlos on it, though she thought it could use more salt, more garlic, more spice.

As soon as she was finished, she escaped to her room. Her stomach felt uneasy. She lay on the sofa bed and stared at the cracks in the ceiling, fighting an urge to cry. It was all wrong. A mistake. She had hoped that she and Tamar could pick up where they had left off years ago, that Tamar would make it all better somehow. It was something they had done for each other since childhood, when their parents were preoccupied in their battles, and Naomi and Tamar had to rely on each other for comfort. As teenagers they had helped each other through heartbreaks and letdowns, spent long hours talking, stealing cigarette puffs outside the window, breaking into fits of laughter and tears and more laughter. Naomi turned to her side and watched the sky darkening outside the window. When did it become so difficult to just be around each other?

Tamar leaned against the patio railing, sipping tea and staring into the forest. "Oh, hey," she said when her sister stepped through the sliding doors. "Tea?"

"Sure." Naomi helped herself to a cup in the kitchen and came back, standing next to her. "It's so beautiful out here."

"I love it," Tamar said.

"You're really thinking of staying here? On the island?"

"We hope to."

"Won't you get bored?"

Tamar laughed. "Here? I'll never get bored."

"Not much to do."

"There's plenty to do."

"No, I mean like culturally."

The muscle in Tamar's cheek tensed and released, tensed and released. "You know, most people think this is paradise," she said.

Naomi looked at her. "Why are you upset?"

"It's just typical," Tamar said. "I've been here for thirteen years and you still think it's just another phase."

Naomi placed her mug on the railing and looked at Tamar, puzzled. "I never said that."

Tamar's jaw ached and she realized that she had been clenching it. This was exactly why she lived away from her family, away from Israel. It made her anxious, irritable. She didn't like herself this way.

"You can't blame me for hoping you'll come home one day," Naomi said quietly.

Tamar rocked her tea mug. She wished she hadn't lost her temper. It had taken her years to call this place home. At first, she'd always assumed she'd return to Israel eventually, but after that last visit, she had decided it was time to commit. She couldn't live like that, torn between two places, didn't want to end up like their mother, who had never let go of Tunisia, had never stopped talking about their family home on the little island of Djerba, pining for it the way she had longed for their father. Some nights, when their father was out, she'd play old Arabic love songs and sadness would wash over her, a longing for the place where she grew up, for her childhood.

Her accent became heavier, her gestures theatrical, sweeping. When Tamar and Naomi were little, she'd take their hands and dance with them around the living room, her hair down, her lips painted red. As teenagers, Tamar and Naomi avoided her when she started playing her crackly records, finding the whole ritual embarrassing, overly dramatic. Their mother danced alone, one hand wrapped around an imaginary lover, the other holding a glass of red wine she would nurse for the entire evening. Even after thirty years in Israel, their mother remained removed from Israeli culture, always a little critical of Israeli bluntness and informality. Only in her later days, with the second intifada, when suicide bombers blew themselves up not far from her home, did her mother start saying "us" and "them." It took a threat to her life to make her feel as if she belonged. But even then, her nostalgia hadn't faded. "The Arabs in Tunisia," she'd say, "they were different. They were good people. They were our best friends."

Naomi sat at the edge of the lounge chair. She looked defeated, and it sucked the anger out of Tamar.

"I left Ami," Naomi said.

Tamar turned too fast and spilled some of her tea. "What? What did you just say?"

Naomi nodded.

"Oh my God, Naomi," Tamar said. "But you guys have been married for what . . ."

"Fifteen years next month," Naomi said.

Tamar scratched her head. "I don't know what to say. I mean, is it final?"

Naomi gave a half-hearted shrug.

"But why? I mean, you were like the most solid couple I've ever known."

"He cheated on me."

"Ami? No way."

Naomi shot a cold look at her. "Why is it so hard to believe?"

"Because he loves you. And he's such a good guy. When did it happen?"

"A couple years ago."

"So . . . why now?"

"Because I just found out."

"So he was having an affair?"

"Well, no—"

"It was just one time?"

"Does that make it better?" Naomi glared.

Tamar bit her lip. "Well, sure. I mean, it's still terrible of course, but . . ."

Naomi stood up and turned to walk away.

"Hey, hey." Tamar grabbed Naomi's wrist, pulled her in and embraced her. Naomi resisted but eventually gave in, standing sullen and stiff in Tamar's arms.

"I'm sorry," Tamar said.

Naomi let go, her body slowly relaxing. She began to cry.

"Who was she?"

"I don't know," Naomi said into her sister's shirt. "Some Rona from Haifa."

"Sounds like a slut to me," Tamar said and Naomi laughed through her tears.

Tamar tucked her sister's hair behind her ears and held her by the shoulders. "I know exactly what you need," she said, and Naomi looked up with wet eyes, sniffling.

Tamar led Naomi to the kitchen, where she opened the cupboard, gazed into it and then grabbed a cup missing a handle.

Naomi's face brightened. "No, Tamar. These are your dishes."

"How about a plate?" Tamar swung another cupboard door open. "Here, this one is cracked anyway."

"Seriously?" Naomi said. "But where?"

"We'll find something." Tamar stuffed another cup into her handbag.

Tamar circled the Co-op building searching for a spot and her sister followed a step behind. Though there wasn't a soul around, they slunk along the shadows, past the darkened café, the stacks of metal patio chairs chained to a wooden pole in the courtyard, looking like a giant centipede. Finally, Tamar stopped by a blank wooden wall, next to a row of green garbage bins piled with remnants of the day: rotten lettuce, damaged fruit, plastic bags. She offered Naomi a cup and jerked her chin.

Naomi looked at the wall. "This isn't Mahane Yehuda Market," she said. "People know you here."

"People knew us there," Tamar said.

Naomi fiddled with the cup, passing it between her hands. She gazed up at the wooden building, turned to look at the empty road behind her, the glowing ring beneath the lone street light.

"Come on," Tamar said. "There's no one here."

Naomi tossed the cup at the wall, underhand, as if she were playing catch with a toddler. The cup glanced off the wall and plunked onto the pavement, unscathed.

"For God's sake." Tamar picked the cup up and handed it back to Naomi. "Imagine it was Ami's favourite cup."

Naomi breathed in deeply. She kissed the cup like a basketball player before a foul shot and squinted to focus on her aim. She extended her arm behind her and wheezed as she flung it forward, working her entire body into the motion. The cup shattered into tiny pieces against the wall. Naomi laughed, covering her mouth with her palm.

Tamar pulled another cup from her handbag and Naomi snatched it from her hand. She took a step back and leaped as she smashed the cup against the wall. It exploded on impact, a fountain of pottery. The shards glittered on the pavement like ice. Naomi clapped. A car slowed down on the road, and Tamar and Naomi froze, waiting for it to pass.

"Okay, hurry up." Tamar waved a plate in her direction.

Naomi threw the next two dishes quickly, one after the other. The car turned around and crept past the Co-op again, and Tamar and Naomi squatted behind a bush, giggling, giddy with the adrenalin. Naomi clutched Tamar's hand. Tamar felt now as she had twenty years ago: proud that she knew how to make her sister feel better, take care of her, as though she were the elder of the two.

The car outside the Co-op drove off, and Tamar hurried to her truck, grabbed a brush and a dustpan and started sweeping up the shards. Naomi watched her, laughing. "I'm a member." Tamar shrugged.

On the way back to her sister's house, Naomi watched the silvered moonlight rippling on the water, reflecting white and glossy on the large flat rocks along the beach. She looked up in awe: stars crowded the night sky, so much brighter than they were in Jerusalem.

Tamar turned into the driveway and stopped the truck. She

turned off the headlights, the backyard reclaimed by ghostly, bluish shadows. "So tell me," she said as Naomi put her hand on the door handle. "Why don't you like Carlos?"

Naomi sat back, giving her sister a startled glance. "I don't not like him."

"Come on." Tamar lowered her chin.

"I like him fine," Naomi said.

"He's a good guy, amazing actually," Tamar said. "I wish you'd give him a chance."

Naomi stared at the forest at the end of the driveway. She hadn't realized how transparent she'd been. "You know," she said finally, "I think I had this image in my head of you and me, two single, carefree gals, going on road trips, picking up hitchhikers . . . I guess I just didn't expect . . . this."

Tamar chuckled. "Funny. Here I thought: maybe she'll take me more seriously now that I'm finally in a proper relationship."

"I'm sorry," Naomi said. "I'm happy for you. I am."

Tamar placed her hands on the steering wheel and squeezed. "He wants kids."

"And how do you feel about it?" Naomi said carefully. She had always avoided talking about children with her sister. Tamar had made it clear in the past that she might not have children, that she didn't appreciate the pressure, that she was aware of her ticking clock, thank you very much. "Israelis are obsessed with babies," she had said. "Like it's the only thing that matters."

"I'm thinking maybe I'm as ready as I'll ever be." She leaned her head back and beamed at Naomi, and as they sat there side by side in the dark cab, Naomi felt an intimacy she'd been missing in her friendships, which over the years, with marriage and children, had turned into calculated meetings over salads and cappuccinos.

It had been so long since she'd felt this close to anybody, even Ami. They'd gotten caught up in the routine of everyday life, kids, mortgage, bills, work. Somewhere along the way somebody had turned on the autopilot and they hadn't even noticed.

"You can't break up with Ami," Tamar said, as though she could read her thoughts.

Naomi looked at her sister and sighed. She was so tired of hating him. It took such effort and it was wearing her out.

"You guys are my rock," Tamar said. "You're the story I tell whenever people say marriage doesn't work. You're my only proof, my happy ending."

"So you want me to stay with him for your sake," Naomi said.

Tamar grinned. "Well, yeah."

Naomi smiled, swallowing her tears. "I'll see what I can do."

ACKNOWLEDGEMENTS

I am immensely grateful to Camilla Gibb, who mentored, inspired and guided me throughout the writing of this book with the utmost commitment and dedication.

Thank you to Jane Warren, my editor at HarperCollins Canada, for her enthusiasm, and to Iris Tupholme and everyone at Harper-Collins for believing in this book.

My first readers, Sean Brereton, Eufemia Fantetti and Becky Blake, read numerous drafts and provided useful feedback and some tough love. Thanks also to the following readers: Anna Chatterton, Janet Hong, Jan Redford, Nazanine Hozar, Amanda Leduc, Kathy Friedman, Leslie Hill, Clarissa Green, Rachel Knudsen, Alev Ersan and Hilda Ragnars (my very first reader in English). Love and thanks to my friends in Israel, Vancouver, Toronto and elsewhere for being supportive, encouraging and generally awesome.

I was fortunate to be a part of the MFA Program at the University of Guelph, where I wrote this collection as my thesis. Thank you to my classmates and teachers, especially Catherine Bush and Russell Smith. I'm greatly indebted to Betsy Warland and Wayde Compton, my mentors in Simon Fraser University's The Writer's Studio, and to the TWS community. I also extend my gratitude to the Canada Council for the Arts for their generous assistance, and to the editors of *Grain* and *Prairie Fire* for publishing "Warplanes" and "The Poets in the Kitchen Window," respectively.

Love and thanks to my family: my four brothers and my sister for their everlasting faith in me; my mother for the love and the food; and my father, a poet in his own right, who once promised me he would publish my first book but passed away before he had the chance. This book is in his memory.

And finally, to Sean, ahuvi hanitzhi. I couldn't have done any of this without you. This book is for you.